Playmaker

The Toronto Blaze Series
Book 2

Kim Findlay

ISBN 978-99904-5-505-2 (digital)

978-99904-5-504-5 (paperback)

Editing by Kristi Yanti (Edits by Kristi), Peter Senftleben (PES Editorial), and Julia Ganis (Julia Edits)

Cover by megan barker designs

Formatting by Heather Creeden (CreedReads)

*To Beck and Liv, and everyone else who wanted
Cooper's story*

"Fashion is the armor to survive the reality of everyday life."
– Bill Cunningham

Toronto Blaze Roster

1	Ivan Petrov	Petey	Russia	Goalie
8	Cliff Royston	Royster	Canada	Winger
10	Devin Oppedisano	Oppy	Canada	Winger
12	Corwin Cashman	Crash	US	Defense
17	Josh Middleton	Ducky	Canada	Winger
18	John Deeker	Deek	Canada	Center
22	Gerber	Gerbs	Switzerland	Winger
23	Brian Barnes	Barnes	US	Winger
25	Phin Collins	Bongo	Canada	Center
32	Braydon Mitchell	Mitch	US	Goalie
33	Lars De Vries		Netherlands	Goalie
44	Justin Johnson	JJ	Canada	Defense
57	Whittaker Cooper	Coop	US	Defense

Coach Osgood — Canada
Coach Salo — Sweden

Scout — Trainer

Chapter 1

This dress might have been a mistake

In front of me was the eighteenth green of the most beautiful golf course in Canada, but all I could see was the arena. Overtime, Stanley Cup Final, and the puck was on my stick in the Minnesota zone. Their goalie moved to block my shot, so I passed to JJ—

But JJ was on the bench getting stitches, and my pass to Crash was intercepted. Minnesota raced to our end, and I exerted every bit of strength I had left in my legs, but I couldn't catch them. Was I getting too old? Were my twenty-nine-year-old legs not fast enough? The goal lit up and—

"I'm going somewhere they've never heard of hockey." Oppy, my teammate on the Toronto Blaze, frowned as he took a long gulp of expensive beer.

I blinked back to the here and now. Briarwood, a week later, golfing with my teammates. Several of the men at the table agreed with Oppy's sentiment as they unwound after eighteen holes. I raised my glass with them. We all wanted to forget that loss, but we couldn't.

I hoped Oppy had a great time. Me, I wasn't going anywhere this summer, aside from one family obligation I'd prefer to ignore. My sole focus would be next year.

Umbrellas shaded us from the noonday sun, our view from the terrace that of lush grass, trees, water hazards and foursomes still working their way through the course. Briarwood was one of the most expensive clubs in the country, and it showed. The eight of us had finished our round an hour ago, and after eating, we were enjoying beer and relaxation.

"I'd be there now if we didn't have this damned charity event tonight," Oppy continued.

"Who the hell schedules a team event after the season is over?"

Silence fell across the table, because of how our season had ended in heartbreak.

"Shit. Sorry."

It wasn't Barnes's fault. It was impossible to avoid hockey. We played hockey professionally, we lived in Toronto—a city that supported hockey above other sports—and we'd just lost the fucking Stanley Cup.

That was the reason I'd invited my teammates out to Briarwood. It hit us all hard, so as captain I'd been checking in, using my membership here to tempt the guys out where I could see how they were doing after that brutal loss.

I knew the answer to Barnes's question. "Radner, the VP of PR, is the guy who set this up, and he's retiring. They shouldn't try it again."

The guys wanted to go to their respective homes or getaways and lick their wounds. They didn't want to sit around tables with adequate food making small talk with people who would undoubtedly ask what happened in that last game. No one who was on the ice that night wanted to rehash it.

"They'd better fucking not. I need a month where I never have to think about hockey, let alone talk about it."

I wanted to warn Oppy that it was a short summer. Training camp started in September, and our bodies fell out of peak fitness quicker than we could get it back. But the long playoff run was draining, and rest was a weapon too.

"Am I the only one who keeps replaying that last overtime?" JJ asked quietly.

JJ was my partner on defense. We complemented each other perfectly—he stayed back, closer to our goal while I was more often in the offensive zone, making plays. Normally, I didn't need to look to know where he would be on the ice.

But that last game...

JJ had been getting stitched up because he'd fallen onto our goalie, Petrov, on a previous play. Petrov's backup, Mitchell, let in the goal. There was a lot of blame to claim.

"No one isn't replaying that." I assured him. "We just have to use it to move forward, not doubt ourselves." It was easier said than done.

"I'm taking a month in Fiji. Then I'll worry about moving forward." Oppy looked around for our responses.

"That sounds awesome." Ducky was our first line right winger, and hands down our most enthusiastic player as well as one of our top scorers.

"You want to come?"

Ducky shook his head. "I have to do something with my mom, and then I'm focusing on making this body"—he waved a hand down his five-foot-nine torso—"a lethal weapon."

We laughed, as he'd intended. He was the shortest player on the team, but fast, with incredible hockey smarts. He'd had a great playoff run, but he blamed himself for not scoring in regulation, before overtime started.

"Laugh all you want, but you'll see come training camp. Petey is gonna fear me."

Ivan Petrov, our starting goalie, was a Russian behemoth. He was afraid of no one.

"I'd pay to see that." JJ gave one of his rare grins.

"You won't have to pay. Just show up. What are you doing in the offseason?"

"Some family stuff in Victoria. My grandmother isn't doing well. The rest of the offseason I'm back here to work out—maybe I'll become a lethal weapon too."

Ducky held up his hand for a high five. "You know it. Next year…"

Next year was going to be different. Coach had told us to use the pain of the loss to push through to win next season and we were damned well going to do that.

The rest of the guys shared their plans: family, vacations, working out. Most would be out of the city and come back in September. Our long playoff run made the offseason short. If we'd won the Cup, it would all have been worth it. Without that…it felt like a waste.

Ducky nudged me with his elbow. "So, Captain, you spending the summer with a special lady?"

I rolled my eyes.

Oppy chuckled. "Nah, that would be many special ladies."

"They're all special." More laughter.

Two guys didn't speak up. Crash, still blaming himself for missing that pass, and Mitchell, the backup goalie who'd let in the winning goal. Those two and JJ were the ones I was most worried about. JJ had been on my radar since he was traded to Toronto, but he was so quiet and self-contained it was hard to get him to open up. I knew him as well as anyone on the team did, and on the ice we were in total sync. Not after our skates came off.

"You've got your camps, right Mitch?"

Mitchell nodded. I wasn't sure if he was holding back because of the loss, or because he was new. He'd been called up from our farm team when we lost a goalie after the trade deadline. Now, he didn't know if he was staying up or playing with the Inferno next season. Part of that depended on whether our regular backup was returning. Also, once the draft at the beginning of July rolled around, the Blaze could trade for a new backup, or move Mitchell elsewhere.

"Yeah. Gonna head back to Montana with Jayna and work out and try to help some kids."

Mitchell hadn't been drafted, partly because of the absence of opportunities where he grew up, so he and his new girlfriend Jayna Templin were running some free camps in small towns in Montana. I'd have helped out in person, but being so well known would have shifted the focus off the camps, so my contributions were only financial.

"Crash?"

He shrugged. "I'm hanging out here, family and training."

I'd make sure to reach out to the guys staying local. We had our own training systems and places we liked to work out, but doing some sessions together would help maintain those team bonds.

"How formal is this thing tonight?" Ducky asked.

"Formal," I smirked. The kid groaned, but he knew the answer. This was a *dress in a suit or tux, sit at a table with white linen and an inflated amount of cutlery while talking and dancing with the people who could afford the cost of the event* thing. We were encouraged to bid on the silent auction items, but at least we weren't being auctioned off. "And we'd better get our asses in gear. Some of you need time to look good."

Lots of chirping back at that, but I was the best-dressed player on the team. My looking good was a given. I'd worked on these guys, and we were finally approaching the best-dressed team title that existed only in my head. Some of the suits these guys wore when they'd started... I'd had the privilege of money growing up, so I was sympathetic to the guys who'd never been able to pay for quality tailoring. But once they were with the team, it was time to level up.

Mitch hung back as I signed for the bill. "I wasn't invited?"

I'd missed that. But it made sense. He, however, was reading more into it than existed, as far as I knew.

"This was arranged before you were called up. Don't overthink it. You know how the PR department has been shaken up lately."

His eyes widened. Thanks to how the people at the top of the Blaze organization's PR department had handled some issues with Mitchell and Jayna, we had new people being put in position. It wasn't surprising that some things had fallen through the cracks. And the outgoing people might have been happy to "forget" updating the new staff about Mitchell.

"Okay." He smiled. "Sounds like I'll have a better evening than you all will anyway."

* * *

CALLIE

THIS DRESS MIGHT HAVE BEEN a mistake.

I tried to slide the hem down, moving my hands discreetly under the table. That only made the fabric press against my breasts, and it was already tight enough there. Buying one-piece garments was brutal when your boobs were the size of mine.

I glanced around the table, finding more than one set of eyes on my bustline. *Shit.* I was trying to make a good impression. I'd been working for Anderson, Krys and Chan for five years after qualifying, and this was the first charity event the law firm had invited me to. I didn't want it to be the last. Invitations to events like this were a step on the path to my goal of making partner. But being conspicuous for the wrong reasons was a problem.

For the office, I had a wardrobe of neutral, loose-fitting suits that were businesslike and functional and didn't draw attention to my body. When I was working I didn't need anybody talking to my boobs. But for events like this, a brown suit wasn't going to cut it.

The speaker was still talking at the front of the room. I shrugged my shoulders, making the dress marginally less binding about my bustline. While I was sitting down, no one would see how the dress was sliding around my hips.

And wrinkling. Was it supposed to do that? It didn't look great. But it was one of those designer labels, so it was supposed to be good quality. At least it was green. Lots of colors didn't look good with bright red hair and freckles, but green was a safe color.

Next time, even if the consignment shop didn't have much privacy for changing, I was trying the damned thing on before buying it. And next time I'd make a note to get a dress before the last minute.

People were applauding, so I turned forward again, clapping my hands together quietly and hoping at long last this was over. I didn't know anyone at the table, and I wasn't good at small talk.

We'd all been introduced to the man and woman across from me, John Deeker, and his wife. He was a hockey player for the Toronto Blaze. There were hockey players sprinkled among all the tables. They were the bait, bringing in the wealthy donors who would pay money to the charity in order to rub shoulders with the athletes.

Darcy was going to be very disappointed that the one at my table was married. None of the players were out, as far as I knew, so it wasn't like I was going to give my roommate's phone number to any of them, but he'd been pretty excited when he heard about this dinner. There was a player at the next table I could tell Darcy about—he was the only non-Caucasian on the team as far as I knew. He had an odd nickname...

"Please enjoy dancing with the band, conversing with your neighbors, and don't forget the silent auction along the north wall. Thank you for your generosity in supporting our world-class children's hospital."

Finally!

I stood, murmuring polite nothings to the couple who'd been seated beside me. We'd made painful conversation on the weather and how the local baseball team was doing. I stepped back, checking for the partners of my firm. I wanted them to know I was here, doing the polite, so I could make my escape.

Before that though, the silent auction. I had plans.

Once I was away from the table, I smiled vaguely at

people I passed. There were a few other associates from the firm, but no one I knew well. I said hello to a woman I'd been at an ethics seminar with last month.

"Nice to see you, Callie. Are you enjoying yourself?"

An honest no was obviously not the proper response. "Very interesting. You?"

"We were sitting at a table with Ducky, and he's such a fun young man."

Ducky? What kind of name was that? "We had John Deeker and his wife at our table."

"She's lovely—she did a lot of the work for this event."

I made note. If I bumped into her again, I'd comment on that. "Everything has gone very smoothly."

"It has. And it's so fun to meet the hockey players. Are you a hockey fan?"

Inwardly, I shuddered. "No, but my roommate is. I've promised to tell him about them."

She leaned forward. "Talk to Cooper. If anyone could make you a hockey fan, that man could."

That was doubtful. On the other hand, if he could help me become partner, I'd follow him around like a puppy. But I'd keep that thought to myself. "Did you meet him?"

She sighed. "No, not yet. He's much too popular."

"Well, good luck."

"Thank you. And that's such a...striking dress, Callie."

The hair on the back of my neck rose. I hadn't been trying for striking. "How kind of you to say. I think I'd have done better to emulate you. That's a lovely outfit."

It was, but since it was pink, it wasn't anything I'd have even considered. But it fit better with this group than what I was wearing. I made a mental note *again* to prep earlier. It would be good to have a few event-worthy outfits ready if I was going to get these invitations now.

She said goodbye to join her husband, and I wished her luck on her Cooper hunt. I finally made it to the silent auction items, quickly scanning through the options. I believed in the charity, but normally I did my giving directly and got a tax receipt for the full value of my donation. These things, where one was required to pull out the personal benefit from any money given, if it was even worth trying to claim, felt like a wasted opportunity. And a headache for your accountant.

But *there*, that was the thing I'd make an exception for. Ten lessons with the golf pro at Briarwood. If the bids didn't go too high, that was what I wanted. Surely most of these people already knew how to golf. This wouldn't be that desirable.

I wrote down a bid that made me cringe, but if I wanted to win, I had to take a risk.

"Learning to golf, Callie?"

I stiffened and turned to find Benson, another associate at the firm who for some reason had taken a dislike to me. He was wearing a tailored suit, and it didn't have any wrinkles, unlike my dress. I forced myself to smile instead of answering.

"Is someone hoping to be invited to the partners' tournament? Sure you want to spend so much money on a long shot?"

Asswipe. I kept the insult inside because I wasn't stupid, but it was tempting to let go sometimes. I reminded myself that I *had* been invited this year, for the first time, which was a sign of approval from the partners. It would take years to make it to partner, but there was a track successful associates followed, and I'd noted each step.

I lifted my chin. "This is for charity. If it was just about learning to play, there are other options."

Theoretically, that was true. But realistically, learning to play golf at Briarwood, where the tournament was taking place? That added extra value.

"Take all the lessons you want. It won't help. What you need to know to fit in at the club, to be partner material, doesn't come from golf lessons."

That jab hit home. There was a lot I needed to figure out, but at least if I was at Briarwood I had the chance to watch people there and learn. I'd overcome a lot of my past doing that. I hadn't been brought up with money and country club memberships. But I'd been invited here, and to the tournament, because I did add value to the firm. "What you need to know to win cases and maintain clients doesn't come from the country club."

Benson shrugged. "We'll see." Then he smirked and walked away.

Asshole.

I didn't know why he loved to harass me. His area of intellectual property didn't overlap with tax often. But ever since I'd joined the firm, he'd done his best to make me feel unwelcome.

I saw a quiet corner nearby and made my way over. I preferred to watch at events like this, and I wanted to keep an eye on the bidding on the golf lessons. I didn't know why Benson was such an ass to me. It wasn't my gender—he seemed to get along with other women. I'd heard a rumor that he'd wanted to work in tax but hadn't been able to keep up with the courses. He might have thought I was a threat, since I was pretty sure he wanted to make partner as well.

Maybe it was just a personality thing. Because I disliked him more than anyone else in the office, including the man who brought in egg salad sandwiches for lunch.

Then a voice spoke behind me. "I can help you."

Chapter 2

That's legal 101

CALLIE

MY HEAD WHIPPED up to see who was talking. How had I not heard him approaching? A tall man, with blue eyes and blond hair, wearing a tux that looked made for him, hands shoved in his pants pockets. He was gorgeous and vaguely familiar.

I narrowed my eyes. "Are you talking to me?"

He smiled, showing a dimple, confidence oozing out of every pore. He and Benson—did they take classes to learn that? He clearly expected the smile was going to get him something. I crossed my arms and frowned.

He waved his hand around us, since for the moment there was no one else within ten meters. "Yes, I'm talking to you."

"What do you want?"

"You heard me. I want to help you."

Was he a client, or one of the hockey players? He was

certainly tall and fit enough. Better to be careful with what I said. "What do you think I need help with?" I forced a polite smile while I tried to work it out, but I didn't think I succeeded.

"Golf lessons."

I stiffened. I could see where this conversation was going, and that was a hard no. With his large body between me and the room, he'd made a private corner for us to talk. Yeah, the dress was a mistake.

Then he added, "And country club lessons."

Shit. I needed that. Benson had been right, and this guy knew it. Not hard to guess what he wanted in return. Still, in case he was a client, I couldn't tell him to fuck off the way I'd like to. "I'm not having sex with you."

Instead of getting angry or offended, he just smiled more. Another dimple popped out. "See, you've just proven my point. Golf doesn't include sex on the greens." He pursed his lips for a moment, losing the dimples. "At the country club, maybe, but it's optional."

Part of me wanted to laugh, but I still didn't trust where this was going. "I'm not going to have sex with you in return for any kind of lesson."

Something flashed in his eyes, and his mouth turned down. "That's not what I'm offering."

Oh now, with the frown, I placed him. He had a kind of sexy frown on his face in the billboards that were plastered across the city. No dimples. This was Cooper. Captain of the Toronto Blaze. The man everyone wanted to meet. I raised an eyebrow. He wanted something. No one made an offer like that out of the pure goodness of their heart. I waited, and he rolled his eyes.

"I didn't like the way that smug asshole talked to you. I'm offering to give you lessons in playing golf, and since I belong to Briarwood I can also show you the ropes around the clubhouse."

Excitement fizzled in my chest. What the— That would be perfect. I imagined Benson's face if I showed up, competent at golf and able to navigate the club. I'd do a lot for that...

Yeah, experience told me there would be strings. "What do you get out of it? Do you know Benson? You want to get back at him?"

"Never met him, but I know his type. Not a fan."

"Then why would you do this?"

He looked over his shoulder, but no one was that close. Looking this way, yes, but not within hearing distance.

"I need a date."

I tried, really hard, not to laugh. He looked sincere, but someone that good-looking could be a serial killer and he'd still have women begging to go out with him. This guy needed a date? With someone like me? I broke into a snort of laughter and had to cover my mouth with a hand before everyone turned to look at us.

I got myself under control. He was still smiling. Maybe this was some kind of prank?

"No, seriously," I said when I could finally speak.

"Sorry to disappoint, but I was serious. I still need a date."

He should be giving up by now. "Is this some kind of joke to you?"

"Why would you say that?"

"Because you don't need to barter golf lessons to get a date."

He raised his eyebrows. "So, you want to go out with me?"

What? "No!"

"Then I guess I do have to barter golf lessons."

I wasn't laughing anymore. I crossed my arms again. "You get lots of 'dates,' I'm sure."

He shrugged. "True. But not what I need."

"I don't know what you need, but the answer is no."

He wagged a finger at me and I wanted to snap it off. "You should hear what I'm offering before you turn down the deal. That's legal 101. I need a date to my sister's wedding."

I blinked. *What the hell?* "A date to your sister's wedding. Right. Is the wedding in Antarctica?"

"No, Connecticut. Bringing a lawyer would be perfect. But if I invite a woman to my sister's wedding, she's going to have certain...expectations."

I bit my lip. That was something I could actually believe. If Cooper wanted to avoid romantic entanglements, maybe he did want a date he could control. Make sure she wasn't posting stupid shit on social media about them being serious together. Those looks, money, that charm he was throwing out like it was trash? Some people wanted that.

No sex, he'd said. A date to a wedding. This sounded like one of Darcy's romance novels. "You want me to pretend to be your girlfriend?"

He shook his head. "No, I want you to come as my friend."

That made me feel...warm and sad at the same time. I didn't have many friends. Would this guy, with his perfect clothes and perfect world, have anything in common with me? "But we're not friends."

Full smile again. "We will be after I show you how to play golf."

Out of nowhere, an image popped into my brain.

Cooper and me, on the deck I'd seen in pictures of Briar-wood, laughing and talking. He'd smile, for real, and I'd...

No. That wasn't happening, and I should just say no, right now. That charm was potent.

He studied me, as if he could read my mind. "How about I give you a lesson or two, you see how it goes, and then, after I've proved that I'm not a lunatic, we can make it official."

"Official?"

"I'll send in the RSVP."

This was a crazy idea, and I didn't do crazy, not anymore. I bit my lip as I weighed the undoubted benefits against the risk to my mental health.

Behind Cooper's shoulder, I saw Benson, talking to one of the partners. They were both laughing. Something I couldn't do. When it came to hard work and knowledge and ability, I was perfect partner material. But all this other networking, making-connections bullshit? I was terrible at it.

"I should introduce myself. I'm Cooper. I play for the Blaze." He held out his hand.

This was the guy who was supposed to make me like hockey. I faked a smile and shook his hand, making sure my grip was firm but not so firm it was threatening. He'd have won a dominance contest, his hand callused and strong. Warm. For a moment, I forgot to pull my own away.

I cleared my throat. "I know who you are."

"I don't know who you are though."

I'd opened my mouth to answer when a voice broke through. "Calliope! There you are."

A blush warmed my cheeks. *Damned fair skin and freckles.* I quickly jerked my hand back. What did this look like, standing in a corner holding hands with the hockey player? "Mr. Anderson." He was the partner who oversaw the tax department of the firm. His silver hair was perfectly coiffed, and his suit looked expensive. Like Cooper's.

"I didn't mean to interrupt, but I have someone I'd like you to meet."

"Of course." If Anderson wanted me, I was there. Introducing me to someone at the event? *Yes.*

He waved a hand. "Finish your conversation. We're at table three. Stop by when you're ready. Thanks for coming tonight, Cooper. I'm sure you and your teammates are making this a success."

I should say...I didn't know what. Partners normally expected associates to jump when they called. He was still smiling at Cooper though. *Holy fuck.* He thought Cooper and I were...something. And he didn't look pissed. He looked impressed.

"Of course, Mr. Anderson. I'll be there in just a minute."

I was still working through that when Cooper interrupted my thoughts. "See? Just talking to me is impressing your boss. Imagine what taking lessons together would do."

If anyone knew how to navigate these social waters, it was this man in front of me. I still wasn't sure what he was up to and what other motives he might have, but this, even if it ended up being just one lesson? It would be more valuable than lessons with the golf pro.

"Okay. We can give this a try. You need a friend date for your wedding who won't assume that means anything. I need to fit in for the partners' golf tournament, and you won't assume anything."

His grin this time was less charming, less perfect. But no less effective. "What's your number?"

I hesitated. This was a risk. There were too many

unknowns, and I didn't want to ignore my instincts simply because there could be a lot of upside. But one lesson...that wasn't a lifetime commitment.

He pulled out his phone from his jacket pocket and I gave him my personal number.

"I'll message you this week, Calliope."

I shook my head. "Callie, please."

"Callie." He changed something on his phone. "Oh, and one other thing."

I tensed. Was this the poison pill?

"For the wedding?"

I nodded, warily.

"I pick the dress. That thing you're wearing? Is a disaster."

Then he walked away, leaving me to question whether I could find something else to wear before meeting this someone with Mr. Anderson. *Shit*.

Chapter 3

I can't report on his abs

CALLIE

THESE RIDICULOUS SHOES were killing my feet. I kicked them off as soon as I was safely in the door of my condo. *Thwack. Thwack.* They hit the wall and slid to the floor.

"That you, Callie?"

I rolled my eyes. Who else did Darcy think would be coming in the front door? "No, it's the ghost of your last hookup." Darcy had a much more exciting sex life than I did. I came around the corner of the living room and found him stretched out on the couch, still in his work clothes. His polo shirt had the cinema logo on it, and there was a smell of burnt popcorn. He was watching something on TV, but he paused it. "How was work?"

Darcy didn't even acknowledge I'd spoken. "Holy shit, Callie, is that what you wore to your thing tonight?"

I'd had enough insults on my dress, thank you very much. "Yes, it is. It's designer. It's fine."

Darcy sat up and stared at me in horror. "Seriously, Callie, that is a fucking awful dress."

I looked down, trying to understand why two guys had such problems with the dress. "It's green. That's a good color for me, right?"

Darcy finally closed his jaw but shook his head. "No, goose-turd green is shit for anyone. Why didn't you let me help?"

Because I was a grown-ass woman. I wanted to make partner, and needing someone to pick out my clothes was infantile. I crossed my arms. "I'm not a child."

"Sweetie, I picked out better clothing when I was a child. I mean...it doesn't even fit you."

"Yes, it does. It's my size."

"If it's your size, why does it only touch your tits and ass? The rest is like a sac."

I blinked. This had been an important event. If I'd looked as terrible as Darcy thought, I might have hurt my chances of impressing the partners. I bit my lip. "Is it really that bad?"

Darcy sighed. It was.

"Why didn't you take me shopping with you?"

I looked at the floor.

"Callie?"

"IkindaforgotitwascomingandIhadtogetsomethingfast."

Darcy held up his hand. "Breathe and say it so that I understand."

I puffed out my cheeks. "I forgot it was coming up and I needed something fast. You were working, and I should be able to buy a dress. I'm thirty years old."

Darcy rubbed his forehead. "Where did you go? Did you go to Eaton Centre? Bloor Village?"

I squeezed my eyes shut and shook my head.

"Call-i-o-pe." When Darcy stretched out my name like that, I knew he was upset.

I gave in. "I went to that consignment shop."

"Callie!" he yelped.

"I know, but I hate spending so much money on clothes. And this was in my size, and it was green..."

I'd messed up, and it was my own fault. My own, stupid, penny-pinching fault. I had money now, but it was difficult to change after never having had it. I had loans to pay off. And a savings account to build. When you grew up with nothing, it was hard to take money for granted.

Darcy stood. "Let's both get into something comfy. I'll dig out the ice cream and you can tell me all about it."

I felt the tension draining, leaving me loose and tired. "That would be great, Darce."

He gave me a push down the hallway to my room, turning into the chaos of his own.

Darcy and I met in foster care. We were opposites in almost every way, but somehow we'd bonded and become friends. When we aged out and were on our own, we teamed up. I trusted very few people, but I trusted him.

We'd been roommates for years. When I'd saved up the down payment for this condo, I'd asked Darcy to keep rooming with me. I charged him less than I would anyone else, and while it helped with the mortgage, I mostly wanted my friend around. I didn't want a roommate I didn't know. Growing up, I hadn't been able to control my circumstances and I'd lived with too many people who were happy to steal my stuff, or worse, when I was asleep and vulnerable. My condo was my haven.

I curled up on the couch in loose shorts and a baggy sweatshirt. June meant the weather had warmed up, but we had AC on. Darcy had put on sweats, leaving his polo and khakis in a pile on his floor, I knew. I had no idea how he always looked so put together when he went out, since his possessions were scattered all over his room. My room was painfully tidy, and I never looked half as good as he did.

He brought over a pint of ice cream—store brand because it was much better value, especially if you poured name-brand chocolate sauce all over it—and two spoons, as well as the chocolate sauce. He dribbled chocolate on top of the ice cream and passed me a spoon.

"Okay, spill. You went to the big dinner with the hockey players."

I nodded. Invitations to the charity events, like this dinner and the golf tournament, were the first steps to making partner. I wanted a job where I couldn't be fired on a whim, and to have my home paid off. Enough money saved up to make sure I'd always have a safe place to live and food to eat.

Darcy took a spoonful of chocolate-covered ice cream and asked, "How hot did they look in person?"

I considered while I licked my spoon. I wasn't a hockey fan. I wasn't any kind of sportsball fan. It wasn't something I'd had time for. "We had John Deeker at our table, and his wife."

Darcy put on an exaggerated pout. "He's not one of the hotties, and he's straight. Come on, who else?"

"I think they're all straight."

Darcy shrugged. "Maybe. But if they're not married, I can dream, right? Some of them statistically are bi or gay, but not out. It's math. In my mind, those guys are single. So, did you meet any of the single players?"

My cheeks felt warm. Why should I be embarrassed about whatever had happened with Cooper? Who I thought

—hoped—was single since he'd talked about me being his friend date. "Cooper was there."

Darcy sat up, ice cream forgotten. "Seriously? Cooper? That man is incredible. So ripped, and those eyes..." Darcy pretended to swoon.

I rescued the ice cream, only half full now. "He was wearing a suit, so I can't report on his abs."

"You don't need to. I've seen the ads."

I didn't ask him what ads because they were everywhere. Six-plus-feet of mostly naked man reclining on something, blond hair perfect, blue eyes giving a sexy frown at everyone passing by. I hadn't studied them but they were impossible to ignore. I didn't remember what brand of underwear was being advertised, but I did remember Cooper. Even if it had taken me a minute to recognize him in a tux, I'd have recognized him right away if he'd been mostly naked.

"I talked to him. A bit. And..."

Darcy's eyes were wide. "And what? Did he ask you out?" Before I could answer, he shook his head. "No, he wouldn't have when you were wearing that dress. Damn it, Callie, this could have been your chance."

I wasn't looking for a chance. Not with Cooper. Or any of the other players, or any guy. I was better off on my own. Safer. But part of me wanted to rub it in. Let Darcy know that even with the dress he hated—to be fair, Cooper did too —I'd gotten a date. Sort of.

Now that I was back in my place, not staring at that gorgeous face, I didn't *really* expect to get a call from Cooper. He had his choice of women, and probably did that whole golf lesson/wedding date thing to get my number as a dare or something. It had happened before. But if he'd helped me with golf and the country club...that would have been great.

I scooped up a big spoonful of ice cream, swirled it in chocolate sauce, and spoke just before stuffing my mouth with yummy goodness. "Cooper asked me to go to his sister's wedding."

Darcy was an attractive man, but the bugged-out eyes and dropped jaw did not make him look his best. It was revenge for his assessment of my dress.

Of course, I got a freezie headache from the big bite of ice cream I'd taken. I rubbed my head and grimaced, while I pressed my tongue on the roof of my mouth. "Damn it. Why did I do that?"

Darcy pointed his spoon at me. "That's karmic revenge for trying to fool me like that."

I blinked, tears threatening. I blinked harder. I didn't cry. I certainly didn't cry because my best friend couldn't believe Cooper, the hockey player, had wanted me as his date. Hell, I didn't believe it, and I'd been there.

It was hard to fool Darcy. He'd known me too long, too well. "Shit, that was a horrible thing to say. I'm sorry, Callie."

I shrugged. Just more proof that I shouldn't expect a phone call from any hockey player. I needed to find another way to prepare for this golf thing. I'd lost out on the silent auction. I couldn't blow all my money on golf lessons any more than I could on fancy dresses.

Darcy stared at me. "You weren't joking, were you?"

"*He* probably was. He won't call."

Darcy leaned over and grabbed my hand, preventing me from getting more ice cream, damn him. "Wait, Cooper has your phone number?"

Now I was worried. "Should I have made one up? He's not going to do something horrible with it, is he?"

Darcy squeezed my arm and let go. "I don't think NHL superstars get phone numbers to prank people." He squinched up his nose. "Well, maybe their teammates, but not people they don't know. That wouldn't be cool."

Or nice.

"So, just tell me what happened."

I relayed the story: the golf lesson auction item, Benson, the offer of help.

Darcy's eyes were wide and he'd forgotten to eat any more ice cream. "Seriously? What did you say?"

I grabbed another spoonful of cold deliciousness. No sense in it going to waste. "I told him I wouldn't have sex with him."

Darcy laugh-snorted and covered his mouth with his hand. "And he asked for your number after that?"

I licked my spoon. "He said he wanted a friend to be his date for his sister's wedding, someone who wouldn't have any expectations about what going to a family wedding would mean." I should have asked more questions. Now that I was telling Darcy, it seemed even less plausible. He'd said something about a lawyer, but still.

Darcy's eyes were a little glassy, so I waited while he considered.

"You gave him your number, and then..." He waved his hand, ready to move on now.

"Then I went to meet a potential new client Mr. Anderson was courting. He said some complimentary things about me, and I'll look up some of the tax information this guy needs, see if we can help him."

Darcy nudged me with his shoulder. "What happened with Cooper?"

"I don't know. After he got my number, I went to meet Mr. Anderson's client."

Darcy opened his mouth, closed it, then sat back, ignoring the ice cream. "That was...that was something. But yeah, not sure he's gonna call after that."

I ignored the jolt of disappointment. Obviously, a big hockey star wasn't going to call up and give me golf lessons. I'd take care of the golf lessons myself. But that was okay. I'd learned a lot of lessons in my life. And one I clung to was to rely on no one else. If I earned something, it was mine, and it was a lot harder to take it away. Gifts were too easily taken back.

I'd earned my law degree. I'd earned the money for the down payment on this condo.

I'd earn the partnership and then they'd have a difficult time getting rid of me.

Chapter 4

You could keep some clothes on

Cooper

"Kook!"

A finger poked my face and I blinked out of sleep. One of my favorite people in the world was beaming at me. "Kook!" she repeated.

I covered a yawn. "Are you poking me, Hails?"

"You sleep."

Impeccable toddler logic. "That I was. Does your mom know you're in here?"

Her blue eyes moved around the room. Her wispy blonde hair was falling out of the ponytail on top of her head, and she hugged a striped stuffed cat closer. "Wanna play?"

I held back the grin that threatened to cross my face. Hailey was a handful, and I knew damned well she'd been told not to wake me up. I was glad I wasn't her parent because standing up to her was impossible.

I pushed myself up till I was sitting in the guest bed at

Hunter's place, careful not to let the bedding slip too low. "Faith! Come get your spawn!"

Faith's footsteps sounded in the hall. Hailey's eyes widened and she turned to face her mother.

Faith stood in the doorway, arms crossed. I'd closed the door when I settled in here last night, but Hailey had obviously opened it. Toddler brain didn't remind her to close it again.

"Hailey! What did I tell you?"

Hailey fidgeted. "Play with Kook when he awake."

Faith narrowed her eyes. "What else did I say?"

"B'ekfas?"

"I told you not to wake up Cooper." Only Hailey got to call me Kook.

"He awake, Mommy."

"Was he awake before you came in this room?"

Hailey turned big eyes on me for the save.

Faith pointed a finger at me. "Don't encourage her or I'll take her to your place to wake you up every day."

No, she wasn't going to do that. But I got the message. "Why don't you take your devil daughter so I can get up?"

Faith came into the room and leaned down to scoop up Hailey. "You know, you could keep some clothes on when you stay here." She headed out of the room, reaching a hand back to close the door.

Hailey's eyes stared at me over her mother's shoulder. "Kook has no clothes?"

"Every morning, Cooper!" Faith repeated before she slammed the door.

I finally let the smile loose.

Faith and Hunter were my best friends, and I adored their daughter, Hailey. I crashed in their spare room often, when Hunter and I were both playing for the Blaze and arrived back in the city late after away games or celebrated too much with the team. He'd been a little over-juiced last night after the charity dinner, so I'd brought him back. After pointing him to his own room, I'd stripped and climbed in the bed here.

I pulled on the pants from last night and the shirt, carrying my tie and jacket with me.

Hailey was at the breakfast bar in her seat, bright gaze on me. She pouted. "Kook has clothes."

Faith frowned at me. I raised my hands. "This one's not on me. You're the one who mentioned clothes. It's not my fault everyone wants me naked."

That eye roll must have hurt her. But hey, there were pictures of me in nothing but my underwear across the city. They paid me for that for a reason.

"Not everyone, Cooper." Faith snorted as Hunter joined us in the kitchen.

"Daddy!" Hailey almost knocked her stool over trying to launch herself at Hunter. He caught her, used to her enthusiasm.

Most of the time I was happy to be Hailey's godfather, without the constant responsibility that Faith and Hunter bore. Sometimes, though, the three of them together made something in my chest ache. This little family unit made it seem worth the effort. It would be nice to have that kind of bond. But that wasn't for everyone. These were some of the lucky ones.

Hunter leaned over to kiss Faith and I passed by them, opening the fridge to see what I could make for breakfast. "Omelets?"

Faith looked over. "You cooking?"

"Like you two are gonna? Someone has to feed Hails."

"Right. She's a neglected child."

I ignored her and pulled out the eggs, milk and cheese. "What have you got to put in them?"

"Anything you find is fair game. I'm gonna dress my spawn."

Faith took Hailey from Hunter. The girl started to tell her mother what she wanted to wear today as they headed back to the bedrooms. I heard *pink* and *sparkles*.

Faith already had the coffee going, so Hunts took out mugs for us while I arranged my ingredients and pulled out the pan and some bowls. I knew this kitchen almost as well as my own. I pursed my lips. Cooked more in this one too.

"Thanks for bringing me home. Oppy made us do shots while you were off doing...whatever."

I shook my head. "Hunts, you're a lightweight. You have to learn to say no."

"Yeah, yeah. How come you brought me home? Didn't find anyone?"

I whisked eggs while butter melted in the pan. "No one interesting."

"Not even the woman in the dress?"

I looked up at him. Was he talking about Calliope, the ugly-dress woman? "What do you mean?"

Hunter set down his mug. "Well, after griping about that green dress forever, I saw you over by the auction table with her. She turned you down?"

As if. She had said she wouldn't sleep with me, but I hadn't asked, so technically... Anyway, that wasn't why I'd wanted to talk to her. "I didn't ask her to fuck, no, but I have her number."

Faith returned, fortunately without Little Miss Big Ears. She peeked over my shoulder to see what I was making. "No single hotties for you last night, Coop?"

Hunts pulled her back against his chest. "No, just a redhead in an ugly dress that offended his taste."

Faith shook her head.

"He got her number." Hunter had his chin on Faith's shoulder and looked content.

Damn it, something was wrong with me if I was suddenly getting spooked by these two. They'd gotten together back in college, thanks to me, so I should be used to them.

"Are you gonna call her?" Faith asked, breaking out of her husband's arms to grab plates.

I took my moment and flipped the omelet. Perfectly. "I told her I'd give her golf lessons."

Faith paused while passing the plate to me. There was a moment of silence, and without looking I knew they were exchanging glances. I took the plate from her and slid the omelet on before giving it back to her.

"Golf lessons," Hunter repeated.

"Yeah, she needs to play to make partner or something, and a dickhead was hassling her about it." Silence again. I turned my head and this time I caught them carrying on their wordless conversation. "What? I can do something nice for someone. I don't have a lot going on this summer." *Especially after losing the finals* but I pushed that thought aside.

Faith took the plate to the table and started to cut up some of the omelet for Hailey.

Hunter put a hand on my shoulder. "You do a lot of nice things. But you're not sleeping with her, just golfing? You don't do that. Or is that why you're giving her lessons?"

I shook my head and poured in the eggs for the next omelet. "No, I'm not doing this to get her into bed. She's a lawyer and not my type." I wasn't even sure what kind of body she had hidden under that ugly dress. "But we made a deal. I'll teach her golf and she'll go to my sister's wedding with me."

I could give her other lessons that would be a lot more fun. She'd frown, and have that crease in her forehead, but when I took her apart—

"What?" Faith was staring at me like I'd grown another head. Good thing she couldn't read my thoughts. I tried to explain. "It's an excellent deal. I'll take a lawyer to my sister's wedding and freak out my family, and she won't think it means anything serious." They were doing the looks. Again. "Come on, spit it out. What's your problem?"

"She's going to pretend to be your girlfriend?"

Shit. I'd almost burned the omelet. I pulled the pan off the heat, checking that I hadn't ruined it. I turned to see my friends still staring at me like I was a new zoo exhibit. "No, we're not pretending to date. She'll just be my plus one, as a friend. It's a straight exchange of assistance. Come on, you know taking someone to a wedding can give that person ideas."

I didn't mention that I still had to convince Callie of this plan by doing well at golf lessons. It was a technicality, after all. I'd ace that.

I had to grab the next plate myself because Faith and Hunts were still staring at me. I slid the eggs on and jabbed the dish at Hunter who roused himself enough to take it.

Hands on my hips, I glared at them. "Or I can just not call her and then you two don't have to freak out about this."

Faith poked Seb. "No, sounds like you've thought this out. You're old enough to know what you want."

That was a quick change. What was she up to? She avoided my gaze, carefully setting out the cutlery on the table. She was getting some kind of weird idea about this whole thing, but that wasn't my problem.

"Seb, can you get Hailey out to eat? She was setting up her stuffed animals to play with Cooper."

I let whatever Faith was worried about slide. I had my best girl waiting to play with me after breakfast. Things were good.

* * *

CALLIE

I JOTTED DOWN A QUICK NOTE. The latest CPA opinion on the appropriate presentation of tax liability for environmental obligations and the penalties for refusing to follow them was supposed to make things clearer, not add more gray areas. A noise disturbed my concentration. With an impatient huff of breath, I looked up.

I wished I hadn't. I set my hands on my desk, sighing internally while I kept my expression blank. Benson would use anything he could find to complain about me.

I'd had three firms competing to hire me when I graduated. Because of that, I'd been able to negotiate a good contract for my employment here. There weren't that many people willing to commit to the time involved in being a tax attorney. There was a lot of demand, so that was why I'd chosen this specialty. My ultimate goal of using it to become partner would take a while, but I had the brains, and the willingness to put in the time, and they needed me. My weakness was people skills, but I was working on that.

Benson had been on my case since we both were employed here. I did my best to avoid him and didn't give him any ammunition to use against me. I took care of my own shit and did my best to ignore everyone else's. He'd tried to throw shade my way in some meetings, but I'd been able to hold my own. Fortunately, he didn't handle tax issues, so we didn't run into each other often.

"Did you enjoy the benefit?" he asked.

What the fuck did he care? I didn't need to waste valuable time chitchatting about a party, of all things. "Yes, it was fine." I didn't ask him if he did, because that would only encourage him to keep talking.

"You didn't win the golf lessons, did you? Too bad." The fake sympathy in his voice was almost comical.

A petty part of me wanted to tell him a hockey player had offered to teach me. But first of all, I didn't want him to keep talking, and that would definitely have him asking questions. Secondly, I didn't think the hockey player was going to call, and wouldn't Benson just love to bring that up as often as he could? "No, I didn't."

I looked back down at my computer, wanting to be sure I got this penalty issue right before I answered the email I was working on.

"No golf tournament this year?"

Why the hell did he have a stick up his ass over that? I'd shortlisted places I could get lessons. It should be a quick decision, where to learn about golf, but Benson and Cooper had made me aware that it wasn't just the game itself that mattered. And I wasn't sure how to add that behavioral aspect into my decision. The "fitting in at a country club" part.

My cell phone rang, so I offered Benson a fake smile and picked up my phone. "Callie Smith. How may I help you?"

Benson oozed out of my doorway as I spoke.

"Calliope! Glad to catch you."

I blinked. Who was calling me Calliope? "Who is this?"

"This is your own personal golf pro. We need to set up a date."

My jaw dropped, and I was glad this wasn't a video call. Also glad that Benson was gone. "Um...Cooper?"

"Exactly. My schedule is fairly open right now. I'm tied up for the next couple of days with a sponsor thing, but I'm available all weekend. Should we start Saturday? I assume you're at the office on weekdays."

I was. I worked most weekends too, at least one day. There was a lot to keep up with in tax, and I needed those billable hours if I was ever going to make partner. Taking Saturday off? "I don't know..." I rolled my eyes at myself. I didn't dither. I knew what I was doing, and I had my time planned out. Cooper was disrupting things, and I didn't like disruptions.

"Come on, Callie. I have no idea how much I'll need to teach you, so we should get started now. And you're going to need to book some time off for the wedding."

"You're going too fast." I hadn't promised about the wedding. And I didn't like being pressured.

"I always go too fast. That's what they pay me for."

He was trying to fluster me. He wanted to push me into agreeing to something before I was ready. Not happening. They paid *me* to be calm and prepared and never taken by surprise. This guy was already pushing my buttons.

"I have work to do this weekend." I absolutely did.

"Are you saying this golfing thing isn't important?"

Damn it. It was. For all kinds of idiotic reasons involving networking and social interactions that shouldn't affect my job and my chance of being partner but did. "I'm not saying that it's not important. It's just not the only thing that's important."

I heard him sigh. "Okay, Callie, how about Sunday? That give you enough time to work?"

I wanted to say no. He was too confident, too sure. I didn't know this man. Just that he was a hockey player, had an ego the size of a hockey rink, and was a member of the country club that the firm's golf tournament was played at. I could guess at a lot more things.

Like, I doubted he'd ever worried about whether he'd be able to have his next meal. Or a bed. Or if he'd be robbed or worse if he fell asleep. He had the confidence of the privileged. Something I was working on. But I'd never forget my past, and that would always shape my future.

I needed to be able to fake some of that confidence. I had no idea why it amused him to offer to teach me to play golf, but I should take advantage. He might flake after, but it was a start.

There would be a price for this, because he wasn't asking out of the goodness of his heart. Everyone wanted something. I could go this once and find out. I'd at least get to see the place, even if I decided his price was too steep to do this again.

"Callie? Are you there?"

"Yes. I was thinking."

"Do you have to think that much about a golf lesson?" He was teasing, but this was serious.

"Going to this much effort for someone you don't know doesn't make sense."

He paused, recalibrating his plan of attack. "I told you, I need a date for the wedding."

"Still seems excessive."

Another pause, and then he laughed. "Yeah, you're

right. But you're not the one I'm trying to make pay. That make you feel better?"

I wasn't sure. "Is it going to jeopardize my position at the firm?"

"No, it's not going to hurt your job."

I wasn't sure he'd know if it would hurt my job, but Mr. Anderson had been impressed that Cooper talked to me. Pushing him like this instead of agreeing was probably too much my own insecurities talking, and not the smartest option. I could gamble on one lesson. "Okay, then. Sunday. What time should I be there?"

"Oh, no. That won't work. You're my guest, so I'll pick you up and drive you."

I didn't like the idea of not having my own transportation. But I didn't know all the rules of a country club, and I didn't drive. I doubted buses went up to the country club doors, and as exclusive as the place was, I'd never get in on my own. I had to set aside this defensiveness.

"I could meet you somewhere." Did I want him to know my home address? *No.*

"Uh uh. I need to make sure you look right."

What the hell? "What do you mean, look right?"

"Callie, I saw that dress. We can't have another disaster like that."

I drew in a breath, ready to tell him what he could do with his judgmental attitude, when I remembered Darcy's horrified reaction to it.

"What size do you wear?"

I looked around my office, hoping no one was close enough to hear even my side of this conversation. "That's none of your business."

"It is if you're my guest. Are you going to tell me your size, or do I have to guess?"

I sat up straight at my desk. "Don't worry. I'll find something appropriate to wear." And then I could have smacked myself. Where would I find the time to hunt down and shop for something to wear to an exclusive country club?

"If that's how you're going to play it, fine. Text me your address. I'll pick you up at seven."

Wait, what? "Seven in the morning?"

"Bring sunscreen." He hung up.

I stared at the phone for way too long, trying to process what had just happened. I was getting at least one golf lesson at the country club. That was good. No matter what happened after, I would have some valuable information.

But I was very suspicious of what was going to happen when Mr. Cooper showed up at my place on Sunday morning.

Thank goodness I had Darcy.

Chapter 5

That dress wasn't hiding any ugly

Callie

I gave Cooper the address of a nearby coffee shop to meet at. I was still suspicious—which could be a me issue—but this whole thing was odd. Hockey superstars didn't just offer this kind of help to random people. I wasn't a kid with cancer, or the guy who'd worked at the arena since he was sixteen. In case something went wrong today, I didn't want him to know where I lived.

As a manager at the movie theatre, Darcy's shifts were variable. He'd worked closing at the theater last night, but he still got up to make sure I would pass muster. We'd looked at some golf clothing online, and I'd ordered something to wear. It arrived yesterday, while I was at work, and when I tried it on, it didn't fit.

Clothing was a constant struggle with my figure. Too much bust, not enough of the rest. To get a top to fit around my breasts, what I'd ordered was so baggy that I looked like

I'd borrowed someone else's clothing, and the skirt was too short. So I'd scrambled in my closet to come up with something that would pass the club dress code.

Darcy frowned, but admitted it was a lot better than what I'd worn to the benefit. The skirt was long enough, even if it was a drab brown that didn't look like anything I'd seen on the Briarwood website, and there was a collar on the white polo shirt. It was a little grayish after a lot of washes, but no one could say the outfit was too loud. I ironed the skirt and shirt, so I should be good. My hair was pulled back in a ponytail, my moisturizer had SPF, and I'd packed a water bottle and more sunscreen, along with a visor and a sweater in a tote bag. Prepared for any eventuality.

To make sure I'd be ready on time, I'd set my alarm early, so I still had twenty minutes before I needed to head out to meet my golf pro.

I'd promised Darcy, again, that I'd use lots of sunscreen —I was about as pale as a human could get between freckles —when there was a knock on the door. I looked at him, in case he was expecting someone. He shrugged from where he was sprawled on the couch under a blanket and let me do the honors. Was it a neighbor complaining about something? This early?

I opened the door and froze. There was a big hockey player in the doorway, with a smirk on his face and a large shopping bag in his hand. Blond hair, blue eyes, and according to Darcy, awesome abs. None of which were supposed to be here, at my door.

"Cooper?" Had I missed something? I definitely wouldn't have invited him to the condo. Darcy sat up on the couch, eyes big with shock.

"Yep. Step back, we have work to do."

I did just that before I realized what I was doing, and he passed me, heading inside with a glance around. He spotted Darcy, hair disheveled, staring at Cooper like he was a ghost. A hot ghost. Darcy looked like he wasn't sure if he should scream or drool. I was thinking instead about slapping Cooper upside the head.

But I followed Cooper like a mindless sheep till I pulled myself together.

"Hi, I'm Cooper." He headed to Darcy as he spoke.

"I know." Darcy's eyes were even wider as he shook the hand Cooper held out, holding his blanket up like a blushing virgin in a Gothic horror story. Darcy was wearing a T-shirt and boxers, for fuck's sake. What did he think Cooper was going to do?

"And you are?"

None of your business. Before I could blurt that out, Darcy responded.

"I'm Darcy. Callie's roommate. I'm a fan."

"Of Callie's? Glad to hear that." Cooper's big smile was still on his face as he turned back to me. "Okay, Callie, let's get moving. We've got a tee time to make."

"How the hell did you find this condo? I didn't give you my address."

He shrugged. "When you bid on the silent auction at the benefit, they asked for some information, like an address."

"And they gave it to you?"

"I might have told them that I wanted to surprise you with flowers."

"You lied?"

"I'll send flowers. But not when you expect them. Surprise, remember?"

That had to violate some laws but what was I going to do? Mr. Hockey here wouldn't be the one hurt, and now he had my address. "I'm not happy about this, but it's obviously too late. Don't bother with the flowers."

I reached for my canvas bag, glad I was ready so I could get Cooper out of here.

I frowned at him so he knew I wasn't happy with him coming up to skooch me along. "I'm ready. I was just heading out for the coffee shop now, if you hadn't barged in here." I turned to my roommate. "Not sure when I'm back, Darce, so I'll probably see you tomorrow."

I felt a hand on my shoulder. I whipped back around, stepping away from that grip.

"You're not ready." Cooper held out the bag he was still holding. I recognized the name on it. A high-end sporting goods store. I hadn't even bothered looking at their website.

"What's that?" I was already frowning, but I upped the wattage.

"Clothes. You know, the stuff you put on over your naked body so that the country club lets you in."

Behind Cooper, Darcy put a hand over his mouth. I'd deal with Darcy later.

"Believe it or not, Cooper, I do understand what clothes are. In fact, I'm wearing clothing. And I checked and this meets the rules for your country club."

Cooper set the bag down on the coffee table and crossed his arms. "First, it's not my club." He shuddered. "Second, we're not just working on golf lessons, are we? We're learning how to fit in at the country club. And whatever that is you're wearing is not going to cut it. Truthfully, the cleaning staff wear better than that."

Darcy choked down a laugh. I turned to him with my best killer glare, while Cooper gave him a smile.

Cooper turned back to me. I don't know what he saw on my face, but his voice softened. "At this club, you don't just satisfy the rules. You'll be ever so politely run off even if you follow every rule that's written down because what you need is to follow the *unwritten* rules. You have to look like you belong there. Otherwise you might as well forget your golf tournament."

He stopped and ran his gaze up and down my body. I felt it, and I didn't like that. I stared back. I wanted to tell him what he could do with his country club and his rules and his bag of clothes and his judgment. It would feel really good. But I'd learned a long time ago that indulging in what felt good didn't get me anywhere. I needed to use my head. And my head told me that the guy was probably right. Ego big enough to need its own postal code, but still, right.

I shot another look at Darcy. He nodded.

"Fine." I didn't ask what was wrong with what I had on, because Cooper was just waiting to tell me. And as much as I wanted to learn, I didn't want to hear him tear apart my choices. "What did you bring?"

He picked up the bag again and passed it to me.

"I guessed on size, but golf skirts and tops, and a couple of dresses."

"Dresses?" I needed a dress? What the hell for?

"For the dining room."

I stopped myself before I repeated *dining room*, since he'd probably tell me it was a room where people sat down to eat. "I didn't know we were going to be there for a meal."

He shrugged. "Part of the country club lessons."

The man was infuriating, and way too sure of himself. But again, my head kept my temper in check. The golf lessons I could get elsewhere, and I would definitely look something up after today. But being familiar with the clubhouse, and the dining room, and what was expected there was something I couldn't take lessons for. He was right.

"Receipt in the bag?" Because I was damn well going to pay for my own clothes.

"Receipt?"

I took my opening. "The piece of paper they give you when you buy something, listing the items and prices. I can pay for my clothes." The corner of his mouth curved up and I wasn't going to like what he was going to say. But I would fight him for the right to pay for anything I wore.

"I don't have a receipt."

"What did you do with it?"

"Nothing. They don't charge me."

This made no sense. "What do you mean, they don't charge you?"

"They're one of my sponsors. When I tell them I want something, they just send it over."

My mouth fell open and I knew I looked shocked, but this...this was not anything I was familiar with. "They just give you stuff?" I heard my voice, high and squeaky. The tax issues that would cause...

"That's cool."

I turned my glare to Darcy, who at least lived in the same universe as I did. "It's not cool, it's—" I couldn't finish the sentence. Not without sounding priggish or stupid.

Darcy grinned at me. "It is cool, but go on, get dressed." He dropped the smile, mirroring Cooper. "You have a tee time, Cal."

I gave him my middle finger, then picked up the bag and went to my room. I might have flounced.

Once there, I set the bag on my bed and looked inside to see what Mr. Cool had asked for. The fabrics felt silky in my hands as I pulled them out.

A top, with a logo on the pocket, in a buttery yellow color. In two sizes. Skorts, in a green and yellow pattern. A matching sweater. Three dresses, two in different sizes of the same copper color, one in green.

Ha! I knew green was my color.

I looked for tags, to find out how much this stuff cost so I could repay someone for it. But there were no price tags. Nothing but the care and washing instructions. Not even a bit of plastic or a stretched-out hole from where a tag had been pulled off. Expensive, but to find out how expensive, I'd have to look online or go to the store. I tried to imagine walking in with cash and asking for a manager to give the money to. No, that wasn't going to work. I'd have to come up with something else.

I tried on the first copper dress and went into the en suite to see how it looked. It fit, which was the first shocker. And it flattered me. I wasn't good at clothes and fashion shit, but even I could see that I looked...well, more like women did who cared about how they looked. I sniffed.

The first top was too small. The second fit perfectly. When I pulled on the matching skort and checked the mirror...again, it looked good. Not just that the colors were nice and the fit was right. It looked like something rich people would wear. This I could wear to the golf tournament, and I'd look like everyone else. Well, not the shoes, but I'd buy some.

I carefully folded up the copper dress to put in my tote bag—for the *dining* room—and returned everything else to the shopping bag. I'd repay Cooper somehow, but for now I could be gracious and take advantage of this opportunity. Even if it killed me.

I opened my door and stepped out, only to hear the two guys slagging on my dress. The one from the charity dinner.

"I didn't see her before she left, or I'd never have let her walk out in that."

Oh, was that so, Darcy? How were you going to stop me?

"I spent the whole night fixated on that ugly piece of shit. How did she end up with something like that?"

I blinked back unexpected tears and marched out to shut them up. "I looked for the most horrible dress I could find just to get your attention, *Cooper*. Would have hated for you two not to have something to gossip about. Feel better now?"

Darcy's cheeks flushed. "Sorry, Cal, but you're hopeless with that stuff, and you didn't let me help you."

I ignored him. I didn't need him making me look even more hopeless in front of Mr. "they give me stuff" Hockey Player.

I looked at Cooper, finally, noticing that he also looked a little embarrassed. *Good.* "We have a tee time?"

"Right. Nice to meet you, Darcy."

I picked up my tote and then stalked to the door, Cooper following closely. I didn't wait for him to open it, just pulled it back and marched through. I heard it close as he followed me down the hallway.

"I'm sorry, Callie. I didn't mean to insult you."

I whipped around. "Then tell me what you *did* mean to do."

He stood, saying nothing for a moment. "Okay, I'm sorry that I insulted you. Clothing is a thing of mine. It frustrates me when someone doesn't take advantage of what they wear to make themselves look good."

"Looking good is not the primary goal of life."

"Sure, but it can smooth things over."

"Or hide ugly things below."

He let his gaze drop, slowly moving down my body and

back up again. And this time too, swear to god, I could feel it like a touch. Then the smirk was back on his face. "That dress wasn't hiding any ugly."

I felt my cheeks warming and turned for the elevator without responding.

Chapter 6

Define sports

COOPER

CALLIE WAS one of those people I just didn't understand. It wasn't that hard to use clothing to enhance your looks and positively affect how people interacted with you. Sure, my career in hockey was about a million miles from Callie and her law firm. But I grew up with lawyers. My family was as obsessed with their appearance as anyone. Presentation was important in court or a law office. Especially if you were hoping to make partner.

Watching her stalk down the hallway ahead of me proved my point. In these clothes, she carried herself like someone successful. I'd been right that she had a good figure under that fucking ugly dress. She wouldn't want the girls spilling out at work, but at parties like we'd been at the other night? That was a time to put on a show.

Not what I needed to focus on now. These clothes looked good on her and would fit right in at the club. Except for the shoes, but I had some pairs in the car for her.

She didn't say anything as the elevator took us down to the lobby. I let her walk out first and followed her through the doors. She stopped, her head turning as she checked out the cars parked in front of her building. I led the way to my Bentley, chirping the lock and opening the passenger door for her.

That little frown was between her brows again.

"Not what you were expecting?"

She moved her gaze to me. "Not exactly."

I smirked, probably annoying her, but it was fun, upending her expectations. "Disappointed it's not a Ferrari?"

She shrugged. "Just surprised."

She slid inside and I moved around the car to the driver's side. I wasn't telling her, but I had exactly the car she'd expected, and it was in the other parking stall at my condo. I'd put two sets of clubs in the trunk of this one, and that wasn't something I could do with the Ferrari. Plus, driving it to the country club was an asshole move. I didn't need to impress anyone or compensate for my cock size. I had the Ferrari because it was a blast to drive.

And yeah, it was part of the image.

I turned on the car and checked the mirrors before pulling out. "I wasn't sure what your shoe size was."

She shot me a glance. I jerked my head at the back seat before changing lanes.

Her head whipped around. I had a few pairs of shoes there, in different sizes. Again, something the sponsor had sent over. She turned her glare on me. "I prefer to get my own things."

I checked her from the corner of my eye, and then turned my attention back to my driving. What was her issue? I hadn't paid for these, and even if I had, it wasn't like

I couldn't afford it. Was it a pride thing? Was she afraid I would make assumptions if she took things from me? "No expectations, Calliope."

She let out a breath and crossed her arms. "I don't want you to give me things. I'll get my own."

Okay, if that was what she wanted. But there was no way I would take her to the country club in what she'd been wearing, or anything like that ugly dress. "Here's the problem with that."

She upped the glare with a frown. Someone was used to getting her own way.

"You want to fit in at the club like the members, not have them decide you don't belong. And so far you're failing that one big-time."

I was pretty sure she growled. My eyebrows shot up. I could imagine that sound in another context, and hell if this was the time for those kinds of thoughts.

Her voice was precise and icy. "I focused on important things. I dress appropriately for whatever situation I'm in, but I'm not going to spend all my time and money trying to impress people."

Sadly, she believed that. "You picked the wrong career, then."

I caught a glimpse of her as she turned to me. Her cheeks were flushed and her eyes lit up. Calliope had passion buried underneath her sensible outer layer, and I liked igniting it.

"Do you really think the Canada Revenue Agency gives a shit what my clothes look like when I'm arguing a filing with them?"

"CRA isn't a person, Callie." There was that growly sound again. I held in my grin.

"But I deal with *people* who work for CRA, and when

they're reading something I wrote, I don't include a photo of an expensive suit to impress them."

I understood her point, but she was ignoring that appearances did matter. If she spent her whole life working remotely, then sure, no one would see her or care what she wore. But she worked in an office. She wanted to go to a golf tournament and make partner. That meant people would see her and judge her. She needed to up her game for that. "Why did your asshole buddy at the dinner last weekend think you couldn't fit in with this golf tournament your firm is hosting?"

There was a pause. No growl. I stole another glance, and her mouth was pressed tight, and she was staring out the window.

Damn. I didn't want to be like Benson. But she had to admit she needed help before I could do that. "Callie, you might find clothing and shoes and all that shit superficial. You might find it intimidating. But if you're going to be in court, or your office, or impress other people at events, all that superficial shit matters."

I took one hand off the wheel to point to myself.

"That's something I'm good at." I'd grown up with it. "And I like to make people look good. I work on my teammates all the time. I don't know if you noticed Hunter the other night, but he desperately needs help or he dresses all wrong. Even that guy, Benson? Wrong shirt color."

Callie turned to me when she heard that. Her lush lips were no longer pressed tightly together.

"Think of this as another tool you need. I am very good with this tool."

This time I heard a snort.

Glad she was feeling better and taking me up on that comment. "I get that you want to pay for your own stuff.

Fine. I'll let you do that from now on. But if you really want to be seen as partner material, I can help you choose the right clothing for the job."

"I get it, Cooper. I just...this isn't something I'm good at. If you are willing to advise me, I will listen to you. But I buy my own stuff."

I could live with that. But another question nagged at me. Callie was smart. Probably brilliant, if she was doing the kind of law that dealt with the tax department. She would get paid a lot for that. But why was her goal to become a partner when the whole "dealing with people" part that was so essential seemed to be something she hated? "Why do you want to be partner anyway?"

The lawyers I'd known who were partners, or wanted to be, were all ambitious, greedy, competitive. I didn't really know Callie, but she didn't throw off that vibe. Ambitious, yeah. But not greedy and competitive, not that I'd seen.

She was looking out the window again. "I deserve it. I've earned it."

Ah. Something was behind it that she didn't want to share. And since I wasn't an asshole, I didn't ask her any more. Instead, I turned on some music and changed the topic.

"So, Callie, why don't you tell me a little bit about yourself." Damn it, I sounded like I was starting a job interview.

She turned to me, eyebrows raised.

I shrugged. "I don't know anything about you. Probably should."

"I don't know anything about you. Well, except that you play hockey and have strong opinions on clothes."

I held in my grin, but I preferred her sassing back rather than making me feel like a shit. "I know you're a lawyer and have terrible taste in clothes. I think it might be good to be a little more familiar with each other before we meet other people."

A frown. "Why?"

"Because we should at least look like we're friends. I mean, I've invited you to Briarwood. No one needs to know that I'm giving you golf lessons to impress Benson or the partners you work for. So, for example, are you married?"

"No. Never married, never want to be. You?"

I grinned at her. "Never have been, never plan to be. Who's Darcy?"

"My roommate. We're friends."

I hadn't thought they were anything else. Unless I was very wrong, Darcy was gay. "Okay, I don't have a roommate."

"I would have guessed you didn't."

I wasn't sure what she meant by that. But I didn't want to know why, so I moved on. "Where are you from?"

"Toronto. Grew up here, never went anywhere."

I wanted to ask why. But I didn't want her to give me grief over my privileged upbringing or current circumstances. I knew, based on the clothes, the lack of golf experience, and her attitude, that she hadn't grown up with money. I had, and I had it now, and I didn't need to justify it.

She was waiting for me to respond. I'd let her ask.

She huffed. "Okay, where are you from?"

"Family's in Connecticut. Went to university in Burlington, drafted by the Toronto Blaze, been here ever since." I didn't say I'd never been anywhere, because I'd been a lot of places.

"Did you want to come to the Toronto area?"

She was curious. *Good.* "No."

"Afraid of the weather?" She had that patronizing attitude that people who lived with "real winters" could get about anyone they thought enjoyed a soft life in the warm.

"Don't you know your geography? Vermont is farther north than Toronto and gets hella worse winters."

Her mouth made an O. "Oh, Burlington, Vermont. You're right. That would be pretty wintery."

It wasn't like even Connecticut was the balmy tropics. "My turn. Do you play any sports?"

"Define sports."

I checked that she was serious. She was. God help me, she was one of those. "Do you do anything that makes you sweat?"

"Interesting definition. I run, but it's not a team thing."

Yeah, she wasn't a team person. She wouldn't be doing any March Madness brackets with her coworkers. "How much do you run?" It would be nice to have some idea of her fitness level. Not that golf was likely to put her in danger of a heart attack, but I didn't usually bother with a cart.

"Three miles. About half an hour."

"How often?"

She did that growly thing again. "How long do *you* run, and how often?"

"You do remember that I'm a professional athlete, right?"

"Are you avoiding the question?"

"I normally run five miles a day, but can do ten or so, if needed. Shall we compare our speed now?" I let my foot off the gas. "Maybe you want to grab a pair of shoes now."

She gasped. "Is this the place?"

The gates for Briarwood were ahead of us. "Yep, this is the place."

"Holy fucking shit."

Chapter 7

The theory of hockey

CALLIE

THE WEBSITE DIDN'T DO it justice. The place was... incredible. Like something out of a movie about billionaires and princesses and people I'd never hang out with in a million years.

There were those white fences, the kind they used for horse farms, around the greenest grass I'd ever seen. It would cost a fortune to keep grass that verdant, and probably leave a carbon footprint the size of Bigfoot, but there was no denying it was beautiful.

Sheltered in a shallow hollow, the clubhouse nestled like it had grown there. A long, low building, with colorful flowers and mature trees. There were big windows, all glistening in the early morning sunlight.

Cooper turned his luxury vehicle down the drive of paving stones. We passed parked vehicles, all expensive—I might have seen a Rolls Royce emblem. *Holy shit.*

We pulled up at a valet stand, because of course we did.

A young man opened my door and I stood up, grateful I wasn't getting out of one of those low-slung sports cars where I'd have to climb upward and risk flashing the poor kid.

"Nice to see you back, Mr. Cooper."

"Nice to see you too, Brad. Just let me get the clubs from the trunk."

"Are any of your teammates coming today, sir?"

"No, it's just me and Callie. Callie Smith, this is Brad, my favorite valet here at Briarwood."

The kid blushed. "Nice to meet you, Ms. Smith."

If we were anywhere else, I'd tell him to call me Callie, but was that a faux pas here? He'd called Cooper *Mr. Cooper*. Was Cooper the man's last name? I should know that.

I waited, awkward and out of place. This club set off my nerves more than any place I'd been in years. I didn't normally worry about fitting in—I'd never fit in, so I mostly tried to stay in the background, not draw attention, and watch everyone else. Then I did whatever they did. Made sure I was so good at what people needed from me that they overlooked my...me-ness.

But this wasn't the office, where I could make value for myself with hard work. This place was all about appearances and connections. The stuff I failed at. I absolutely did not know the rules at this place. Reading a dress code on the website didn't even touch the things I needed to know to fit in around here.

Cooper hefted two bags of clubs out of the trunk. Should I help? Did women around here strive to be equal, or was this a polite gesture I should accept? There was so much I could mess up.

Brad slid into the car and pulled away. I stepped in

front of Cooper, blocking his path. "I need you to be brutally honest with me."

One eyebrow shot up. *Nice trick.*

"I don't want to embarrass you. Or myself. And I will, so you have to tell me when I do the wrong thing."

Now the eyebrows were both pulled down, frowning. "Callie, you're not going to embarrass me."

I huffed a breath. "Yes, I will. I'd have made us both look bad in what I was wearing before. I just...I don't know what I don't know."

He was still frowning. Shouldn't he look less attractive that way?

"Like, if I walk on the wrong grass will I be kicked out?" I smiled at him, trying to reassure him. It was weird to see the man without that cocky attitude.

"Callie, I'm sorry, I didn't mean to—"

I held up my hand. "No, I'd rather you told the truth. I don't want to make mistakes, and I will if you try to sugar-coat things. Other people will judge me, I know that. Please help me avoid that." I hadn't liked it, the way he'd over-ridden me about the clothes, but I got it now.

He rubbed his hand over his face. "What you were wearing would have made you uncomfortable here, because people would have stared and talked. Me? I'm expected to be a little 'unconventional' but I'll be on my best behavior today so that it doesn't reflect on you."

That made me blink, and something inside me warmed. There was no way this guy would reflect poorly on me, but he was putting me at ease. And something in the way he said that... Had someone told him he had been an embarrassment?

"For the most part, just follow my lead, and I'll let you know if you're doing anything that's a problem."

"Thank you. I'm not here to get my ego stroked. I'm here to learn."

He cocked his head, still looking at me, and I wasn't sure what he was thinking. Maybe the women he was with normally were upset if he criticized them? They probably already knew this stuff. Not me. If something went wrong today with Hockey Stud and me, I might not get back here before our corporate event in September. And in that case, I needed to understand everything I could about this place.

"Okay, let's go." He started walking toward a smaller extension on the side of the building.

I scurried after him. "Should I carry one of those bags?" One set of clubs looked spotless, new, and my skin itched at the thought they might have been sent over for him like the clothes. But I kept my mouth shut. I'd learned early that I couldn't afford pride. Why had I been so upset back at the condo? Actually, maybe I didn't want to know.

We went into the pro shop. It was full of clothes, clubs, and other things that presumably helped with golfing, but I had no clue what they were. Everything was clean, tidy, and smelled of new and rich. More expensive materials and packing? An accumulated miasma of expensive colognes and perfumes? I didn't know, just that it was a rich smell.

Cooper was greeted by almost everyone in the shop. He was polite and charming and didn't flinch when people mentioned that the team lost their championship. But I watched him, the way I watched people to try to fit in. And something—a crease around his eyes, a slight rigidity with his smile—made me think he wasn't as unbothered as he seemed to be.

I was paying more attention to the people around Cooper and how he responded than what he was actually doing, so I didn't realize until he left the building, me trailing along behind him, that we weren't headed to the greens. We took a path to a fenced-in field. Well, the netting on the fences rose about two stories high. The grass was gorgeous, like the rest of the property, but there were markers, and some golf balls scattered around.

"Okay, I don't know golf, but this doesn't look like what I've seen on TV or in movies."

He dropped the bags of clubs. "This is the driving range."

I squinted my eyes at him. Since we were both wearing sunglasses, I wasn't sure he could see. "You said we had a tee time."

He shrugged. "Saying we had a practice time didn't have the same flair."

"I thought we were preparing for the tournament in September."

He pulled out a club, swung it in his hands and let it rest on the grass. "You've never golfed before, correct?"

"Correct." I crossed my arms.

"Do you have any idea how to swing a club?"

I stared at the club he was holding. The theory seemed pretty simple. Hold it, swing back, and whack the ball. Then again, the theory of hockey seemed simple—get on skates and hit a puck with a stick. I couldn't do that. Some professional golfers made a scandalous amount of money, so obviously not everyone could do this either.

"But if we were swinging it out there"—I waved a hand toward where the other people were moving around —"I'd be learning that part as well as how to swing a golf club."

"And you'd be distracted, watching everyone like you were back in the pro room, while also trying to figure out how to handle your club. As well, you'd take a long time and hold people up, which you really don't want to do if you can help it."

I considered. "How long am I going to look stupid?"

He shook his head. "Not stupid, but you're going to look like you don't know what you're doing."

I'd hoped to do the real golfing thing in case this was the only time I got to Briarwood. But what he said sounded logical. And if I was going to do something embarrassing, better here where it was just the two of us. "Okay, if this is how learning golf goes."

He looked down at the grass, and back to me. "I haven't actually taught anyone how to play, but I googled some shit. I thought you could learn how to stand and swing while we work on the long game."

"Long game. That's shooting the ball far."

He grinned. "There's that sharp legal mind." I was tempted to flip him off, but that would probably be a no-no. "When you tee off, you want to move the ball a long way, so we'll work on that first."

I shrugged. Made sense.

He pulled a tee from his pocket and pushed it into the grass. Then he passed me the club he'd been playing with. "I guessed on some clubs for you based on your height. This is a driver, so we're starting with it. It's meant for distance."

I took it gingerly. "So I use this and hit the ball as hard as I can?" I eyed the fenced field. At least there wasn't any risk to other people if I didn't hit it straight.

He didn't grin, but it was close. "Let's see how that goes."

Next thing he'd pulled a golf ball out of somewhere and bent to place it on the tee, pants stretching over his muscled thighs. He stepped back. I stared at him, golf club dangling from my hand.

"Go ahead."

"Aren't you going to tell me how I'm supposed to do this? How to hold the club and stand and whatever?"

"I thought I'd see what your natural swing looks like."

I didn't have a natural swing. I didn't have an unnatural one. The only swing I had was with a broom.

I shuffled up to the tee, the ball resting on it. I held the club in my hands, checking that the big head would hit the ball. I looked over the grass where I hoped it would go. It seemed pretty straightforward.

How did those golfers on TV do it? I'd only seen them while I was channel surfing, so I didn't have much idea, but I lifted the club behind me and brought it down hard. It smacked the earth behind the tee, the ball untouched.

I jerked my head sideways to get Cooper's reaction. Again, I couldn't see his eyes behind his sunglasses. But his mouth—the corners were twitching.

Okay, I needed to shorten the length so when the club moved to the tee it didn't hit the grass first. I adjusted my grip and tried again, this time catching just the top of the ball and knocking it off the tee to roll by my feet. I knelt down to pick up the ball and put it back on the tee. I didn't look at Cooper again—he wasn't offering advice. I adjusted the length of the club in my hands and took another swing. I did hit the ball, but it went up and sideways, and I jumped out of the way.

I huffed. "Aren't you supposed to be teaching me?"

"Figured you'd want to try it for yourself first."

He had a point, but I didn't have to admit it. "Well, I obviously am doing something wrong."

He nodded. "Watch me."

He pulled a club out of the other bag and crossed over to the tee. I moved several feet away, where I was out of range of his swing and where I could get a good look at how he moved. He stopped in place, shirt stretched over broad shoulders and his hands sure on the club. He shuffled his feet a bit, adjusted his grip, swung back. And next thing the golf ball was sailing straight down the...green? Fairway? Range? *Whatever*.

His motions were smooth, graceful, and controlled, and a familiar wave of inferiority swept over me. I would never be able to do that. But I shoved my chin higher. And when he stepped away, I took my place at the tee, where he'd set up another ball, and tried again.

And again. No matter how I tried to recreate his smooth and effective swing, I missed the tee or chipped the ball too high, or too far sideways.

Throwing the club across the grass would have been satisfying but wouldn't help. Cooper was still standing there, calm and patient.

"So teach me!"

A smile crossed his face, bringing out the dimples and adding charm to his already lethal good looks. I was too frustrated for that charm to affect me. "Now you're ready."

I almost growled.

"I'm going to have to touch you, put my arms around you to show you how you're supposed to do this. It's not a move. You understand why I have to do it?"

I wasn't sure it wasn't still a move, but he was right that I'd have resisted his attempt to do that earlier. All I had to do was imagine Benson sneering to give in.

"Right. Show me."

Chapter 8

I didn't die from it

COOPER

SHE WAS STIFFER than the driver. To reassure her, I was as professional as possible, wrapping my arms around her slowly and gently. I had to wonder what had happened in her life to make her react this way. Her body was lush curves and her citrus shampoo tickled my nose. Tempting, but I reminded myself to focus. *Professional!*

"Try to relax."

She huffed but dropped her shoulders, only to tense them up again when I moved. She couldn't let go. After a few aborted attempts, I came up with something different.

"Okay, I have another idea." I stepped back and her posture relaxed. "You put your arms around me and I'll swing the club. Maybe that way you can get a feel for the motion without tensing up."

She bit her lip. "I'm really not trying to make this more difficult."

I shrugged. "Everyone learns differently." I grabbed my

club and positioned myself in front of the tee. I looked over at her, still biting her lip.

"Do people learn like this?"

I grinned. "I've never seen anyone do it, but maybe I can start a new school of golf. I'll earn a fortune."

She shook her head, and I knew her eyes were rolling behind those big sunglasses. But she dropped her club and wrapped her arms around me.

At first, she barely touched me. "That's not going to work. You need to feel how my body moves. I trust you not to take advantage." A joke to loosen her up. But Callie reacted differently.

"Do people do that to you?"

Of course they did. Part of the job. I was the face of the team, so people thought they knew me, and made assumptions—about what I wanted and what I'd allow. "I can handle it."

I heard her mutter that no one should have to, but she moved closer, pressing against my back and putting her hands over mine where they held the club.

It was hella awkward trying to swing with Callie enfolding me like a coat, but I focused, telling her what I was doing as I moved.

One golf ball sailed down the range. Callie backed away and returned with another ball, passing it to me, and once I had it resting on the tee, she wrapped herself around me again.

The feeling of those full tits pressed against my back was a distraction. It felt good, and since golf had never been a passion of mine, I was more interested in Callie's body than the swing I was supposed to be demonstrating.

I swung again, and felt her moving with me. Less tension, less resistance.

She passed me another ball. This time, as we moved together, she was anticipating what to do. When her defenses dropped, her mind picked things up quickly.

I heard voices and stepped away from her. What we were doing was pretty unorthodox, and I didn't want anyone remembering this if they came across Callie again. With that vivid orange hair, the freckles covering her skin, and those tits, she was memorable.

"You ready to try again?"

She turned her head, noticing the men setting up a few places over. "Okay. I think I have a better idea of what to do now."

She dropped a ball on the tee and stood beside it. "This where I should stand?"

I squinted at her feet. "Spread a little more." She did that. "Give it a try."

Her face was set in lines of concentration, and I could almost see the instructions she was reviewing in her head. She nodded to herself and swung the club back. She let it swing by the tee, checking how it moved. Already she was doing much better. Then she swung back again, and brought it down, hard. The head of the club met the ball, and it sliced forward. Not too far, but it went in the right direction.

A smile split her face, and I grinned too. "Good job."

She nodded. "Okay, now what did I do wrong?"

"What do you mean? That was a good shot."

She cocked her head. "I hit it as hard as I could, but it didn't go that far. So what did I do wrong?"

I shook my head. "There are a couple of things you could refine."

"I don't need you to sweeten it up. Just tell me."

"You're not gripping the club right."

"So show me."

And I did.

Callie was never going to fool anyone into thinking she could have gone pro. Being a tax lawyer? Yeah, that took brains, and she had that. But she didn't have muscle smarts. Her coordination was average, and her balance and vision were only so-so. Pretty well what I'd expected.

She was determined though. If she'd had any talent at all, that determination would have helped her get a long way. It probably drove her through law school at the top of her class. With enough practice, she'd survive her company's golf tournament. Not with a low score, but she wouldn't be an embarrassment to herself.

By the time we had to call it quits on the lesson, she looked like she'd been through a workout. Tendrils of hair were coming out of her ponytail and her face was flushed. I didn't know if that was from exertion or the sun—she'd put on sunscreen, but she was also really pale.

"Ready to eat?" So far our lessons today had been all about the sport, not the behavioral aspects that didn't have rules to follow.

She looked back at the building, chewing her lip. "This would be the country club part of the lessons, right?'

If she was too tired or wanted to wait to try this next time, we could do that. It wasn't like being on display here was my favorite pastime. "This part is all brains, no muscles. But if you've had enough for today, we can grab something to eat back in the city."

She shook her head, jaw set. "I don't have a lot of time, so let's eat here." Her chin went up again. "What's wrong with me?"

Other than wanting to be part of this pretentious, elitist cult? "What's wrong with you?"

She looked down at her clothes and then back up at me. "Is there anything I need to fix? I have to comb my hair. Should I change to that dress?"

A chivalrous instinct hit me to assure her she was fine. That had been ingrained in me. Be polite, be charming, make the other person feel good. But she didn't want that. She wasn't arrogant, but she had some kind of inner strength that could take the truth and not flinch. "Your hair is a mess. And your face is flushed."

"I can fix the hair. I have makeup in my bag. If I take care of that and put on the dress, will that be enough?"

I picked up the bags with the mostly unused clubs. "Dress would be better than what you're wearing. Men don't usually change, but the women do. There are locker rooms just inside. Let's go."

* * *

I put our clubs in a locker, greeting some more people we met on the way. I could see speculation about the woman with me, but I didn't pause for chitchat. I steered Callie toward the women's section and promised to meet her outside when she was ready.

I took a quick trip to the men's myself, checking that I was still looking good. Since the most effort I'd exerted had been to refrain from laughing at Callie, I was fine. I waited in the hallway, not sure how long she would take. Some of the women I'd been with invested a lot of time in their appearance. I pulled out my phone, in case something had come up while we were out shooting balls.

There was a message for me in the family wedding chat. I didn't want to look at it, but if I didn't respond, my sister or mother was likely to call.

We're planning the bachelor party for the weekend before the wedding.

It was my brother. Of course his primary involvement was in the bachelor party. Something I really wanted to miss. He continued.

You don't have anything to do till after, so you can help with that.

My family chose to believe that my career involved nothing but showing up at the rink for three hours on game days. After all, I played hockey. And right now it was the offseason, so I wasn't even doing that.

I'll check my schedule.

I didn't want to commit to anything before I had a chance to get out of it.

What schedule?

Dealing with my brother was enough to ruin my day, but I knew how to do the same to him.

I may be doing another photo shoot.

Nothing bothered my family more than the underwear campaigns I'd done. I used to keep a map, pinpointing the places my family would be exposed to those. I got to be petty *and* make a shitload of money, so it was a win-win for me. It was also something that would shut my brother up, at least temporarily. I didn't have anything scheduled with them this summer, but I did have commitments to other sponsors and I needed to check those dates.

You still trying to get attention by posing naked for everyone to see?

I don't try. I do.

You're a spoiled brat.

No, I wasn't spoiled. At least, only by money. I turned the phone off before my mood tanked. I'd find something to keep me busy until I had to go back for the wedding. I should just tell him to fuck off. I'd do my duty, but the less time I spent with my brother, the better.

Just in time, Callie came out. I shouldn't be surprised that she was quick, but she was also startlingly efficient. She was wearing one of the dresses I'd asked for and had brushed her hair. For the first time, I saw it down. The color was still bright orangey-red, but it was thick and wavy, resting just below her shoulders, softening her face and bringing attention to her hazel eyes. Her makeup was discreet and minimal, but effective. Plus, the dress was absolutely the right color and fit and made her look good. Really good.

She met my eyes, brows raised. "Will this pass?"

It was exactly the way she'd asked about her golf swing. She didn't want a compliment, just reassurance. "More than pass. You look like you belong here."

And she smiled. Hell, when she smiled like that, it packed a wallop.

* * *

CALLIE

"MORE THAN PASS. *You look like you belong here.*"

I grinned, enjoying his praise. Till he spoke again.

"I was right about that dress, wasn't I?"

I rolled my eyes. "Yes, the dress is very flattering." I straightened my spine. "So, now are we ready for the dining room?"

The golf part was straightforward. Sticks—no, *clubs*—balls, and walking around on the grass. Presumably we'd get to that. I wanted to keep this arrangement going if I could, because it was invaluable to me. There were rules I could memorize for actually hitting the ball, but social events didn't have straightforward rules, and they weren't codified. If I was going to be a partner, I had to learn how to play that game. Not that I expected I'd be very good at golf, but if I didn't do anything spectacularly stupid, I'd just be a not-so-good golfer. Messing up the social game could leave me ostracized.

Cooper put a hand on my back to guide me and I almost flinched. His hand was warm and big and possessive. Unfamiliar, and not something to get accustomed to. Instead of heading to the dining room, he found a corner out of the way and stepped back. "Are you sure about this? You look like I'm taking you to dine with zombies."

I crossed my arms, but that just brought more attention to my boobs, so I uncrossed them again. Damn it, I was so nervous. "I'm not good at this. Which utensil to use and when it's okay to sit or eat or whatever. You can check out videos and books, but there's so much—who you can talk to and what you shouldn't say."

Growing up, I'd had other priorities, things like food and clothing and a safe place to sleep. At school, I'd learned I was smart. Once I stopped trying to find someone to love me, education had been my focus. Getting good grades, so I could make good money. Social skills, friends—none of that had been as important as surviving. And I'd done that. I was playing catch-up on the people stuff, and it wasn't easy.

"I can tell people I haven't played golf," I said, "and they'll make some allowances. Give me tips, or well, just not care because not everyone plays sports. But I can't tell people I've never eaten. Obviously, I have. All my life. I just haven't learned the right way for places like this." I waved my hand to indicate the clubhouse. As Benson had made all too clear, this part was important. This was more than knowing what fork to use. I pursed my lips together. Enough word vomit.

Cooper didn't laugh, or sneer. "I grew up in places like this, but I never liked the way people used manners as a weapon. I'll make sure you do it right. Can you trust me for that?"

I bit my lip. Could I?

So far, he'd kept up his end of the deal perfectly. He hadn't been handsy while trying to get me to swing the club properly. He hadn't focused all his attention on my breasts. And if I did something wrong in the dining room? Well, I'd been embarrassed before. I didn't die from it.

I drew in a long breath after that mental pep talk and nodded. He held out his arm. After a moment, I realized what he was doing. My cheeks heated as I set my hand on it. I'd seen people do this in movies for fancy balls, but I'd never been in a situation that called for it. I let him guide me, keeping a close eye on everything around me.

There was a host. The way his eyes ran over us, he was checking to make sure we belonged. Cooper gave his name, and the guy nodded. We passed. No, I passed. Cooper had already been through this.

As the man led us to our seats. I noticed people watching. Cooper, not me. He was the celebrity. My shoulders relaxed. If they weren't looking at me, then I wasn't sticking out enough to distract them from the hockey player. So far, so good.

The table the gatekeeper led us to was in the center of the room. Even among these rich and powerful people, Cooper was someone. The club was flaunting his presence. Did he notice? His eyes followed mine, flicked to the watchers, and his warm expression was replaced by a pleasant mask as he pretended to ignore the eyes. Like in the pro shop. He had a public persona, one that was different from the guy I saw when it was just the two of us.

He didn't like this. Which meant I was even more in his debt.

A waiter held out my chair, and we did that awkward shuffle as he pushed it in. The first time I'd been in the kind of restaurant where it happened, I'd almost wrestled the guy for my chair. Now I knew better. But just when I thought I was safe, he picked up my napkin and put it on my fucking lap. I jerked away, hands fisting, before he did the same to Cooper.

It took me a moment to calm down. I'd almost flipped out there. Rich people, not worrying if someone got in their personal space. I had to remember the napkin move was a thing. I reached in my bag for my phone to take notes. Cooper's hand landed on mine. I shot my glance up.

"No phones." He barely moved his lips, his voice almost a whisper.

I dropped the phone into my bag, and the bag at my feet. I looked around, checking the other tables. I didn't see any phones. *Shit.*

"Seriously?" I hissed.

A corner of his mouth quirked up, his expression relaxing. "You wanted to know how to fit in here."

My shoulders dropped. "How am I supposed to take notes?"

The grin faded from his face. "You're not supposed to take notes. You're supposed to learn this from the time you're in diapers."

Of course. And I didn't. "Like you did?"

That expression on his face, was it mocking? Mocking himself, not me. "I did."

I nodded.

"Okay. Do you drink?"

"Yes. I don't know much about wine, and I hate gin." My mother had loved it.

Cooper turned to another waiter who approached the table. He ordered a Briarwood lemonade and some kind of beer I wasn't familiar with. I'd learned to drink with cheap beer, but I'd never gotten into all the crafty types that Darcy liked.

After the guy left us with menus, I leaned forward. "Is the beer for you?"

He nodded. *Good.*

The lemonade must have alcohol in it, but as long as it wasn't gin, I'd be okay. I hoped. I leaned back to look at the menu. I'd just opened it when I felt Cooper kicking my shin.

I sat up, dropping the menu in front of me in case I wasn't supposed to read it yet. "What is it?"

"Sit up straight."

I glanced around. Everyone was sitting upright. *Heaven forbid we be comfortable.*

I sat up, making sure my back was straight.

"And don't cross your legs. Ankles if you must."

My jaw dropped and Cooper leaned over, a finger on my chin, closing my mouth.

"Why the hell would anyone want to belong to a place like this?" I asked softly, checking that the waiter wasn't sneaking up on us.

"How else could you ensure you weren't eating with someone who crossed their legs?"

It was a stupid answer, but it had been a stupid question. It was all about being exclusive. Setting up rules to identify and keep out anyone different. Someone like me. I needed to bluff my way through until I was a partner.

I opened the menu, making sure I wasn't the least bit comfortable. Sitting up like this meant I had to hold the menu away from my boobs. I forgot about that once I started to read—the prices made my eyes widen. "I'm paying for the meal." Cooper might have provided the clothes in a way that meant I couldn't repay him, and this club wouldn't take my money for lessons even if I offered, but this I could do.

Or not. Cooper was shaking his head. "You don't do anything as plebian as pay at the end of the meal here, Calliope."

I squinted at the use of my full name. "Then why are there prices?"

"It goes on your member account." Which meant Cooper's account.

Okay, they might not let me use my phone, but I would memorize the prices of our meals and force that much money on Cooper. But I didn't know the prices of the drinks. I'd take the most I'd ever paid for a cocktail and triple it. That should cover it.

He seemed to read my mind. "Don't even try. I have to spend a certain amount on food every month, or I get charged for it anyway. I don't come here a lot, so I usually end up paying for nothing."

This was too much. Way too much. I had to find a way to balance this deal. I earned things, so I knew they were mine. With this big an imbalance, I owed Cooper, and how could I repay him? Something inside me rebelled at the idea of taking advantage of this man the way others did.

Chapter 9

Ganging up on me

COOPER

CALLIE'S JAW HAD LIFTED, and her lips were pressed together. I sighed. People were weird about money. In my case, about being with someone who had money. Maybe they were weird when people didn't have money as well, I didn't know.

"What about tips?"

"Not allowed. The members take up a collection twice a year and that's distributed to all the employees."

"That sounds good for the members, but not so good for the employees."

"Another reason I don't really enjoy this place."

She looked down and rubbed her finger on a knife. "You're doing this just for me?"

"I come here for other reasons, normally a few times a year, with my teammates or sponsors. I was here before that charity dinner, because golfing is a way to check on the guys without it looking like I'm checking on them. Since I'm in town all summer, except for the wedding, I'll probably be here more often."

She rubbed the knife a little faster. "I'm even more in your debt."

"Callie, which one of us is currently making more money?" My hockey contract was publicly available. If someone wanted to know badly enough, they could probably work out the kind of cash I got from my endorsement deals.

Some asked me for "loans" or gifts. Those people I quickly removed from my life. Some were aggressive, like I owed them. A lot of people thought that if we were out at dinner, I had money and should pick up the check. I wasn't cheap, and didn't mind spending my money, but I didn't like being an ATM.

Then there were people like Callie, who wouldn't accept *anything*. The people who were terrified of taking advantage were almost as much of a pain as the takers. It was a minefield to tiptoe through. It made me nostalgic for school, when a group of hockey players had been living in a big old house together. Everyone chipped in equally to pay for pizza and beer. We were all on the same footing.

I leaned toward her. I didn't give a fuck if someone thought my posture was a problem, but I had money and celebrity to let me get away with things. Callie was desperate to fit in, so I'd corrected her to protect her.

Her lips tightened. "Which one of us is getting the most out of this arrangement?" she countered.

I didn't want her to be keeping a tally on this. "You have no idea what my family is like, so you shouldn't assume you're getting off easy."

There were those wrinkles in her forehead, reshaping the freckles.

"Callie, if you're going to be a human calculator through this, it's not going to work. I offered this deal freely, and of sound mind." Close enough. "I don't like lawyers, at least lawyers like that Benson guy. I'm happy to help you, for my own personal reasons. I would like you to come to my sister's wedding. It's an easy solution to something that's a potential problem. Lots of stupid shit has happened in my family, and you are the perfect person for me to take."

She swallowed and her cheeks turned red. Wasn't sure what she was going to say, but it wasn't going to be *Yes Cooper, that's going to work out great.*

"Am I the perfect person because I'll embarrass them?"

The waiter delivered our drinks before my jaw dropped on the floor. Callie didn't look at me again as she ordered—the chicken, cheapest dish on the menu—and I took the easy out with a steak.

Callie had herself under control by the time he'd swanned away. I took a quick scan of the dining room, saw a few gazes drop when I looked, a few that wanted to catch my eye, but none close enough to hear us. "Hey."

She moved her attention from her drink to me. Her cheeks were still flushed. *How far does that go?* I wanted to give my dick a punch. *Not now. Not with her.* She'd be sure this was part of some negotiation.

"I'm not going to be embarrassed by you as my date. It's exactly the opposite."

She didn't need to say a word. Her skepticism was broadcast by that little frown on her brow and the set of her lips.

I didn't like to talk about my family, but hell, if all went well, she'd meet them, so I might as well tell her. "I come from a long line of lawyers."

Her mouth formed an O and I reminded myself not to think about her lips and what they could do like that.

"Yeah, mostly family firm, very proud of themselves, very stuffy. I'm an outlier."

The only one not to focus on law or finance as a career. I'd gone about as far from that as possible. And I was even more successful than they were, which I loved, and my father and brother were totally pissed about. It was one of the many perks of my job.

"When I decided not to go to Harvard, but to a school that launched a lot of NHL players, they weren't impressed. My career, especially that I'm so good at it? That's what embarrasses them. They like to think I'm a dumb jock, because the idea that I was smart enough to follow the mold and didn't just chaps their asses. Showing up with an intelligent, successful lawyer, exactly the kind of person they hang out with but the kind of person they assume I could never meet playing hockey? Totally on point. You are absolutely perfect for my wedding date."

Her eyes were wide as she took all that in.

"The fact that we're not dating? You're not with me to marry me for my assets? Totally fucks with their expectations. I would pay you to do this, but I'm pretty sure you'd refuse. So, we do each other a favor."

I hadn't spent that much time talking about my family since...I had no idea. Not my favorite topic, not something that came up a lot in conversation.

"You want me as your date, as a friend, so you can tell your family to get fucked. That's what you're saying?"

That summed things up quite nicely. "That's it."

She moved her cocktail over a fraction of an inch. "And your family is like Benson? Not all lawyers are the same."

"Aren't most of them?" I was perhaps a little jaded on the topic of lawyers.

Callie shook her head. "No, not all of them. But I've had to work very hard to get where I am, harder than Benson has ever had to. So I get what you're saying. I'll be your date."

I grinned. *Yes!*

She held up a finger. "I'm not going to be an asshole to anyone. Not Benson, and not your family. I have my own future to think about. But if you need a tax attorney to impress them—"

She smiled, and holy hell, that smile did something. It took away the tension in her expression, lit up her eyes. "You have a deal." I held out a hand to shake on it.

"One thing." Her smile left and her voice was serious.

What was she going to freak out over?

"I pay for the dress for the wedding, and any more clothes."

She looked good, totally right at the moment, wearing the clothes I'd picked out while she laid down her ultimatum. I couldn't let her wear something like that green monstrosity she'd worn to the dinner. "Only if I choose the clothes."

She was frowning again.

"Clothes matter. Here at the club and with my family. Remember, they're like Benson."

"You choose, I pay?"

I could live with that. She was a tax attorney, for fuck's sake, at a big firm. She had to have money. "I choose, you pay."

She finally held out her hand and we shook. Her palms were smooth, the hands of someone who didn't use them hard. Mine were callused. But she didn't flinch, didn't comment.

"So, when exactly is this wedding?"

"The end of August."

Her hand jerked, and I knew she wanted to get her phone out to mark it in her calendar.

"I'll send you the details."

She nodded, but there was still a little frown between her brows. I wished there was some way to make Callie understand that by the end of this arrangement, I'd be owing her. The money I'd earned playing hockey, the endorsements, my condo and cars and investments—it wasn't enough to impress my family. Having someone like Callie with me would make a bigger impact than any amount of cash.

But something of what I felt must have gotten through because she finally relaxed. Not totally. Whenever she realized she'd started slouching she jolted upright like she'd been prodded, and she kept fidgeting in her chair as she started and stopped crossing her legs.

Our meals arrived, and our water glasses were topped up. Callie refused another drink or a glass of wine and I did as well. I was driving.

She watched as I started to eat, then mimicked me, cutting into her chicken with the correct cutlery. "So, you pay an amount every month for food, even if you don't use the restaurant."

I nodded. Typical for a country club.

"And a portion of your dues goes for meals and entertainment, even though the expense may not be for a meal."

"Are you planning to rearrange the billing system here?"

Her cheeks pinked. "It's a hazard of the job. Meals and entertainment have a personal benefit to them, so theoretically, if you're claiming a membership here as a business expense, you'd only be able to claim half of those costs. But if you don't actually pay for food, should you be able to claim the whole amount?"

My steak was good. Callie didn't seem to be tasting her food, her mind busy on this problem.

"I can't help you there, but you could talk to my accountant if you want and see how he handles it?"

She set a forkful of rice back on her plate. "Who does your work?" I told her. She nodded. "They're good."

I'd asked around before I'd hired them, but it was nice to get confirmation from someone who knew.

Callie continued to pepper me with questions between checking out what everyone was doing. She must have trusted me with any protocol issues, because her questions tended toward the organization and management of the club. Things I had no knowledge of. My ignorance made her more confident, which was all to the good. I didn't care about those things.

I signed for the meal, ignoring her frown, and we walked out into a beautiful afternoon to get my car from the valet.

The ride back to Toronto was a lot better. Callie, when she'd loosened up, was an entertaining companion. She knew nothing about sports. I asked how she was going to handle that in her partnership campaign. The firm she was working for was very involved with the local sports clubs. The partners were big fans and participated in a lot of the team charity events.

She smirked. "That's easy."

"Really? If a partner or client is a big fan of baseball or basketball or hockey, you're just going to say you don't care and hope it doesn't bother them?"

She rolled her eyes at me. It was cute. "I just have to

know when the sport seasons run. Hockey and basketball in the winter. Baseball and football in the summer. I ask what team they like, and if it's the offseason, question what they think the team needs to do. Everyone has an opinion, and they're happy to share it. I just listen. Remember the names of the players they like. Or I can ask them who was the team's best player ever. They like that too."

Huh. Had people done that to me? I would always support my team, so I wouldn't offer opinions on the current roster, but asking about my hockey idols? That would distract me. I couldn't underestimate this woman. She didn't know sports or dressing or golf, but she had an incredible mind, and it was sexy. "What about in season?"

"Which player is having a good or bad season. If it's a local team, if they see the games live. What team is their biggest challenge. Just generic stuff, but if I listen and pay attention, it usually goes well."

That technique wouldn't work on a golf course, or in the club. You could ask someone who their favorite golfer was, but it wouldn't help you navigate the dining room, or make sure you didn't try to take your next shot out of turn. Smart as she was, she needed my help. And that made me feel good.

We talked about movies and TV shows. Her roommate, Darcy, was a manager at a movie theater so she saw a lot of popular films. On the team jet we had downtime while traveling to away games, so we'd both seen most of the new releases and shared some tastes in common. There'd been a popular legal thriller out this year and her opinion on that was scathing. And a hell of a lot of fun to listen to.

I stopped in front of her condo building. She turned in her seat. "I should get you those clothes I can't wear."

I turned off the car. "I'll come up and get them."

She frowned.

I raised my hand. "Just saving you a trip. Show me what else you have to wear to the club, so we can work out how much you're going to need."

The furrows in her brow deepened. She picked up her bag, with the skirt and top she'd worn to practice in. "I'm good with this. I can clean it between golf lessons."

"Callie."

She lifted her chin again. The woman was *so* stubborn. "What?"

"You can't wear the same thing every time."

"I don't need a whole lot of clothing like this. When would I wear it again? No one is going to even remember what I had on."

There was a lot to unpack in this. But I didn't want to have this discussion in the car, so I agreed to see what she already owned.

She was tense again as we headed up to her condo. That ease we had while talking at lunch and on the way back to the city was gone. She opened the door with jerky movements and dropped her bag on the coffee table in the living room.

"Stay there."

I stayed, standing in where I'd stopped and checking out her place. It was nothing like mine, either in space or design, but it looked comfortable. I wondered which parts of the decor, if any, were Callie's. Based on the sounds drifting down the hallway, and the swearing, she was having problems rummaging around in her room. I heard someone at the door, and her roommate Darcy came in.

He stopped when he saw me, arms full of groceries, face showing surprise. "Uh, hi." He tried to wave, but that just jostled his bags.

I stepped over and reached for a couple.

"Um, thanks. Uh, I can leave again. Really. Just put the milk in the fridge and—"

Callie stomped down the hallway then, arms full of clothes. "Darcy—you got food. Sorry, I meant to—"

"No problem." He looked between us. "I'm, um, just going to put the milk away and I'll be gone."

"Why?" Callie asked.

I kept quiet, enjoying the show. Darcy thought I'd come up here for more than clothes, and Callie was so oblivious it was funny. She was a strange mix. Super smart about some things, and totally missing out on others.

"We could probably use your help," I added, and Darcy's eyes widened to almost full circles.

"I don't need the two of you ganging up on me."

I watched Darcy blink as he processed the clothes in Callie's arms, and the lack of any closeness between us.

"Why are you carrying around your running clothes?" he finally asked Callie.

She dumped them on the coffee table. "He"—she pointed at me—"thinks I need to buy a bunch of clothes for this country club."

Darcy was up to speed now. "He's right."

"This is what I mean. The two of you ganging up on me."

Darcy finally moved to the kitchen and I followed him, carrying the two bags of groceries I still held and setting them down on the counter. Callie stomped back down the hallway, muttering.

"So," I asked, leaning against the doorway. "You don't do threesomes?"

Darcy's face flushed. "Sorry, but I thought..."

I smiled at him. "I know. Just playing with you. But if

you can help Callie understand about the clothes, it would be great. She wants to make the right impression, and this is important."

Darcy put the milk in the fridge. "I know. I've tried to explain it to her. She just lives so much in her head that she doesn't understand why this external stuff is so important."

I had one concern that I hoped he could help with. "Can she afford it?"

He balanced on one foot, the other toe twisting on the tile. I'd overstepped.

"I don't mean to cross a line. I can help with the clothes issue, but she was upset about the stuff I brought this morning."

He sighed. "She can, but it's not her first priority."

I heard Callie returning, so I stepped back into the living room. I didn't want her to think we really were ganging up on her. For her sake, I wished she had some clothes that would work. But the things I saw on the coffee table were old and worn, and not up to the code of the club.

Callie and I were going to need to go shopping. And this could be all kinds of interesting.

Chapter 10

Mr. Fussy

Cooper

We'd set up a date, after Darcy and I convinced her that this was important. I knew she got it, empirically, but there was something inside that was refusing to listen to reason. My guess? Money. Especially when I heard she got that horror of a dress for the charity dinner from a consignment shop. And didn't try it on before buying it.

I'd invited Darcy to join us on our expedition. He had good taste, at least enough to know that green dress was impossible, and he might make Callie more comfortable. But he was working the couple of nights I had free this week, and Callie needed something new for our next lesson.

I was tempted to pick her up in the Ferrari this time, just to see the expression on her face, but it had no storage room so I stuck to the Bentley. Another time.

We pulled up behind the main store of my sponsor and I turned off the car. Callie looked at me suspiciously.

"What?"

She looked at the back door. "Why aren't we going in the front?"

The back door opened and the brand liaison woman I worked with poked her head out. Seeing us, she waved, inviting us in.

"Did you tell them we were coming?"

Duh. "Of course I did."

"I don't want a lot of attention." She looked ready to crawl into herself.

"That's why I called ahead."

She stilled and blinked at me. I could see the gears moving in her head as she finally worked it out. Part-time genius, and part-time totally oblivious.

Her chest began to rise and fall, her breathing picking up. "I can do this on my own."

"Callie, we talked about this. You want to fit in with these people, so you can't go cheap and you can't pick the wrong stuff."

I wasn't sure if she had no taste at all, or just was so freaked about spending money that she refused to think about what looked good. How could I calm her down?

"Let's make a deal. We'll go in there, check out what they have. You promise not to look at price tags, and we'll see what you choose. If you can pick out something on your own that works, then you won't need me the next time."

The way she jerked in her seat told me she hadn't thought there would be a next time.

"But if you can't pick out the right things, then you need to listen to what I tell you looks good. I know what will work at the club. There's no point in learning to play and learning what to do in the dining room if you don't look the part, because these people will notice."

She ran her teeth over her lip.

"Do you want this, or not?"

The brand woman had disappeared out of the doorway, obviously picking up that we would be a few minutes. Hopefully not too many.

Finally, a long, capitulating sigh. "Okay. But you have to be honest. No pretending my taste sucks just to prove your point."

Didn't think any pretending would be necessary, but I offered her my hand to shake. It was just a handshake. No big deal. But when our hands met, there was a spark. She felt it too, snatching her hand back like I'd shocked her.

I reminded myself that we weren't going there. Callie would think I'd set this up to seduce her, and I wanted her with me at the wedding. I didn't do relationships, so even if she was interested, sex would mess things up.

* * *

CALLIE

THIS WAS SO over-the-top it was ridiculous. All I wanted was to walk in the store, look at some racks of clothes, reminding myself that I was spending money to make my future secure. Pick some things out that were my size, and if I absolutely had to, try them on for Mr. Fussy.

Of course, that was too simple for said Mr. Fussy.

Cooper introduced me to the woman who'd put this together.

"Valerie, this is Callie. She's looking for something she can wear at Briarwood. She works for Anderson, Krys and Chan, and we've been practicing for their tournament this fall."

"It's so nice to meet you, Callie. Did you like the things I sent over earlier?"

"Yes, they were lovely."

"I'm so glad. Well, I've pulled a couple of racks of options that might work for you, Some of this isn't available yet, but for our best sales ambassador we're more than happy to share items from our new lines."

Valerie led us through the back storage room to the retail space. In front of the dressing rooms were two racks of clothes, like I'd hired a personal shopper. I didn't think the store was open, since there were no customers, but there were still a lot of people wearing the store polo shirt, folding clothes or swishing hangers. A lot of people. Like everyone who'd worked for the store, ever, was in there somewhere. All watching Cooper.

Some of them were watching me. I understood the surprised look on their faces. I didn't get it either.

"Why don't you see what you like?" Valerie suggested.

I smiled, like this was no big deal. Internally, I sighed. Legal issues were so much easier to figure out.

I wasn't here to impress Cooper or pick things out that he liked. I was paying for this, so I would choose things that lasted. I knew what I liked. Basics. Neutrals. Classics. Clothes that would stand the test of time, wouldn't come in and out of fashion, wouldn't attract attention. Too many people talked to my bustline, so I did my best to minimize it.

I started flicking through the hangers, but what I was looking for wasn't what was on offer. I wanted black and brown and maybe some navy blue. Instead, there were colors, everywhere. "I don't see anything in neutrals."

"Neutrals?" Valerie asked.

"Brown, black, navy..."

Valerie looked from me to Cooper. "Um, our golf line is

more...varied in color. Our clients prefer bright shades, or pastels. Because it's usually summer, sunny and hot."

Right. If you were out for hours on those greens, black would swelter. "Of course. I was thinking about work clothes."

I slowed down, checking the clothes more carefully. This was going to be a little more difficult than I'd hoped, but I could do it. No pinks or reds. That much had been drilled in over the years, so I skipped past those. I'd thought I was safe with green, but apparently not.

I paused on the greens. There were some really pretty shades. But that dress, the one that'd started this whole thing, was green. I headed to the blues. They should be safe, right? Despite the fact that so many of these pieces of clothing were bright, I didn't want to attract a lot of attention. So I grabbed a powder blue top, with a skirt that mixed blues and yellows. I held them up together. Yeah, that should be good.

I turned around and refused to look at Cooper. Instead, I looked at Valerie. She was frowning.

Damn it. I'd gotten it wrong again? I flicked a glance at Cooper. He was smirking.

Obviously I didn't have an eye for color. I knew some colors clashed, and avoided putting them together. But the other side, finding whatever color was supposed to make you look better? I'd never really tried. I'd been aiming for professional, respectable, maybe even trustworthy. Background clothes. Nothing here was that.

I put the top and skirt back. "Okay. I give up. You win."

I waited for Cooper to gloat and tell me I wasn't good enough to do this on my own. I'd had a lot of people tell me I wasn't good enough, so I was braced and ready.

He dropped the smirk. But he didn't say *I told you so.*

Instead, he headed to the racks and started pulling things out, holding them up to me. Sometimes he'd frown, or purse his lips. Other times he nodded and passed the item to Valerie. Most of the time there was a light in his eyes, his lips tilted up into a half smile. He liked this. Maybe he should have had a Barbie doll as a kid. Hell, maybe he had.

"What do you think, Val? Is this going to work better with her complexion, or this?" He was holding up two tops, in different shades of yellow. He didn't say *freckles*, which was considerate. He waved me over and held them up against my face, and one top went into the reject pile.

I was sent into the dressing room with the clothing they'd settled on. I hated trying on clothes, but no way were they letting me go without seeing what this looked like on. I read the price on one of the tags and swallowed hard. Okay, I couldn't afford to make a mistake with anything that cost that much.

I pulled on the first sleeveless collared shirt and a skirt/short combo. My hands smoothed over the fabric before I realized I was petting myself. The fabric was soft, with a thickness to it that wouldn't stretch out or fade. I turned to check the fit in the mirror and stopped in surprise.

Was that me? My hair had always been a bright red, almost orange, and unlike Anne of Green Gables, it had never faded to auburn. But instead of glowing like a beacon, now it looked—kind of pretty. And my freckles didn't overwhelm my face.

"You ready in there?" Valerie asked, and I realized I'd been staring at my reflection.

I never did that, unless I was checking for makeup smears. I didn't like looking at myself. And yet...

I came out and stood in front of them. Cooper twirled a finger, so I did a 360 so they could see the whole effect.

"That's pretty good, flatters her figure without being too much."

Slutty. That was what they meant. When you had big boobs, that was always a problem. He paused, and I waited anxiously. I liked this. I wanted it. I wanted him to like it.

"I think the skirt is verging on too short. Can you try the next one, Callie? We don't want to push the rules."

Something inside me warmed. What he'd brought for that first lesson hadn't been an outlier, as I'd suspected. I'd been worried he would pick tops with deep cleavage, too-tight skirts. Guys I'd dated in the past had always skewed that way. But he didn't. Maybe the difference was that we weren't dating. This wasn't a sex thing. And I was not disappointed about that.

I could trust him. For *this*, I reminded myself. I could trust him to pick out clothes that would look good, so that I fit in. It was a hell of a lot more than I'd trust Benson.

THEY FINALLY SETTLED on three things to wear while golfing, and two more for the dining room. Only one was a sample item that had no price tag. They'd rejected things I'd have taken just because of the way they felt and how they made me look like someone different. But the final selections? I couldn't argue with them. They did look and feel good. I didn't want to get back into my old clothes.

The colors they chose made a huge difference. It was some kind of voodoo, and I didn't understand it.

I left the store with things I loved. I wouldn't waste this lesson. I'd use these clothes as a guide and buy more things in those shades. I might not have the perfect eye they did to pick colors out, but I could use the information they'd given me to my advantage in the future.

It would take some time to get used to the fit though. I'd learned that the looser the clothes, especially around my chest, the fewer the comments. I was trying to succeed in a competitive world as a woman with big breasts, and I didn't want to accentuate them. I didn't want anyone to credit my boobs for my success. Or to decide my IQ diminished as my cup size grew. My neutral colors and loose clothes did that. People noticed my work, not me.

I didn't dare look at the receipt, just passed my credit card over. I'd open a bottle of wine back home to fortify myself for the ridiculous amount I was sure I'd spent. No, I'd *invested*. This was an investment in my career. And Benson would not be able to criticize anything.

After my purchases were bagged up and Cooper had done the kissy face with Valerie, we went back through the storeroom and then into Cooper's car. He carried out the bags for me, ignoring my rolled eyes, and stored them in his trunk after holding the passenger door for me. Despite my wine plan, I mentally added up my purchases. I didn't remember how much that one skirt was, so I doubled the amount of the other one. Then add tax... When I turned, he was staring at me, the car quiet. Was there a problem with his expensive car?

"Are you okay? Did we push too hard?"

That was...sweet. "No. I actually enjoyed that more than any other shopping trip I've been on."

"Really?"

I nodded.

"I know it was a lot of money for you."

"It was. But you're right. My stuff wouldn't have fit. And this is...actually, really nice."

His smile lit up his face, both dimples out. He was handsome, maybe even beautiful, all the time, but this... This was relaxed and open. None of the tension I'd noticed when he was on for hockey fans.

I wanted to make him smile like that again. It felt good to have that power. No one except Darcy smiled to see me. Well, Darcy and my clients when I had good news for them relating to their tax situation. "So, are we done?"

His smile dropped. "Yeah. Won't need to take up more of your valuable time."

My time was valuable. I knew my billing rate. But his? His was much higher than mine. "Thank you."

"No trouble. I enjoy that."

"I could tell. But still, thank you for being patient, and kind. You're not like I expected, in a good way."

"I can say the same, Callie. It's nice to be surprised."

I wanted to preen—I had beautiful clothes, and I'd surprised this man, in a good way. He was letting me in, underneath the famous hockey player exterior.

It gave me a contented, warm feeling. Another surprise.

This arrangement might be one of the best decisions I'd ever made.

Chapter 11

I don't think he likes you

WITH THE CHARITY dinner that we'd been required to attend over, the team had dispersed for the summer. Most of the guys had gone to see family or unwind on vacations, but there was a group of six of us who were planning to make the most of this offseason. Because next year we weren't losing the finals.

I'd arranged for us to use the facilities at our practice rink for the summer. Team management was just as keen as we were to make next season different. Today was the first day of our workout sessions. I'd employed Scout for the last couple of offseasons for training and arranged with him to work with us to get in condition. The workouts wouldn't be too intense until we'd had a chance to rebuild from the stress of the playoffs. But the longer we let our bodies go, the harder it would be to get back into shape.

I was the first to arrive at the rink. I changed into shorts and a T-shirt, then let Scout in and did warm-ups while he set up the exercises he would use to test our current fitness levels as a starting benchmark.

Ducky arrived next, the youngest in our group, almost bouncing in place with excitement. Petrov, the big Russian goalie, strode in with a nod. Crash and Royster carpooled together, and JJ slipped in last.

We shared an intensity that was rare for this time of year. Coach had told us to hang on to the feeling of that loss, the brutal pain, and use it to propel us in the next season. Everyone here was doing that.

Assessment took about an hour. Scout was big on flexibility and stretching, and he made sure we could do all the movements he assigned to us for the week. For the next three weeks we'd meet with him here on Monday and get our assignments. After that, in July he'd work with us Monday through Friday, upping the intensity until August, when we'd get on the ice again.

Gathered together in the locker room after our session, it was almost like the season, except there were a lot fewer of us.

"So what's everyone doing when they're not here?" Ducky asked.

Petrov lowered his brows. "Training. Resting. Rebuilding."

Ducky nodded. "Cyborg life, right. But don't you normally do all that in Russia?"

"This year I focus on hockey. Also, my family say not a good time to visit."

Crash pulled off his T-shirt. His dark skin stretched over a broad chest. He was a hard man to get off the puck. He was the guy who'd stepped in for JJ on that last shift. If I'd just thought before I'd made that pass...

But I'd told Mitchell not to dwell on it, and I had to follow my own advice.

Crash bent over to untie his shoes. "I've bought a duplex—half for me, half for my mom and sister. We're settling in, staying close this year."

Royster grabbed a towel before heading to the showers. "I'll go home for a week at some point, but it's a small town and everyone is going to ask about the playoffs, so I'm just as happy to stay here."

Ducky sat on the bench in front of his locker. "I'll go home for a week sometime too, but mostly I'm here. We should do stuff!"

JJ frowned at him. "What kind of stuff?"

JJ was staying in town for most of the summer. His twin sister shared his condo, and since she worked a regular job she wasn't leaving. The siblings weren't close to their parents in any case.

"We could go to the beach and swim. Spend a day at Wonderland. Go out to a club or something."

"Do you have any idea what the water temperature is in Lake Ontario? Your balls will pull up so far into your body you'll never see them again. I'll pass on swimming."

Petrov crossed his arms, pale, naked body fully exposed. "We are in training. No clubs."

Ducky pouted. "All right, how about poker nights?"

"Not if Royster is playing," Crash objected.

Royster, Barnes and Bongo were our shutdown line and shared some kind of poker voodoo. They rarely lost.

"We'll come up with something, Ducky," I reassured him. We all wanted to be at our best for the next season, but we couldn't train and do nothing else. As captain, I had to make sure we were all in a good place, mentally and physically.

"You're in town all summer too?"

"Mostly," I agreed. "We'll do some golfing if you want."

"When are you away?"

"End of summer. Family wedding."

"Weddings can be fun."

I wrapped a towel around my hips. "Not this one."

"Do you have to go?"

I'd face incredible pressure if I didn't. I'd considered it. But the same part of me that had mapped out all the billboards where I'd posed mostly nude in my sponsor's underwear made me determined to go and flaunt the success I'd gained in front of my family. By almost any standard, I'd succeeded, and I was proud of what I'd done. Would have been nice to bring the Cup along with me. But not this year.

"There's no one holding a literal gun to my head, but it's family, so." I shrugged.

The guys nodded. They were familiar with family pressure.

"But you can get a killer date. There was that actress you went out with, right? And that model..."

I smirked. These guys—most people—would find a date like that impressive, but not my family. "Oh yeah, I've got a date lined up who will make the perfect impression."

I left for the shower before Ducky asked any more questions. He had his brow furrowed, so something was coming.

I was the last to leave—I'd promised management that I'd make sure the place was left secure. I buckled on my watch and my phone buzzed. I checked, and like he'd been summoned by the previous conversation, it was my brother.

Call the skydive place for the B-party. You're in charge of that.

What the hell? Anything like that was against my

contract. The fucker knew that. I was sure he was just waiting for me to complain about it.

Don't even try to say you're modeling that weekend.

Turned out, I had plans for the weekend before the wedding. Golf lessons with Callie. And my busy tax lawyer date couldn't get that much time off. I'd tell my family she couldn't, anyway.

Date can't get away early. Will only be present for the wedding events.

I turned my phone off before he answered. He could go break his neck skydiving without me. I'd better turn in that RSVP with my plus-one.

* * *

CALLIE

"DID YOU HAVE A GOOD WEEKEND, Ms. Smith?" Leonie, my assistant, smiled at me as I passed her desk.

"Yes, thank you. And you?"

"It was nice to get outside, wasn't it?"

I frowned. "How did you know?"

Her smile dropped. "I'm sorry—your nose is just a little pink and I see you don't have any hours logged for Sunday again."

"That's okay, Leonie. You're right, I did get out. It was good."

She nodded anxiously. I'd worry that I somehow scared her, except she was like this with everyone, as far as I could tell.

"Mr. Anderson wanted to see you when you have a chance."

"Can you ask when's a good time for him? Rearrange anything you need to on my end." If a partner wanted to talk to me, I would make it happen.

We were able to find a time just before lunch. His secretary sent me in. Mr. Anderson had a corner office, with a large desk and a couch and chairs. It was three times the size of mine, but I was happy with my office. Having my own walls and a door felt like my position in the firm was secure. But if I was partner, it would really be secure.

To get that, I had to demonstrate my value to the firm, so I was anxious about what Mr. Anderson wanted.

"Calliope! Thank you for making time."

"Of course, sir. How may I help you?"

He waved a hand at the couch. "Have a seat."

I sat down, perched on the edge. At work I wore suits with skirts. The tops were loose enough that my breasts weren't conspicuous and the jacket and skirt a little baggy, but if I had to struggle up off the cushions, I didn't want to flash Mr. Anderson.

He sat in a chair, crossing his legs and steepling his fingers together. His suit was a light gray, and for once I noticed the color choices and fit of what he was wearing. My own outfit was subdued and bland, but Anderson's spoke of confidence and maturity.

Cooper would approve. I wanted to shove him out of my head, but it was becoming obvious that he had a point. My plan to make partner and *then* worry about how I looked? Might not work.

"I appreciate the information you prepared for Carruthers. He wasn't happy with the firm he was using, and what you sent over gave him the confidence in us to transfer his business over."

I smiled. I kept it contained and polite but inside I was

grinning ear to ear and dancing. *Yes!* The petty part of me wanted to see Benson's face when he heard the news. The anxious part of me was reassured that the stupid green dress hadn't torpedoed my career.

"We'll have to shuffle things around, but you'll be doing a lot of work for Carruthers. We will definitely make note of this when it comes time for year-end bonuses. I hope that makes it worth interrupting your tête-à-tête?"

My—oh right. That talk with Cooper. "Not a problem."

"Is Cooper a friend of yours?"

What the hell was I supposed to say? The curiosity in his expression indicated that he would prefer it if he was. Damn, this firm liked athletes. Did Anderson think I might bring Cooper in as a client? Yikes. That was not happening.

"That was actually the first time I spoke to him."

Anderson looked disappointed. "Ah. Well, I hope he didn't feel we were rude, doing business at a charity event."

I spoke before I thought this through. "He didn't say anything negative about it when we went to Briarwood."

Fuck. Bragging about spending time with the man like he was a trophy I'd scored? I didn't like that. But I wanted Anderson happy with me. I wanted to show I could not only handle tax matters, but also do the people part of being a partner—like networking and hanging out with celebrity athletes.

"Oh, he took you there?"

I couldn't be upset that Anderson didn't think I was a member. He was, and he'd know if an associate at the firm had somehow scored a membership. They probably had a long waiting list. "A couple of times. Since I was invited to the tournament in September, I want to be sure I represent the firm well."

Was that too much of a suck-up? It was the truth, but perhaps I should have been a little less keen.

"I'm sure you will. Are you going again? Might I see you there?"

"I think we'll be there again Sunday." We were, right? Damn, I hadn't done anything but hit the ball on the practice range either week. How bad would I look on the greens?

Anderson spread out his hands. "We won't be there this weekend—we've got guests going out on the boat. Maybe another time?"

"I hope so."

Anderson stood, so our meeting was over. "Thanks for stopping by, Callie. And tell your young man I'm looking forward to seeing him at Briarwood."

"Oh, we're just friends." No way was I letting one of the partners, the one I knew best, think there was something more than golf lessons going on. It was a surprise that he thought there might be.

"Ah." He nodded. "Mr. Cooper does seem to go through a lot of dates. Friends probably last longer."

I nodded and left his office, taking a shaky breath. I wasn't sure what was going on with Anderson and his expectations, but I'd better not mess up my career.

When I got back to my office, Benson was talking to Leonie. I narrowed my eyes. I hoped she was being discreet.

She glanced up with wide eyes. Her shoulders dropped. "Here she is now."

Benson turned and raised his brows. "Early lunch?"

My hours were none of his business. I smiled reassuringly at Leonie. She hadn't told Benson where I was, which probably indicated she hadn't been sharing anything she shouldn't. I crossed my arms. "Why, did you want to join me?"

I brought my own meals and ate them at my desk. That way I could keep on top of updates and notices without impinging on my billable hours. I didn't know what Benson did for lunch, but I doubted it was a turkey sandwich and an apple.

"Krys had a question that I thought you might have some advice on, but you weren't here, so…"

Was he going to run back and tell someone I was slacking off? Was that why he kept dropping by my office? "Not that I need to clear my schedule with you, but Mr. Anderson asked to talk to me. I feel so special, with two partners both wanting my input."

Benson's mouth turned down. "I'll send you an email about that question."

I nodded. "Probably a more efficient use of your time than dropping by in person."

He shrugged. "I was passing by anyway."

I lifted a brow. The lawyers in this section of the office had very little to do with Benson's area of intellectual property.

He turned and left.

"I don't think he likes you," Leonie whispered.

"I know. I'm not sure why."

"If I hear anything, I'll let you know."

The offer surprised me. It seemed out of character. Maybe Leonie wasn't a total mouse. Maybe she was all about girl power, or maybe Benson had been unpleasant. In any case, I was happy to have an ally. I wasn't good at making those.

Chapter 12

A nicely dressed disaster

Cooper

IN THE OFFSEASON, my sponsor commitments increased. Between the workouts with the guys still in town and those obligations, the week went quickly, and I was looking forward to seeing Callie again. I expected she'd be prickly to start, but once she relaxed, she was interesting.

This week we had an actual tee time. I'd booked it for late in the day. I wanted the keen golfers to get through their rounds so we had time for Callie to learn without being rushed by the group behind us. It would have been better to go on a weekday, but she'd never agree to that.

When I pulled up in front of her building in the Bentley, she was already waiting. She was wearing one of the new top and skort pairings she'd bought and she looked exactly right for the club. She had a new bag over her shoulder, holding probably her dress and makeup and whatever. Her hair was pulled back in a ponytail. She started toward the car before I'd stopped it.

"You look nice," I told her once she'd slid in and buckled her seat belt. I checked for traffic and moved north.

"Thank you." She looked down at herself, as if to verify that she did look nice. I held back a grin. "Oh, you do too."

Of course I did. I'd made sure of it before I left my condo. Growing up, I'd had to earn my mother's approval before leaving the house, until I got good enough to not require her final check. "Thank you. How was your week?"

She drew in a long breath. "I need to apologize to you."

My brows flew up. "What for?"

"One of the partners, Mr. Anderson—the man who came over at the charity dinner?"

I nodded, remembering the man.

"Well, he was talking to me, and said something about knowing you and, well, I kind of boasted that I had gone to Briarwood with you."

Disappointment. That was what I felt. I hadn't expected that of Callie.

"I don't know what got into me, but he was just so pleased at the thought I knew one of the hockey players, and I was feeling uncomfortable about how I might have messed up at the charity dinner with that dress, and I wanted to make a good impression."

"It's okay." It was done. I should be used to people taking advantage by now.

"No, it's not. It's what Benson would do."

That made me laugh. "Is that your guideline—if Benson would do it, it must be wrong?"

"That might work more often than not. Again, I'm sorry. He thought we were maybe dating, but at least I didn't try to claim that. I told him we were just friends. That's okay, isn't it? You said we'd go to your sister's wedding as friends."

That's what I'd said. And it was what we were doing. "I can live with being friends."

"And I have something else I should apologize for. But it's mostly your fault."

Callie could learn some things about apologizing. "You're going to say you're sorry I made you do something?"

"No, of course not. But earlier this week, Mr. Anderson wanted to see me and I noticed how nice his suit was. I hadn't paid attention to that before, and you are right. My idea of earning a partnership by hard work and worrying about appearances afterward may not be feasible."

Her firm was one of the most conservative in the city. Appearances would matter a lot to them. Whatever she wore to work must be better than that green dress or she wouldn't have come as far as she did. "So, I've converted you to dressing well?"

"Maybe. My ideas and yours might differ a lot, but I'm going to have to up my appearance game. I apologize for fighting you on that."

"I'm happy to help, if you need any advice."

She shot a glance at me. "You know what to wear on the golf course, I accept that. I'm not sure you understand how I need to dress for work."

I stiffened. "What do you think I'd want you wearing? Miniskirts and low-cut blouses?"

She sighed. "No, but even this." She waved down her body. "It's too snug."

"It's not too snug. It's not slutty, it's classy."

"I understand that. But the first thing people are going to notice about me? Is my chest."

"Maybe not the first thing."

"It's either the boobs or the hair. Guarantee it."

"And you don't want that."

"I need people to believe I have a brain. That I got my job because I'm smart and I work hard. All my life people have dismissed me because of how I look."

"Seriously?"

"When I wear my 'fade into the background' clothes I look a little frumpy, but then people believe I'm a boring tax expert. I've spent years learning what I know. I want people to trust my advice, not second-guess me because I have a large bustline."

I'd never considered that. I'd never had to.

"Now I need to find a way to look less frumpy but still find something that's not going to distract people by empha-sizing my boobs."

I might have missed something important with how Callie had to operate, but I could make up for it. "Let me see what I can come up with."

She shook her head. "You're doing enough. I'm going to start changing the colors I wear and get better quality. Then maybe I'll get some things tailored, a little, so they're not quite as loose. But I don't want people to notice the wrong thing."

I wanted to insist I go with her. To pick the things I knew would work. I claimed it was easy to look good, but that didn't mean everyone knew how to pick the right clothes. That was what personal shoppers and advisors were for.

But Callie was a grown woman, a successful tax attor-ney, and she was smart. I couldn't push in and insist on her doing things my way. A dress for the wedding, sure, because then she'd be facing the judgment of my family and their circle, and I didn't want her to go in unarmed. "If I can help, just let me know."

"Thanks." She paused, and I heard a laugh in her next words. "Did it hurt, not asking to pick out the clothes?"

I smiled, delighted that she was relaxed enough to joke. "Truly painful. But I do get to pick the dress you're wearing to the wedding."

She sighed. "That's going to be worse than the golf clothes."

But there was a little grin on her face as she said it. Callie had a sense of humor under those prickles. Which were mostly lying flat today.

We turned into the club driveway again and pulled up to the valet. It was a different kid, but he called me Mr. Cooper and I gave him a warm smile. Some club members thought it was okay to be an asshole with the staff, and I did my best to treat them like the people they were.

Once he drove off with the car, and Callie and I were standing by our clubs, she asked what the plan was for today.

"We're going to hit the greens."

"Am I ready for that?"

I shrugged. "Probably not. We're going to do a little bit of putting first. I didn't want a bunch of the more serious types rushing us, so I booked a later tee time. It might be a little hot, but we can take time to talk you through it. You have sunscreen, right?"

"Of course."

I checked in at the pro shop. I'd booked a cart, but not a caddie—I didn't think Callie was ready for anyone to watch her that closely yet. With an hour to kill, we went to the putting greens, mostly empty at this time of day.

I pulled out a putter and a few balls. "Have you played mini golf?" It was as close to putting as she was likely to have done.

She eyed me suspiciously. "Are you saying there's a windmill out here to roll that ball past?"

I grinned. "No, but the windmill might be less frustrating. Ready to start?"

* * *

C ALLIE

C OOPER WAS PATIENT.

It was probably a hockey thing, needing to be patient to, I don't know, shoot or skate or hit people. But I was so bad at this, and he never lost his calm. If I didn't have a deadline at the end of the summer, we'd have been better staying at the practice place.

I learned, after repeated shots that went in the wrong direction, that you only had so much time to find your ball, and if you didn't, you took the "drop." I didn't care—I wasn't even keeping track of my score after the first couple of holes.

It seemed like cheating to me, but I used the easiest tee box. The first hole, I almost argued with Cooper. Wouldn't it be better to learn the most difficult tasks first? That didn't last because I was so bad at this.

We were slow, so I also learned about letting others play through. I preferred not to have someone watching me as I missed hitting the ball or hit it a paltry distance, or hit it far but in the wrong direction.

We'd let four groups play through before we finished up, and I was so done by that point. My hands were sore from swinging the club. I had aching muscles almost every-where, because it seemed running didn't give you any advantages for golfing. I was sweaty, and pretty sure my nose was turning red in spite of repeated application of sunscreen. Loose strands of hair were catching in my mouth and clinging to my neck.

I held up a hand to Cooper. "I don't even want to know the score."

He laughed and grabbed the golf bags. I let him, too tired to fight him. Now I had to try to pretty up and prepare for the dining room again. I blew a breath up my face to move the hair falling over my eyes.

We dropped off the cart. I didn't want to consider how my muscles would ache if we hadn't had that. I felt Cooper's eyes on me as we walked toward the clubhouse.

"I have a suggestion."

He was going to suggest more practice. I needed it, I knew, and I was the one who'd limited our sessions here to Sundays. But damn it, I was so tired...

"What if we skip the dining room today?"

I glanced down. I must have looked as bad as I felt. But yeah, this was probably not the time for dining room lessons.

"And practice instead?" My voice might have been whiny, but I felt like a kid in that I knew it was a good thing to do but I really, really didn't want to.

Cooper shook his head. "You've already pushed your limit. Practicing now will just risk injury."

I could have kissed him for that— Wait, where had that come from? "Thanks. That was a lot."

"We could grab a bite somewhere else, where it doesn't matter if you use your phone or cross your legs."

"Sure." I remembered those rules, and posture was a big issue as well. No tipping.

I nodded before I realized I'd just agreed to eat with

Cooper. In a non-country club setting. Was this outside our agreement?

We waited by the valet stand for the car. "You don't have to take me somewhere to eat."

He raised a brow. "I thought you could pick up the tab."

Oh. Oh, that? Definitely. "Of course I will."

The valet came up with the Bentley, driving it with caution, and I caught a glint in Cooper's eye that told me he'd planned that exchange. He knew telling me I could offset the financial imbalance would have me agreeing immediately.

I just didn't know why he'd wanted that.

We went to a pho restaurant in the north end of the city. It had a mostly Asian clientele and staff, and no one paid us any attention.

Once we'd ordered beer and pho, Cooper leaned back in the booth across from me. "So what do you think of golfing now?"

I flexed my hands. "It's more physically demanding than I'd expected."

"Are you sore?"

I moved my shoulders. They ached, as did my arms and my thighs, but not too badly. "A little, but nothing serious."

"Take some anti-inflammatories and use heat and ice."

My spine stiffened. I knew how to take care of myself. But that was stupid—he was a professional athlete, and if anyone knew how to take care of injuries, he did.

So I swallowed that reaction. "And stretching?"

"You got it."

"Can you tell me what I need to do to improve? I mean, more than 'everything.'"

He chuckled. "It was your first time on the course, and

only your third time hitting the ball. Don't be too hard on yourself."

I sighed. "Is this worth it? Or am I just going to be a nicely dressed disaster at the tournament? It's almost July, and the tournament is the third weekend in September."

"You can only do one day a week?"

I considered. "It's not just the hours I put in at the office on Saturday. I need time to do laundry and clean the condo. I can't ask Darcy to do all the shopping."

"What about an evening?"

Our server came with our meals then. The aroma had my stomach gurgling. Cooper heard—he held back a grin as he thanked the woman.

I picked up my spoon and stirred the contents of the bowl. I leaned over and took a deep breath in. This was going to be good.

"It's a long drive to Briarwood to try to make it in an evening."

Cooper added some chili sauce to his bowl. "There are places in the city to practice. We could work on your swing and your distance if you aren't at the office late every day."

Damn, I sounded so boring. My life revolved around my job. An unfamiliar voice said I deserved a break. But that could come once I'd secured my position in the firm. I needed that.

Unfortunately, as I was becoming aware, I needed more than an established work ethic and familiarity with the tax act. I needed to show I fit in. And this tournament was my chance to prove that.

"Summers the workload usually gets a little lighter." I used that time to do more reading since tax was a constantly evolving beast. Governments added and changed what was in the tax act, and rulings by the courts affected the interpretation of that. "I can take an evening or two."

"What nights work best for you?"

"Aren't you busy?" Darcy had a social life when he wasn't working. Most people did, right?

He swallowed some noodles. "This is the offseason. No games in the evenings."

But what about dates? Not your business.

I pulled out my phone, checking my schedule. "I'm preparing a file this week which is going to take some extra hours, but as long as it's ready for Monday, I can be flexible about the time I spend on it."

He squinted, looking out the window. "You need a day or two for those muscles to recover. Wednesday and Friday?"

Wasn't Friday— No, not my business. If Cooper was willing to help me, I'd use it. But I should be helpful in return. If only I could think of a way to do that. "I'd appreciate it if you could spare that time."

He gave a lazy smile. "Maybe golf coaching can be my follow-up career when I'm done with hockey."

I held back a snort. Like this guy needed a fallback. Did he?

I'd done some research on him—if I was going to trust a big step to my future with him, I wanted to know about him. He had an insanely large contract to play hockey. There would be agent fees and taxes, but still. And his endorsements. He would have to work hard to spend all that money. But he'd grown up with money, and I felt confident he knew what to do with it.

He could have a secret gambling habit or something, but my bet was that he was taking care of his future just fine.

"I'll book us some time on those evenings."

Chapter 13
Captain Cooper

Scout was working us a little harder now. By the end of our workout Monday, we were all sweating and feeling some burn.

"Fuck. Why is this so hard every year?"

Ducky grinned at Royston. "Cause you're old, dude."

"Easy on the *old*, baby Duck."

"Is matter of chemistry. Eat well, sleep well, exercise well, and body will perform."

A moment of silence followed Petrov's announcement. He wasn't wrong, but it was just...not very encouraging.

Ducky shook his head. "Well, all work and no play makes everyone kind of boring. Who's in for poker Wednesday night?"

"I'm in," Royston said.

"I can do that," Crash agreed.

I pulled off my T-shirt. "Sorry, I can't."

"Hot date?" Ducky asked.

I grinned. "Not quite what you're thinking of, Duckster. I'm going to the driving range."

Ducky looked at the partially dressed men around him. "We could do that instead."

I held up my hands. "Sorry, it's a private thing."

"But you said it's not a date."

"It's not. It's a lesson."

JJ, normally so quiet you could forget him, spoke up. "But it's with a woman, right?"

My cheeks heated and what the fuck was up with that? "Yes, I'm helping her get ready for a golf tournament in September. She's never golfed before."

"She must be hot."

Was she? Not conventionally. She was also blunt, a little prickly, and honest. It somehow made her relaxing to be with. "It's not like that. We're...friends."

Ducky cocked his head. "That's cool, I guess."

JJ frowned at me. "I don't remember you talking about a woman friend."

"I have women friends. Faith Devereaux. Her teammates, like Tempo and her roommate Megan Thomson."

"Faith is different. She's your best friend's wife. And Thomson has a crush on you. Had. I hear she's with someone now."

I shrugged. A lot of people had a crush on Cooper, the face of the Toronto Blaze. "Well, now I have Callie."

"Have you known her long?"

"Not sure why this seems worth discussing, but I am spending Wednesday and Friday teaching a friend, who happens to be a woman, to golf. As a favor. So, I won't be playing poker with Ducky. She's someone I met recently, and she doesn't want half the hockey team watching her learn."

"How about Thursday, then?"

I agreed to Thursday, and conversation moved on to whether Royston was allowed to join.

I was dressing back in the street clothes I'd worn today —dress pants and a short-sleeved shirt—when JJ came out of the showers. The others had gone, and I'd leave once JJ was ready.

"They don't mean anything by it, you know."

I gave him a sharp glance. "No?"

JJ pulled on his briefs. "They know you as Captain Cooper."

"Jesus. That sounds like a cheesy superhero."

"You're our James Bond."

I paused, checking JJ for an unexpected concussion. "What the hell?"

He gave one of his rare laughs. "Not that you're a spy. But you're good-looking, good at what you do, well dressed and always on top of things. You lead us. This group you set up to work out here? You're being the captain, watching over us and helping us prepare for the new season. But that's Captain Cooper. There's another Cooper behind who's a little less perfect, but we don't see him much."

JJ was quiet, but he observed. We'd been linemates for three seasons now. He was guarded, so he knew me better than I knew him.

"Captain Cooper, if you follow the analogy, doesn't have women friends. He has dates, and they don't last long. I know Hunter and Faith are your friends, and I like to think I am too. But these guys, even though they don't know you as well, picked up that this is a little different."

"I'm not completely altruistic. I'm helping her prepare for a golf tournament, and she's my date for a family wedding which will be a shitshow."

He stood up, throwing on a T-shirt. "If she's a friend, that's good. You need people you can be yourself around."

"So do you, JJ. You have your twin and who else?"

"You, I hope."

"Get your shoes on and let's go before we start crying and making friendship bracelets."

He flashed a grin. "As you wish, Captain Cooper."

I threw a towel at him.

* * *

CALLIE

I WORE MORE of the golf clothes I'd bought. A driving range in the city might not have a strict dress code like an expensive country club, but I liked these clothes. They felt good, and I felt good knowing I looked good.

Since Cooper, I didn't even want to wear some of my old stuff. At least I had a few new blouses to wear at the office, in the colors that Cooper and Valerie had picked to make me look good. And they did. I didn't know why, and wouldn't dare try something different on my own, but these colors were now going to be staples in my wardrobe.

I was waiting for Cooper at the door to my building when he pulled up. I managed to get in the car before he came around to help me.

"I hope you won't do that when we're at the wedding."

"What?" What the hell had I done wrong?

"Get in the car before I can open the door."

"But that's just a waste of time. I'm perfectly capable of opening my own door."

"Still."

I closed my eyes and drew in a breath. "Basically, when we're with your family it's like being at the country club permanently."

"That sums it up pretty well."

"What was that like when you were growing up?"

He shrugged. "It was all we knew. All our friends were the same, so I thought it was normal. Until I started playing hockey."

I shot him a glance. He was focused on driving, eyes slightly narrowed, hands relaxed on the wheel. He looked confident, even with buses cutting in and taxis treating yellow lights like greens.

Growing up the way he did was part of that confidence. He knew how to behave in any situation, how to be part of the in group. But despite that, he'd chosen hockey. I was curious about that, but it wasn't my business.

Still, I let the pause linger in case he wanted to share, but instead he told me about the place we were going.

I wasn't sure what to expect at a driving range, but this was a Cooper kind of place. There was parking that he could access with a card. Everything was clean, modern-looking and well cared for. He'd brought some clubs along, and I followed him to the entrance.

"Mr. Cooper, so glad to see you. We have your bay waiting for you."

He smiled his easy, charming smile, dimples in play, and the man's face lit up. He led us to "our" bay, as he called it. Cooper asked him questions as we walked, me following a couple of steps behind. I saw a lot of people do a double take, then watch Cooper.

Apparently the golfing contingent were big hockey fans.

Our friendly guide showed Cooper how everything

worked, which made me think Cooper hadn't been here before. Had he set this up all for me?

"Would you like a picture?" Cooper asked our guide, who was still lingering.

The man's eyes lit up. "If you don't mind."

Cooper posed for several shots, and then, reluctantly, Cooper's new friend left.

Something relaxed in Cooper—his shoulders were less rigid, his mouth softened, and he let out a long breath.

"Tough day?"

He turned to me and forced a smile. "Nothing to worry about."

I held up a hand. "I'm not asking for secrets about hockey or whatever. You just seemed tense. Are you sure you want to do this tonight?"

"Yeah. I do. Did you follow what he told us?"

I rolled my eyes. "What he told *you*. I don't think he noticed I was here."

"Does that bother you?"

"It's fine. Honestly. I'm good at being in the background. You'll just have to explain to me why the balls are going up and down on those tee things, and what's with tapping that card?"

Turned out this was a fancy automated system that would set different tee heights and would keep track of your shots.

"It's very elaborate."

"People take their golf seriously. Another time we can even virtually play Briarwood."

I did not understand that kind of obsession. "Do they insist on a dress code when you do?"

Cooper laughed. Maybe I was thinking too much about

it, but it felt like a real laugh, not one that was part of the Cooper experience he gave his fans.

"I haven't tried it, so I don't know. But you're covered with what you're wearing. Now, let's see if we can improve your swing with a little practice."

Two hours later I'd learned a few things. I was never going to be a real golfer—the kind of person who chose to spend hours hitting a ball with a club. Because it was kind of boring. I knew a little better how to swing a club and hit the ball so the ball went farther, the way it was supposed to. And I knew I'd been right that Cooper was incredibly patient.

Since I was the person with the most to learn, I spent most of the time on deck, and Cooper had to be behind the red line. Which meant people passing by felt they had access to him.

And they all wanted to be in that Cooper orbit. They wanted to share in his charisma and be close to their hero. I learned more about being a public figure than I did about golf. I was starting to believe he earned his inflated salary for playing hockey.

He did his best to balance being polite with fans and helping me. I was getting the hang of what I was doing, so I didn't need as much input from him. But one blowhard with a loud voice started to talk about "terrible loss" and "failure" and Cooper's smile grew more rigid. I wanted to shove the man out of our bay, but if Cooper was working so hard to protect his image, it wouldn't be helpful to undo it. And the guy had money, based on his clothes and an entitled air, so someday he might be a client.

Instead, I straightened, shoved my boobs out a touch, and did my best to sound sweet and flirty. "Coop, babe, I need some help here."

Blowhard turned as if he'd just realized there were more people around than him and Cooper. I tried a pout.

Cooper's rigid smile changed into something real. "Coming, honeybun." He turned to Blowhard. "She needs me." Disgruntled, Blowhard stood while Cooper walked over to me. "How can I help you, babe?" His eyes were glinting.

I batted my eyes. Blowhard was still waiting, so I had to make this good. I wiggled my hips. "How am I supposed to hit this again?" Was that going too far?

Cooper moved behind me. "Do I need to show you, sweetheart?" He bracketed my body with his, firm muscles forming a cage around me. I felt protected, sheltered. For a moment, I let myself relax into the feeling, imagining what it would be like to be someone who could do that. Be taken care of.

"Is he still there?" I muttered, low enough that only Cooper could hear me.

"Is that what this is about? Is he bothering you?" He placed his callused hands overtop mine on the club. Goose bumps pebbled my skin.

"Not me," I hissed. "You."

I felt him stiffen for a moment, then relax. "Now pull back." He lifted the club with our combined grips. We swung together, but I was paying more attention to the man behind me than the ball. That sheltered feeling lingered, and we missed hitting the ball altogether.

"Guess you'll have to keep showing me." I looked under Cooper's arm and saw Blowhard finally give up.

We swung again, and this time I paid attention, and the ball shot straight and far.

"Good job, Callie. You're definitely getting better."

I was. But I knew that a major part of that last shot was

because I'd relaxed. I'd followed Cooper's lead. I'd trusted him.

He stepped back. "How are you feeling?"

I dropped the club and rolled my shoulders. "Like that's enough for today."

"Then let's get out of here."

I nodded and thought that was more relief in his voice than he intended to reveal.

We ran into additional fans as we headed out, and Cooper was patient and charming but insisted we had somewhere to go. I did my best to look like I was eager to get Cooper to myself. I did like the man, liked talking to him. But that was when it was just us, and he didn't have to put on his public face.

I got my wish when we stopped at another small restaurant, one that was blessedly free of hockey fans. I'd told Cooper I was paying for the meal, because the driving range, like Briarwood, was charged to a membership card, and that I didn't have.

Cooper shrugged but it turned out I was wrong that no one at the restaurant cared about hockey. They insisted the meal was on the house.

As we headed back to the Bentley, I frowned at him. "Did you know they wouldn't let me pay?"

He shrugged. "Depends. I think they thought we were on a date and wanted to help out."

At least these fans weren't taking from him. "Friday, we're going someplace I can pay."

Chapter 14

Was I going to have to dress up?

I STEPPED out of the shower at the practice arena and wrapped a towel around my waist. Grabbing another to rub through my hair, I ambled into the locker room, rolling my shoulders to ease what tension remained.

"So how was your golf lesson?" Ducky asked slyly.

I flicked a towel at him. We'd had another hard workout today and I was feeling it. I wasn't twenty-four anymore, like my teammate.

"We went to the driving range and hit some balls. She's improving."

"That's it?" Ducky sounded disappointed. "No kissing? You didn't go out for dinner or anything?"

"We stopped for food after. No kissing." Not that I was opposed to the idea. Wrapping myself around her at the driving range had definitely inspired some non-platonic thoughts. What would Callie do if I tried to kiss her? She'd been more relaxed last night, but other than her flirty rescue from the guy who wanted to explain exactly how we'd lost that last game, she hadn't given any indication that she would welcome anything beyond golfing instruction.

"Maybe we should go out tonight then, instead of playing poker. Go to a club, hook up, have some fun."

My days of hooking up at clubs were over. I'd rather meet someone at a bar than a noisy club, where everyone was sweaty and overstimulated. But it would be Ducky's kind of scene.

"No." Petrov's voice was flat. "We have training in the morning. This is not the night to drink and sex."

"I get your point about the drinking, Petey, but sex—come on, that's another kind of workout."

"You are young, but soon you should be serious. Find a girl who will help you calm down. Not just for fun, no?"

Ducky's face fell. "Yeah, don't know if that's happening again."

Again? As long as I'd known Ducky, he'd been a light-hearted fuckboy.

Before Petey could ask him about it, Crash, JJ and Royston returned from the shower, and Seb Hunter walked in.

"Hunts!" Ducky never stayed down for long. "What are you doing slumming here?"

"Came to talk to your captain. Thought he might be up for lunch?"

"Sure." Something was up with Hunter, but I wouldn't ask him in front of the guys. Seb worked in player development, and he might have some inside news for me that wasn't for the whole team. Or it could be something about his daughter Hailey, my best girl.

We went to a place nearby that I'd found over my years playing on the Blaze. It was a hole-in-the-wall with good food but plain decor that discouraged most diners. The owners spoke very little English and cared nothing about hockey. Once we were at our table, waiting for our food, I found out that Hunts had news about the team *and* my goddaughter.

"They're announcing this tomorrow. Trading two of the Inferno and a high draft pick to Edmonton for Daniel Astrom and a kid named Chromy. Chromy will be playing in net in Hamilton."

"So what's happening to Mitchell?"

"They're keeping mum on that, but with this trade, they're either moving him next, or keeping him as backup for Petrov."

"For Tempo's sake, I hope they keep him. I think he could do pretty well, but that playoff goal is going to be hard to get over."

Our food arrived, and for the next couple of minutes that kept us busy.

"Speaking of Mitchell," Hunts started.

"You're going to see him next week, right? You and Faith are helping with his camps?"

"Yeah, we're flying out Friday. And we've got a problem."

"What's that?" I couldn't help with a flight cancellation, but I could maybe pull some strings if they needed to get there.

"Faith's mom is taking care of Hailey while we're away." I nodded. "But she's at the cottage. She was getting a ride back with a friend, and now that's been delayed."

"Ah, you need a Hailey sitter."

He grinned. "Yep. Grammy should be back about noon on Saturday, but her ride doesn't want to deal with Friday night traffic."

"You're asking if I know of any babysitters? Maybe someone on the team?"

Hunter laughed. "Ducky? Or even better, Petrov?"

"The thought of Petey trying to handle Hailey? I'd give money to see that. But of course I can do it. What time is your flight?"

"We have to be at the airport around three."

"I'll get there by two? How about I bring some lunch and come right after our workouts here?"

Hunts' shoulders dropped, but he shouldn't have worried. Whatever he needed, especially when it came to Hailey, I'd do it.

With that out of the way, we discussed what we knew about Daniel Astrom. He'd been born in Sweden, so played for their national team sometimes, but his family had moved to California when he was young and he'd gone to college there before being drafted by LA. He'd signed with Edmonton a couple of years ago, and now Edmonton had traded him to Toronto.

"Married, right?" Hunter said.

"I hear that's ended."

"Maybe he'll like a new start here."

* * *

Callie

I stood in front of the door to Faith Deveraux and Seb Hunter's apartment and wondered what the hell I was doing.

Cooper had called to tell me he couldn't make our...not really a date, but kind of. He needed to babysit his goddaughter, so I'd have to pick up the meal tab another time. And I could have left it at that.

I hadn't babysat since I'd been in foster care, and I remembered it being a chore. But after the uncomfortable time Cooper had at the driving range, and since I owed him a meal...I'd offered to help babysit and bring food.

I'd still been surprised when Cooper accepted the offer. So here I was, with pizza, including a cheese one for the kid, beer and juice boxes. I hoped that was good. I'd considered finding a toy to bring as well, but I had no idea what this girl would have or want. And that was almost as if I was bribing her to like me. Which was ridiculous. It didn't matter. I was just helping out a friend who was helping me.

I must have taken too long to knock, second-guessing what I was doing, because the door opened and I was not ready for this.

Cooper was a good-looking guy. I mean, he was on those billboards everywhere, so objectively, yes, he was very attractive. Seeing him in the doorway, with those blue eyes and blond hair and that ridiculously fit body, wearing a sparkly pink tiara and a purple tutu? That did something extra, chipping away at shields I had inside and putting a ridiculous smile on my face. Especially when he didn't apologize for it or show any signs of embarrassment.

A blonde head, also in a tiara, appeared around his knees. Narrow blue eyes peered at me suspiciously.

"Come on in. Hailey, this is my friend Callie. The pizza smells good. Step back, Hailey monster." The little girl stayed tightly behind Cooper's legs as he moved back so I could enter.

"I have plain cheese, for um, the monster."

Cooper laughed and bent down to pick up the girl, who I could see now was also wearing a purple tutu. Oh god, was I going to have to dress up as well?

As Cooper carried the girl to the kitchen, I looked around with interest. The condo was a little bigger than mine, but not too much fancier. The kitchen was large enough to have an island, instead of just a counter between the kitchen and living room.

The walls were mostly neutral, with color added in pillows and throws. Everything was chosen for comfort, not show. I could feel my body relaxing as I got farther into the space.

"This is nice," I said as I set down the boxes of pizza and bag of drinks.

Cooper sat Hailey on the counter. The girl was still watching me warily. I tried to smile at her, but I wasn't good with kids. And this one? Was not impressed.

"Hailey likes pizza."

Hailey shook her head.

"What are you up to, Hailey? You always eat pizza."

She crossed her arms. "Not dis."

I stared at the boxes. They were generic pizza boxes, showing a cartoon Italian holding a pepperoni pizza in his upraised hand. How could she hate the pizza without having seen it? Or did they only eat fancy organic pizza shit in different boxes?

"That's not polite. Callie brought you cheese pizza, special."

The little diva shook her head hard enough to jostle the tiara.

"Well, there's pizza to eat, and chicken and broccoli. Which do you want?"

Hailey's lower lip jutted out impossibly far and she shook her head again. This was why I'd given up on babysitting. How the hell was I going to help Cooper?

Cooper stared at the girl who was staring back at him just as hard.

"Okay." He picked her up and set her on her feet. By the frown on the small face, this was not a move she approved of. "Callie and I are going to eat now. You can go play." Cooper turned and reached for plates in a cupboard. "Hope you don't mind, but I'll have to augment the pizza with some boring protein and veg." He gave me a grin. "Training."

I mentally slapped myself. I hadn't considered that. "I'm sorry, I didn't think."

"It's okay. I don't expect the world to revolve around my training regimen."

He opened the fridge and pulled out some prepared containers. "I'll just warm this up in the microwave." Once he'd set it inside and punched some buttons, he headed to the table. "You can find cutlery in the drawer under the microwave."

I turned. Hailey had moved to stand in front of the drawer I needed. She'd done that on purpose.

"I brought juice boxes. If you let me get into that drawer, you can have one."

She shook her head.

But then Cooper was back. "I thought you were going to play, Hails."

She stepped aside for Cooper to open the drawer, giving me a triumphant look. Yeah, I wasn't good with kids, but I didn't remember one hating me like this.

I followed Cooper back to the table, bringing the beer along. "Can you drink beer with your training?" Looked like

I could have come empty-handed for all the good I was doing.

"Absolutely. What did you get?"

I'd texted Darcy for advice, and I'd picked some over-priced labels that he swore were good. Cooper nodded, so at least that part was working.

Cooper opened the boxes and invited me to help myself while he went back for his healthier portion. "What are you gonna do, Hailey? The pizza looks pretty good."

I pulled out a piece of the combination pizza. If I didn't seem to want the cheese, maybe Hailey would eat it and I'd feel like less of a failure. When she didn't respond, Cooper continued as if she wasn't there.

"Faith and Seb flew out to Montana today. They're helping a teammate run some hockey camps."

"Both of them?"

He picked a slice of combination pizza and added it to his plate of broccoli and chicken. Not even cheese sauce to make the plain vegetable more palatable.

"Faith plays for the Bonfire, the women's professional team here in Toronto. Hunts used to play, but he got a concussion, so now he works an office job for the team."

"That's how you met him?"

I took a bite of pizza, and yeah, it was good, despite what little divas might think. Cooper shared the story about meeting his friend in college, and helping the couple over-come some problems they had in their relationship.

The whole time, Hailey crept closer to the table, finally climbing up on a chair. Cooper didn't skip a beat. He pulled out a piece of cheese pizza and put it on a plate. He slid it over to the toddler and opened juice box for her too. I care-fully ignored her as she took a small bite of the pizza.

The whole piece finally disappeared. Neither

Cooper or I said a word, but he kept an eye on her, and when she was done, he turned to her. "So how was the pizza?"

She shrugged.

"You should thank Callie for bringing it."

She crossed her arms and shook her head.

"Don't worry about it." I expected a full-fledged tantrum if he insisted.

"Her mom and dad wouldn't let her be rude," he said, standing and taking the plates to the kitchen. Then he took the tiara off his head. "Sorry Hails, but I can't play with someone who isn't using their manners." He started to wiggle out of the tutu.

I fought to keep back a smile.

"NO!" Hailey shouted.

Cooper set the tutu on his chair. "Now you're yelling? That's not going to fly."

For a full thirty seconds, she struggled. Finally, "Tank you." The glare she shot me proved that she was doing this under duress.

"And the yelling?"

"Sorry," she muttered.

"That's better."

"Dwess up?"

"Maybe Callie wants to dress up?"

Not sure which of us was quicker to shoot down that idea. "Why don't you let me clean up while you do...your dressing up or whatever."

Cooper cocked his head at the girl. "Callie is being pretty nice to offer that so we can play."

She nodded. Then grabbed Cooper's hand and dragged him away.

It didn't take long. I put the leftover pizza in the fridge

and washed the dishes by hand rather than filling up only part of the dishwasher.

Cooper came out with Hailey again. This time the girl was in pajamas, but she and Cooper were now dressed up as some kind of animal, wearing headbands with ears. Hailey's pajamas included feet and a hood. Cooper suggested a movie, so we spent an hour on the couch, Hailey on my side of Cooper, snuggling in tightly against him. I hated to admit it, but it was adorable.

When the movie ended, Cooper said it was bedtime. I asked if I should go, making Hailey's face light up, but Cooper asked if I could stay for a bit. I was tempted to stick my tongue out at Hailey when I agreed, but I refrained. I was an adult, after all.

I scrolled on my phone while I waited. I wasn't surprised it took a while. Hailey did not want to share her godfather, at least not with me. And yeah, she was just a kid, but it didn't feel good, having someone immediately dislike you.

Cooper reappeared without any dress-up accessories. "Thanks for waiting."

"You sure you don't want me to go?"

He nodded. "Appreciate you coming."

"I didn't do much."

"I love the kid. But I can only take so much toddler time before I need some adult company."

I lifted my brows.

He ran a hand over his face. "Hell, that sounded wrong. No adult expectations here. Hailey's grandmother will be here tomorrow morning, but I don't care if we just watch a movie, as long as it doesn't have animated animals."

"Sure." Maybe coming over hadn't been a waste. Maybe I'd helped after all.

I didn't care what we watched, so he picked some action thing with a lot of explosions. This time there was no tiny diva separating us, and I had to fight a strange urge to snuggle up in the space she'd occupied.

It must be a reaction to Hailey, because I didn't snuggle people.

Chapter 15

What I'm doing wrong

COOPER

I'D ASKED Callie if some of my teammates could join us on our next trip to the driving range. I hoped that having more of my teammates around meant I could spend more time with her and less dealing with fans, as well as stopping Ducky from making up a romance. The guys had promised to behave. We'd see how well that lasted.

The extra practice time we'd put in was working—Callie had done better at Briarwood on the weekend but I knew she wasn't happy about having to let people play through while she searched for balls that had vanished in the rough.

This time at the range I booked two bays side by side. The same kid greeted us, and his eyes couldn't have gotten any bigger as he stared at the six of us with Callie.

As he led the way, I introduced the team to her. "The big guy is Petrov, Russian, goalie. He's...intense. Ducky, the short one, is kind of excitable, but wouldn't hurt anyone.

Crash, following Ducky—I'm giving you nicknames because that's what we use—is another defenseman. Royster, the tall redhead, is a forward on the shutdown line, and this is JJ. He's my partner."

Her eyes followed each name, and I knew she'd memorized them all.

"We've been curious about you," JJ said.

Callie shot a look my way.

"I told them about our arrangement, and they're nosy fuckers."

JJ smiled. "Coop is showing layers we didn't know he had."

I bumped my shoulder into him. "Don't freak her out."

We arrived at the bays. I'd brought the clubs Callie and I used, but the others decided to rent something here and save bringing their own. I preferred my own equipment, and Callie needed to be familiar with her clubs for her tournament.

Last time, Callie'd had the bay mostly to herself. I'd only taken a few shots, because she was the one trying to improve. This time, we all took turns.

Callie watched everyone carefully. Probably making mental notes on how they stood and swung and how effective they were. I saw Royston's eyes dwelling on her as she lined up for a shot.

I nudged him. "Don't."

"Don't what?"

"She's not a jersey chaser."

He shot a glance at me. "Doesn't mean she might not want some fun."

"She doesn't do fun. She's a tax attorney, on the partner track. She's only taking time for golf for her firm's tournament."

"She can turn me down herself. You don't need to gatekeep."

"I'm trying to help her here. Don't make it uncomfortable."

"Dude, I've been turned down before." He shrugged. "Doesn't have to be uncomfortable."

"I'm telling you this is not the time."

He smirked. "You're not with her, right? So it's up to her."

I wanted to march the guy right out of the facility and throw him on his ass, but settled for a glare and made sure Royston played in the other bay. Next time we weren't inviting this crew along.

A man with a prominent belly stretching his expensive polo shirt stopped where we were taking turns. "This is how the team is spending the offseason?"

Royston stiffened beside me, so it wasn't just me getting asshole vibes off this guy.

"We need some downtime." I smiled, teeth gritted, being the team rep I was supposed to be.

"After that last game, I think you need something other than downtime. That pass—and Mitchell. Hope he's back with the Inferno where he belongs."

Most hockey fans were great. They might assume they knew us and invade some of our personal space, but they loved hockey, loved the team, and were the foundation of our sport. Without them, I wouldn't be playing the game I loved and getting paid well to do so. But some thought they knew more than we did, more than our coaches did, and that it was necessary to give us their input.

I put a hand on Royston's shoulder before he exploded into speech. He was rash, and I didn't need him to get in trouble. Too many people watching, too many phones ready to catch an encounter.

Ducky was up in the other bay, which was good because he was the most impulsive. Crash and JJ were unlikely to shoot off their mouths. And Petrov—well, he was a law unto himself. He headed over. *Shit.* This could go badly.

Suddenly Callie pushed past us. "Mr. Duffy. How are you doing?"

He frowned at her. "Do I know you?"

"I work at Anderson, Krys and Chan. I was in a meeting to discuss your new expansion."

His eyes dropped and focused on her breasts. My hand formed a fist, and this time Royster was holding on to me.

"Hard to believe I missed you."

A small smile. "Tax attorneys are a necessary evil. We're often overlooked."

"I'll look for you next time."

"Mr. Anderson will be so pleased to hear that. But we have only a limited time here— Do you know Mr. Cooper and Mr. Royston?"

His eyes were on her face now. "Everyone knows them. They're on the Blaze."

"But they aren't here to play hockey today."

"They could do some improving on the hockey front."

Her brows rose. "Oh, you're a coach as well?"

"No, but I know the sport. Better than most."

"I'm sure they appreciate the insight. But that's their job, and I know they've spent most of the day working out and practicing—I think they need some time off. Just like I'm sure you wouldn't want me to start talking to you about your tax issues here, would you?"

He definitely wasn't looking at her bust now. "Are you threatening to talk about private business matters?"

Her eyes went round. "Oh, no. I just assumed you were here to get a break from work, like these men."

By this point, Petrov was standing beside the man, arms crossed. He was frowning. Petrov wasn't our biggest guy, but he was tall enough and solid, and could look scary.

I could see the battle going through Asshole's mind. If things went south got physical, it would look bad for us. But with Callie between him and the team, it would look worse for him, taking on a young woman.

"Of course," he said. "My friends are waiting for me."

"Sure you wouldn't like a photo?" I smiled broadly.

"No. I'll leave you to it."

We watched him walk away.

"He is asshole," Petrov stated.

"Yeah, but we don't need to look like we are. Not with cameras around."

"Did you guys miss that shot I just made?" Ducky hadn't realized what was going on, but he stepped over now.

"No—let's see you do it again?"

"Okay. I think I figured out what I'm doing wrong."

The guys got back to their game. I put a hand on Callie's arm, to stop her for a moment.

"You're not going to get in trouble at work over this, are you?" I appreciated that she'd stepped in. But I didn't want her to risk her career. This whole golfing setup was to try to advance her path, not derail it.

"He doesn't know my name. And I was in one meeting with him, but it was a couple of years ago. I don't work on his file."

"Thanks."

Dealing with fans was part of the job. So was taking care of my teammates. Taking care of Callie? Not in my job description, but I was doing it anyway.

* * *

CALLIE

WHAT THE HELL had I been thinking? Every time an email notification popped up, I dreaded a question about why I'd been interacting with Mr. Duffy at a driving range.

What I'd told Cooper was true—I'd consulted at one meeting with Duffy but he wasn't my file. Still, it wouldn't be unheard of for him to complain to the firm. He was obviously entitled, and I shouldn't have gotten involved. But I'd rushed to Cooper's defense like he needed my help.

But really, to criticize professional athletes about their game? When they were just having an evening out? That was stepping over some lines. Duffy had relied on the fact that these younger, bigger and much fitter men had to be polite because they had a reputation to uphold. That was taking advantage, and it bothered me. Which was unnecessary. Those men dealt with that all the time. I hoped they didn't laugh over my intervention.

I wrenched my attention back to my work. We were replying to CRA about how they'd interpreted the way a client had set up a subsidiary, and I needed to make sure all my citations were correct.

A knock on my doorframe interrupted me. I glanced up. Leonie was away from her desk and oh goody, Benson had stopped by when there was no one to run interference.

"May I help you?"

He leaned on the doorframe he'd knocked on. He was in an expensive suit, but I examined his shirt. Was this one the wrong color as well? I wanted to take a picture to check with Cooper, but I didn't see a way to do that without Benson getting too much information about me.

"I hear you're going to the golf tournament in September."

"That's correct."

"I'll be there too. My third time."

Yes, I knew. Benson didn't keep it much of a secret.

"Too bad you didn't get those golf lessons with the pro at Briarwood."

My smile grew. I think I'd come out ahead on that one. I might have been slightly better off as a golfer with the pro, though the extra sessions at the driving range were paying off. But the golf pro couldn't have given me the inside knowledge of being at the club as a client rather than an employee. "I'll manage."

"My dad is really enjoying them."

I raised my brows. Benson had bid on those lessons just to foil me? Perhaps I needed to get out of my little bubble and find out why he was so determined to make me look bad.

"I'm sure they'll be very beneficial." Some people took golfing way too seriously. I could see Benson's family being like that.

"Maybe you don't want to go to this thing? If you don't know how to play or how to act at the club...I'd hate for you to look bad in front of the partners and some of our best clients."

"I'll manage," I repeated.

"Oh, Benson. What are you doing here?"

Praise be, it was Mr. Anderson. Why he came in person I didn't know, since he normally set up meetings through our assistants. But I really wanted Benson to move along and share his particular charm with someone else.

"I was just checking something with Callie."

Anderson frowned. "I wasn't aware you were working on anything together."

"He was asking for some general tax advice," I said.

Benson stiffened.

Anderson focused his attention on me, and I held myself upright. If Anderson was here to scold me about my interaction with Duffy in front of Benson...

"You made it out to Briarwood again? Someone told me they'd seen you there."

I thought back. I hadn't spoken to anyone, but several of the partners were members and they might have recognized me. Oh, maybe they were in one of the foursomes we let play through. "I've been there a few times."

Benson glared at me. "You're not a member."

I shook my head. "A friend brought me. So I'd be familiar with the place before the tournament."

Anderson nodded. "Excellent. Sound planning. I'm happy to see you're not limiting your education to tax issues."

I had to thank Cooper for helping me see that I had to broaden my focus past the tax act.

"Ah, Benson. You're working on Cartwright's with Palmer, aren't you?" Anderson started back to his own office, and Benson had to follow. "Would you mind passing on..."

I relaxed for a brief moment. I was impressing Anderson, and a petty part of me enjoyed that Benson was going to stew over who my golfing friend was. He'd never guess.

Chapter 16

They had my back

CALLIE

I HAD STARTED to look forward to Sundays at Briarwood. It was good to get out of the office and leave work behind. One week Darcy came with us and pretended to caddy. I'd played better that day, more relaxed with him around. I'd been happy to see him and Cooper getting along. Technically, I was doing this to advance my career, but neither tax nor law were mentioned all day.

I didn't have to worry about how I looked, since that was covered. And now, my game still needed improvement but I knew what I was doing. And I was doing it well enough. This week, no one had played through, which I counted as a major accomplishment. It had been rainy this morning, so people had canceled their tee times and there were fewer people on the course, but I was feeling good about my progress, and tremendously grateful to Cooper.

I'd decided that gratitude was why I'd leapt to defend him from Duffy. It didn't explain that strange urge I'd had to cuddle, but I had enough problems to deal with so I set that aside.

We'd agreed to head to the locker rooms before meeting for dinner. I changed into a dress and fixed my hair and makeup. I no longer ended the day with a pink nose. There was something almost like a tan on the skin visible through my freckles. I looked okay, I thought. More than okay. I looked good. Would Cooper approve?

A woman came into the restroom, nodded at me and continued into the next section. She didn't even raise an eyebrow—she thought I belonged.

I pulled the door open, ready to share my triumph with Cooper, but before I got close to him I heard a Boston accent drawl out, "If it isn't the little Cooper."

My brows shot up, not just at calling Cooper little, since he was anything but, but at how his whole body stiffened. Should I step forward and offer support, or would he rather handle this without me around?

"If it isn't the big Winthrop," Cooper responded.

A man, early thirties, stopped in front of Cooper. He was a few inches shorter than the hockey player, softness around his arms and middle indicating an easy life. No question who would win a fight. Some might call the other man attractive, with dark brows and thick dark hair, a firm chin and straight nose, but something about the eyes and the drawl convinced me this was another Benson.

"I didn't think you golfed." That drawl had to be an affectation.

"I'm with a friend." Cooper looked back and I moved beside him. Was that a flash of relief in his eyes? "Callie, this is a friend of my brother's, Remington Winthrop."

Seriously? What a douchebag name.

"Pleased to meet you." Douchebag's eyes ran down my body, coming back up to land on my breasts.

Yep, douchebag.

"Winthrop lives in Boston. So, slumming it up north?"

He moved his attention back to Cooper. "Something like that. We're working with a firm up here. I came to make sure they're getting their shit done." He looked around the clubhouse, late afternoon sun lighting up the interior. "Not a bad place." He smirked at Cooper. "You don't mind sharing with me, do you?"

I could feel the tension in Cooper's body. This was not the confident man I was used to. What the fuck had happened with Douchington Winthrop?

"What do you do?" I asked, distracting him.

He gave me a dismissive glance. "Finance. Business stuff."

Right. Like I wouldn't understand. Cooper was still stiff beside me.

"All those big numbers, right?" I poked Cooper in the ribs. He jerked, but it finally got him moving again.

"How long are you here for?"

"We're leaving the club after we eat. But if things go well, I might be in Toronto frequently. I should ask about a membership of my own."

Finally Cooper smirked, and it felt like he was back. "I hear there's a long waiting list."

Winthrop narrowed his eyes. "How long were you on the list?"

Cooper shrugged. "I didn't go on a list."

"Because?"

A big smile, showing white teeth and dimples. Actually, more of a grimace. "Lots of hockey fans in the club."

Winthrop's mouth pinched. "Maybe this isn't my kind of place."

"Maybe not. It would be terrible if someone blackballed your application."

Winthrop drew in a sharp breath. Cooper had won a point in whatever the fuck battle they had going on. "Apparently this place has run downhill lately."

"Be sure to tell the PGA that. They'll probably move their event from here."

"I won't keep you." I got a glance again but was dismissed. "I'm sure you're...busy."

"Yes, more...I mean, important things to do."

"I'll tell Pierce I saw you."

"That will make his day."

Winthrop stalked toward the dining room. He joined a group of similar, well-dressed, well-maintained, douchy-looking men.

Cooper stared at the wall, as if he'd forgotten I was there. I could give him time to deal with whatever that had been, since I didn't particularly want to eat in the same room as Winthrop. After a few minutes, though, it was getting awkward.

"Did his parents really name him Remington Winthrop?"

That brought Cooper back to the here and now. "They did."

"Were they determined to raise an asshole?"

A laugh escaped him that he quickly reined in. "My name is Whittaker. Whittaker Zane Cooper."

"I thought Calliope was bad."

He shrugged. "Dining room?"

"Would you mind if we didn't?"

Now I had his full attention. "Is something wrong? Are you tired?"

"I'm always tired after marching around in the sun for the afternoon, but nothing special. I just don't want Remington staring at my chest while I eat."

"Should I speak to him?"

"Like it would change anything?"

That faraway look hit his face again. "Not at all."

"Then let's go. I think I've had my quota of pretentious for the day. At least at work I'm paid for it."

Cooper stalked to the valet, and I had to hustle to keep up with him. Something had upset his deeply ingrained manners, and that something was called Winthrop.

He didn't speak as the young man brought the Bentley around. They put the clubs in the trunk, and I waited patiently as the valet opened my door. Sliding into the comfortable seat was familiar. *Probably best not to get too accustomed.*

We drove in silence for ten minutes before Cooper realized he was ignoring me.

He turned and gave me his polite, public smile. "Sorry, I was lost in thought there. Did you have any questions after today's round?"

That hurt. I'd thought we were friends. Of a kind. He didn't need to tell me what was up with Winthrop, but if he didn't want to make conversation, he didn't need to put on his facade. "You don't have to make small talk."

He shot a glance at me. "Sorry. Not in my best mood."

"That's okay. I'm not one of your fans who has to be placated. If you don't want to talk, don't talk."

"Okay." He shrugged and sank back into his thoughts.

And irrationally, now I wanted to make him talk. To tell me what the tension with Winthrop had been. Was it some-

146

thing about his brother? He had said his family wasn't very nice.

As the car moved through the outskirts of the city, he spoke again. "I don't think I'm going to be a good dinner companion."

"Fine."

"We can do dinner another night. You can even pay."

"Cooper, you don't owe me. If you're in a bad mood, be in a bad mood. Go punch a bag or kill people in a video game or whatever you want to do."

"I want to drive."

"Lucky for you, you've been doing that."

He shook his head. "Not this car."

I frowned, but of course—why would I think the man had only one car? This might be Toronto, where the traffic was insane, but he had more money than he could spend. "Let me guess, a Lamborghini? Ferrari? Porsche?"

That got a smile. "A Ferrari."

"I knew it."

He shot me a glance. "It's not what you think."

"And what do I think?"

"It's not about the image. What other people think. It's about how she feels to drive."

There was no doubting his honesty. His voice had gone deeper, and he almost smiled again. I shivered. Not something I could relate to, but I'd never driven a vehicle. "I'll have to take your word for it."

Something sparked in his eyes. "Do you want to come for a drive?"

Didn't he want to be alone? "When?"

"Now? Do you need to be somewhere? Fuck, you're probably hungry."

I wasn't ready to head back to my apartment alone. I'd

planned to be with Cooper at Briarwood for the rest of the day. I wasn't that hungry, and when would I get a chance to ride in a Ferrari again? Was I trying to justify saying yes? "I didn't have anything planned, and I'm not hungry."

A smile picked up the corners of his mouth this time. "Okay."

I wasn't just curious about the sports car. I wanted to understand this man who was helping me. And his family. I wanted to help him. Meeting Winthrop had shown me that the Cooper family would be a challenge, and I wasn't prepared for what was coming. Those undercurrents indicated problematic issues that could set Cooper off, and I didn't know how to avoid them. Or protect him when they came up.

We pulled into the underground parking of a luxury condo building near the waterfront. It looked like the kind of place Cooper would belong. He pulled into a parking stall next to a sleek, red, low-slung car that was probably the Ferrari. I peered at the back bumper. I thought that rearing horse was the Ferrari symbol.

I opened the door of the Bentley carefully, pretty sure dinging the red vehicle beside me would be considered sacrilege. Once I was safely standing behind the cars, I looked at the gleaming vehicle. "So, this is a Ferrari?"

He nodded.

"It's...low."

He looked at me, as if just remembering I was wearing a dress.

I waved a hand. "It's okay. No one is here to see me flash them when I get in."

I got another smile of approval, and this one—a real smile, not a polite expression—warmed something inside me. Very few people got to see this person beneath the perfect facade. I liked this man, more than I'd expected. And I liked knowing he'd let me see past the mask.

And hell, I was going to ride in a Ferrari. Darcy would be so jealous.

Cooper drove the sports car with the competence he seemed to have for everything. I was confident in my work, but not in all the aspects of being a lawyer—hence the need to learn how to behave at the golf tournament, and how to dress. Today was the first chink I'd seen in Cooper's armor. I hadn't known there was one, but realistically? Everyone had their secrets and weak spots. Some just covered it better.

There wasn't much chance to show how the car performed on the city streets, but he was soon on the Gardiner Expressway, weaving his way through traffic, and the car attracted a lot of attention. We curved onto the Don Valley Parkway, heading north. Then the 401 East, heading out of the city, traffic lighter as few people were exiting the city on a Sunday.

The car was smooth and fast, and with a good driver, exhilarating. Like a roller coaster that didn't need to suspend you on a hill to make your stomach swoop. It was reckless and exciting, and totally unlike me, but I was just along for the ride. Enjoying it more than I'd have predicted.

Cooper eventually pulled into a service center along the 401. He stopped near the doors. "You have to be hungry now. Why don't you get us some burgers or something, and meet me around back?"

He looked out the windshield, and I saw the eyes staring at the car. *Of course.*

"Sure. What can you eat?"

He shook his head. "Anything goes tonight."

I opened the door and managed to exit without flashing the watchers. Those were disappointed sighs I heard as I wasn't any kind of celebrity. *Sorry, people.* The celebrity was still inside.

I was a little overdressed for a service center, but the range of clothing here was broad so I didn't attract attention. I analyzed the vendors available, and got an assortment of burgers, salads, sandwiches, fruit, veggies and drinks. The prices were inflated for their captive audience, but this time I wasn't going to stress about it.

The sun hadn't set yet, so it wasn't difficult to find my way to the Ferrari parked in the back. Cooper was sitting a little distance away on a picnic table. He had his back to the building, and so far had escaped attention. A minor miracle.

He must have heard me approaching, but he didn't react. I climbed up on the picnic table beside him and spread out my findings in the space between us.

He looked down and forced a grin. "You must be hungry."

I shrugged. "I wanted to give you options."

He picked up a burger. It was greasy and had about a zillion calories, but he opened the wrapper and took a large mouthful, groaning in pleasure. "I haven't had something like this in too long."

I rolled my eyes. "Obviously, or you'd be as big as a house." I chose a sandwich. I was worried less about the calories in a burger and more about getting grease spots on what I was wearing.

"Afraid I'm going to get fat?"

"Not my business if you do or not. But I'm sure you'll burn it off, since, you know, you're playing a sport professionally."

"I won't be forever."

That was true, but I'd never heard him mention that before. "Does that worry you?"

"I've got plans. Financially, I'm set for life, and I've been approached about different options when I'm done."

Of course he had. But still... "Will it be hard to not play anymore?"

He was still staring at the horizon. "It'll make my family happy."

He finished the burger and reached for the fries. Apparently, if he was going to eat junk, he was going to eat all the junk. I took a bite of my sandwich. No groans, because it was a barely adequate sandwich, and I looked out across the pavement to the bushes behind the service center. The sun had almost set, so the shadows were long and the evening was cooling. I didn't get moments like this. I'd enjoyed Briarwood, and I enjoyed this. Maybe, once I made partner, I'd learn to drive and explore outside the city. Or take the train.

Cooper picked out some slightly dry carrot sticks. Apparently he could only handle so much grease. "You're still willing to come to the wedding?"

I swallowed. "Yes." I wouldn't renege on our deal now.

"Then I should explain a bit of family history. Remmy will be there, and my brother, and it might come up."

I was as curious as any cat, but I hated the resignation in his voice. "Only if you want to."

He let out a humorless laugh. "I don't want to, but it's not fair to you to go in blind."

I set down the sandwich. "Okay, then."

He leaned back on his hands, watching the shadows stretching farther across the pavement.

"I was sixteen. At that point, my brother Pierce and I had the normal older brother/younger brother relationship people had, as far as I knew. I secretly admired him, and he gave me a hard time. I didn't see him that often. He was at

Harvard and had his own friends he kept busy with. I was going to a private boys' school, but I also played on a local hockey team. It was a lot of fun, and I was good. I'd started going out with one of the girls who came to the games and hung around with us. She was...gorgeous."

Like that was a surprise. The mediocre sandwich didn't rest well in my stomach.

"I was home for reading week. Pierce and his girlfriend were there too. I didn't think much of it, was mostly counting down till I could see Vicky and get back on the ice."

He crunched up the can of sparkling water he'd emptied.

"Pierce's girlfriend made a pass at me. I turned her down, obviously, but somehow Pierce found out. I went back to school, back to Vicky, and began planning, god help me, a promposal."

I pictured a young Cooper, perhaps a little awkward and gawky, but undoubtedly attractive. More so than his brother, I expected. But I braced myself, because this story was going somewhere bad.

"We went to a hockey tournament, were gone for most of a week. I'd taken a couple of days off school because there were some hockey scouts there and I'd hoped they might notice me. Maybe I'd make the team at Harvard—because obviously, as a Cooper, that's where I was going."

He'd also said he'd gone to college in Vermont, so...

"Pierce sent me a picture. Sent me a few of them. He was in a hotel room with Vicky."

My fingers twisted into claws on the picnic table.

"He messaged something about making us even, so I knew it was about his girlfriend. I told him I'd turned her down, but he didn't care. When I got back to school, Vicky came to our next hockey game, crying, begging me to forgive her. She told me a story about him seducing her and I wanted to believe her. So I took her back."

I wouldn't have.

"I didn't realize, back then, that she wasn't interested in me. I was the rich kid on the hockey team. She wanted someone to provide the kind of life she dreamed of. That became obvious a couple of weeks later, again when we had an away game and Pierce sent me a photo of Vicky with his best friend, Remmy."

The fuckers.

"I told my family. My dad said 'boys will be boys.' Vicky wasn't the right kind of girl, and I needed to focus on my future and give up hockey. But my teammates? They had my back. Pierce and Remmy found their cars vandalized while I was at a family dinner and had an alibi."

No wonder he chose hockey.

"I stuck with the people who supported me. My maternal grandmother had set up a trust fund for each of us, and she let me use it to go to a hockey college. My family was offended but I wanted to be with people who had my back."

His family obviously didn't. Benson could only aspire to that level of spite. And the girl? I saw myself in Vicky—growing up poor and wanting to be financially secure. But I didn't lie and manipulate and use people. I made my own security. "I hope she sees your underwear billboards every time she leaves her fucking home and regrets her choices," I growled.

Cooper shrugged. "I learned an important lesson. Not everyone is trustworthy. It was brutal, but it was better to learn that when I did."

This was something real about Cooper. I wondered if

anyone else outside of his family knew about this. Seb Hunter? Was he a teammate back them?

"I got that lesson in foster care. But what a bitch." But there'd been a deeper betrayal. "And your brother deserves an STD. A really disgusting and painful one. What—who would do that?"

"Pierce. And Remington fucking Winthrop."

"Fucking Pierce as well. He was jealous." I understood Cooper better now. "They hate the underwear billboards, right?"

"Immensely."

I frowned. "Was that why you did them?"

He shrugged. "They pay me a shit ton of money." I was about to argue that couldn't be the only reason when he continued. "But yeah, knowing how they feel about it makes it even better."

Families were mostly screwed-up entities determined to fuck up their kids for the future. Even wealthy ones like Cooper's. "I wish I'd known this before I met the fucker. I'd have taken my driver to his balls."

Finally, a laugh. "As your mentor, I have to warn you that behavior like that can get you removed from Briarwood."

It would be worth it. Cooper took care of everyone else, but who took care of him? Someone should.

For now, I was the only candidate in sight.

* * *

We were quiet on the ride back to Toronto. I didn't know if Cooper regretted telling me, or if he was still dealing with the encounter with Remington fucking Winthrop, but I was comfortable in the quiet, enjoying the feel of the car around me.

Cooper stopped in front of my building. "Are you okay going in on your own?"

I rolled my eyes, as if this wasn't something I did all the time. "I'll be fine."

"Thank you." Then he reached over and pressed a kiss to my cheek.

I froze for a moment, and then my face heated. "It was nothing." My voice came out low and gruff.

I scrambled out of the car, a major effort, and closed the door carefully. I waved, unsure if Cooper would see it through the tinted windows, and turned to enter my building.

I wished that kiss had been somewhere other than my cheek.

Cocky Cooper, with his confidence and money and charm, was someone I didn't understand and couldn't relate to. But vulnerable, betrayed and mistrusting Cooper? That was someone like me. That was the person I wanted to defend and snuggle up to.

I was glad I was going to this wedding. He might think he needed someone to impress them with a legal back-ground, but what was even more important in this situation was someone like his hockey teammates. Someone who had his back.

I tilted my chin up. I was more than ready to be that person.

Chapter 17

Be the playmaker

Sometimes I liked to run outside, smell the air coming off the lake and be fairly anonymous. There was privacy from fans when I worked out at the team facilities, but I was still the captain, and I was on duty while I was there. If I used a gym somewhere in the city, even in my building, people watched. Sometimes they didn't just watch.

I was paid a lot of money to represent my team, and with that came the responsibility of dealing positively with the public. But sometimes I needed to be me, not "the captain of the Blaze." Running outside gave me a chance at that. It wasn't foolproof, since my sponsorships had made me recognizable. But even the most intrusive fans couldn't be upset that I was working out—and they couldn't keep up.

I'd asked Seb to join me on my run. Meeting Winthrop, talking to Callie... It had all been unsettling, and after too much time dwelling on that, I needed to shove those uncomfortable things back in a box so I could make it through the wedding. It was a month away, and after that, training camp would start in September.

We greeted each other and stretched. Seb and I ran in silence for a few minutes. It was early, to beat the heat. And with school vacation, enough people were out of town that the boardwalk wasn't too busy.

"How was your trip to Montana?" I asked. "Mitch's program going well? How's he doing?"

Seb wiped a hand over his forehead. "Yeah. The kids and their parents were really excited about having something like this in places without hockey opportunities. And Jayna and Faith there together? There were a lot of girls watching them like they were superheroes. A few boys too."

Mitch wouldn't have realized, when he set the program up, that it might help him as well. "Keeping busy with the camps is good for him. That goal still bothers him, but Tempo has been there, can help him deal with it. How's she doing?" Mitch's girlfriend was a former teammate of Faith's on the Bonfire, the Toronto professional women's hockey team, and had found out in the spring that a knee injury was ending her career.

Seb's brow furrowed, so he was giving this real thought, not a pat answer. "The camps, this whole summer program, it's helping her. But she hasn't processed it all. We talked, and I tried to help." Seb had retired from playing before his daughter was born, after a bad concussion. He knew what Tempo was going through.

"Glad you could help her."

Tempo—Jayna Templin—wasn't my responsibility. But her boyfriend Mitch was our team backup goalie, so indirectly, her well-being affected my team. And I liked her. She'd been a great right winger till this injury took her out.

"She appreciates all you've done to help her too."

I shrugged. I hadn't done much. And I'd been given so much, it was only fair to help others. "Happy to help."

"Speaking of helping…"

"Were we?"

He bumped a shoulder into mine, knocking me slightly off-balance. "How come I hear your workout buddies got to meet your new woman before Faith and me?"

I laughed. "Hey, your daughter got to meet her. And she's just a friend."

"But Hailey won't talk about her."

I bit back a grin. "She didn't like Callie."

He frowned again. "Is that something to worry about?"

"You mean like dogs are supposed to be good judges of character? Don't worry—Hailey was jealous."

Hunter was quiet for a few strides. "Is there something she should be jealous of?"

Maybe. The thought slipped out. Was that the issue? Hailey was my goddaughter and one of the people I loved most in the world. Had she seen something? Callie wasn't a typical friend or date.

I hadn't realized how setting up this agreement would tie us together over the summer. We were…definitely friends. Closer than. I hadn't even told Hunter about my brother and Vicky. But after meeting Winthrop, and his comments, I'd spilled the whole story. I'd rationalized it because I had to tell Callie what the situation would be when she got to Connecticut, but was that the only reason? For the first time, telling someone had made me feel better.

"So there is something?"

"We're…friends."

"Just friends?"

"I'm not fucking her, so yeah."

"You could be dating without fucking."

"Have you ever known me to do that?"

Hunter slowed to a walk and then stopped. I did too, wondering if he'd hurt something. There was no one near us here, so we had the illusion of privacy.

"I'd like to meet her."

I narrowed my eyes. He rarely met my dates, since they normally lasted for one event, and he wasn't always around. Faith loved to name-check who they were, but they weren't part of my life. He knew that.

His jaw was set. My protesting wasn't going to do anything but convince him I was hiding something.

"Okay, come to Briarwood with us Sunday."

His eyebrows shot up. "Really?"

I nodded. "Callie's learning how to navigate the greens and the clubhouse. Extra eyes to see if I'm missing something would be good." The day Darcy came with us had been fun, but he knew less about golf than Callie did. And after spilling my guts yesterday, I was uncomfortable with the idea of more time alone with Callie. Seb as a buffer would be good. Maybe Darcy could join us at the driving range. Make sure this stayed an arrangement.

"Sure." He jerked his head back the way we'd come and we settled into our running tempo again. "And then the two of you can come to our place for dinner. Believe me, Faith is just as curious as I am."

* * *

THAT WEEK I had a photo shoot with a watch company. After our morning working out at the practice facility, I met the crew at a hotel downtown where they'd booked a suite for the shoot. I wasn't going to be showing much skin, but I was pumped up from the workout, which should help with the photographs.

It was an expensive watch manufacturer, putting out a new line called Playmaker. Despite being on defense, I set up a lot of goals and ran the power play for the team, so they thought I was a good face for the product.

They'd promised to provide a wardrobe, but I'd brought my own tux. It would look better than anything they could come up with since it had been tailored for me by one of the best in the city. I was more comfortable in my own clothes.

The sponsor had provided the obligatory partner for the shoot. A willowy brunette, beautiful, poised...my usual type. For a moment I was disappointed that there was no bright red hair. Which was fucking stupid, since there was no chance Callie would be here. We each got ready in one of the bedrooms of the suite, and came out for makeup and to pose on the... Oh hell, they'd decided to put her on the piano, while I sat in front of the keyboard with a glass of fake whiskey in my hand, watch prominently displayed.

I settled in to wait. These things were always slow. Setting up lights, checking the angles for unexpected shadows, perfectionist photographers...it was part of the job.

My co-model, Monique, chatted with me as we waited to be positioned, lighted, touched up and posed.

She leaned a hip against the couch. "I've been looking forward to meeting you. I'm a big fan."

I stood beside her. We didn't risk wrinkling our clothing by sitting down. "I'm a big fan of yours as well." I'd looked up some of her portfolio when this was all set up. She photographed well, and had a reputation for being easy to work with.

Full red lips tipped into a smile. Green eyes peered up at me through dark lashes, and her long, almost black hair moved around her shoulders as she shifted a little closer. "I'm a bigger fan of the billboards than your sport, if I'm being honest."

"It's easier work than hockey. Fewer bruises."

She pouted. "Ever thought of hanging up the skates to do this full-time?"

I barely repressed a shudder. *Never* was the answer, but that wasn't the game we were playing. "I'm only here because of hockey. I'm the 'playmaker.'"

"I'd love to play with you."

I sighed. I knew the moves, but I couldn't be bothered today. Fortunately, we were called to the piano then. Monique was helped onto the baby grand that this expensive suite came with, and once she was carefully draped over the lid, I sat on the piano bench and let them pose me.

I was supposed to look off camera, lost in my own importance and playmaking, while Monique gazed at me with longing. *Buy this watch, and you too will have gorgeous models pining for you.* It was a silly concept, but it worked.

The day dragged tediously. I was uncomfortable, unsettled. I blamed it on Winthrop, and the need to dredge up my past. Normally I'd enjoy flirting with Monique to pass the time, and after, I'd have invited her for dinner and whatever might follow.

Maybe it was the Cup loss, not only Winthrop, because when Monique suggested just that, I declined politely, blaming my grueling training sessions. She looked disappointed but shrugged. She didn't know me, except as an image on the billboard. She'd have liked it if we'd hooked up, to have the story, another name she'd been with.

The thought of Callie popped into my head again, I forced it back. Callie, thanks to that story from high school, knew a part of me that wasn't successful and rich and popular. She saw the real me. But she didn't want anything more, so why was that thought even in my head?

Damn it, I needed to get back on my game. Be the playmaker they paid me for.

* * *

CALLIE

I WAS surprised when Cooper mentioned his friend Seb Hunter was joining us at Briarwood. Except for meeting some of his teammates at the driving range, and Darcy hanging out with us sometimes, it had always been just the two of us. Cooper said it would be good to have some additional eyes on how I was doing. Golf-playing eyes. Between the driving range and his friend today, I would be familiar with guys I didn't know watching me. That should help for the tournament.

Seb was a patient teacher, focused more on the mechanics of golf than the behavior of people golfing. Between him and Cooper, I got a lesson that covered all the aspects of the game that I needed to know. The two men were greeted by a lot of the other golfers on the course, mostly other men, and I was happy to stay back and observe. Blending in was a vital skill, and I worked hard at it.

When we finished our round, I started to head almost automatically to the clubhouse.

"We've been invited to Seb and Faith's for dinner."

I jerked my head around. "What?"

Seb frowned at his friend. "You didn't ask her?"

"I wanted her to meet you first. Otherwise, she would have made an excuse."

My cheeks heated up. Damn, the man knew me too well.

Seb shook his head. "It's not fair, dropping this on her. Callie, don't worry about coming if it makes you uncomfortable."

I smiled weakly at Seb. There was no easy way to get out of this.

"Consider this another lesson," Cooper said, and if my glare could cut, he'd have been bleeding. "This time a wedding lesson."

I crossed my arms and frowned.

"My family will be nosy, just like Seb and Faith. But they'll be more insidious about it. Right, Hunts?"

Seb grimaced. "Yeah, they're not the easiest people."

"This is your chance to get grilled by nice people. So you'll be prepared for my family."

"Will they be worse than your goddaughter?" My eyes rounded as I realized what I'd said. "I'm sorry—there's nothing wrong with Hailey, just she didn't like me."

Hunter's eyes were dancing, and the corners of his mouth tipped up. "Oh, I know what my daughter's like. She's used to being the center of Cooper's attention, so this should be fun. You'd be very welcome, and I know Faith would like to meet you."

Cooper narrowed his eyes at his friend. Maybe he hoped I would say no, because his friends would give him shit. He'd been relaxed all day with Seb Hunter around. I liked seeing that side to him. And it might be fun to see how he was with his friends.

"That sounds nice. Thank you."

* * *

Cooper parked in the guest slot and we took the elevator up. There was an appetizing aroma when Seb opened the door of the condo and announced we had arrived.

Fast-moving footsteps sounded and Hailey rounded the corner.

"Daddy!"

Seb picked her up. "Are you a good girl?"

She nodded. She caught sight of Cooper and immediately stretched her arms out, saying, "Kook!"

Cooper took her from her father. She patted his chest and grinned at him. And then she saw me.

Her face fell and her bottom lip jutted out. "No."

Cooper laughed, while Seb looked shocked. "Hailey, that's rude."

I had no idea what I should do. Leave? Ignore the kid? Try to win her over?

"Hailey monster, if Callie goes, I go. I'm her ride."

The little girl squinted at Cooper. "Down."

Cooper set her on her feet and she stalked away from the three of us.

"You weren't kidding when you said she didn't like Callie." Seb sounded surprised.

Was I the only person in the world the toddler didn't like? "Maybe I should just go..."

Seb shook his head. "No, she's spoiled enough. She doesn't get to decide who's welcome in our home."

Yeah, well, for a small person, she was good at making someone feel unwelcome. Cooper reached out his arm, grasped my hand with his and pulled me forward. His hand was callused and warm, and surprisingly calming. My tension eased.

Faith—it had to be Seb's wife, Faith—was in the kitchen. She was wiping down the counter while delicious smells came from what she had on the stovetop.

"Faith, this is Callie."

She straightened and offered a polite smile. "Nice to meet you, Callie." She was tall, blonde and blue-eyed. Obviously Hailey's mother.

"Thank you for the invitation."

Faith's brows lifted, and I realized I was still holding Cooper's hand. Cheeks warming, I tugged mine away.

"Thanks for helping Cooper with Hailey last week. Normally we meet someone before we co-opt them into babysitting." Faith glanced at Cooper when she said that. He just grinned at her.

"I don't think I was much help. I'm not good with kids."

"Still, everyone survived. How was the round?"

Cooper and Seb held up most of that conversation. I cradled the glass of wine I was offered and we sat in the living room when Faith insisted everything in the kitchen was under control. Hailey reappeared, having decided that pretending I didn't exist was the way to deal with me. I did the same with her.

"So you're a lawyer," Faith said as she curled up on the couch beside her husband with her own glass of wine.

"Yes. I'm with Anderson, Krys and Chan."

"I don't know the law firms in town."

I shrugged. "I don't know much about hockey."

Hailey's head lifted. "Kook play hockey. Mummy too."

"So did I, pipsqueak." Hunter pulled on the blonde ponytail on the top of his daughter's head.

"Daddy a low-yer?"

"He-heck no." He looked up at me. "Golfing is as close as I come to lawyers most of the time."

I tried to hold in a smile. "Golfing is as close as I come to hockey players most of the time."

Hunter laughed. "I guess that's our common ground. But I think you'll do fine in your tournament. I wouldn't have guessed you were that new."

"That's because you're still terrible after all these years." Cooper smirked.

Hailey tugged on Cooper's arm. "Me play golf."

"Sure, Hails." Cooper tousled her hair with his free hand and she ducked away. "As soon as you're taller than the golf club, we can do that."

"Me big," she protested.

"Not big enough yet."

I risked a look at Cooper. He was grinning at Hailey but looked up at me and winked. I felt my cheeks flush and picked up my glass.

Cooper turned back to the little girl. "What are you going to do when you grow up, Hails? Play hockey like your dad and mom and me?" Kid certainly had the genes for that.

The toddler turned to glare at me. "Marry Kook."

Her dad did a spit take, while Cooper threw back his head and laughed.

Faith shook her head. "We're going to talk about this, Hailey girl. We need to get you aiming a little higher."

Cooper pretended shock. "I think I'm pretty high-level there, Blondie."

Faith swiped a hand through his hair. "Watch it, Blondie."

While Cooper protested and carefully rearranged his hair, Hailey leaning up to "help," a pang of envy shot through me.

This—this close-knit kind of family circle—was something I'd never had. I envied Hailey having this environment to grow up in. I envied the adults their closeness, the comfort they had with each other. I only had something like this with Darcy. And someday he'd find someone, even if it wasn't a hockey player the way he dreamed of.

When he did find his person, would I be like Cooper, a welcome addition? Or would I be left behind?

Chapter 18

Your daughter wants to marry me

COOPER

CALLIE WAS QUIET DURING DINNER, but she seemed comfortable enough. We'd gone out on the balcony to eat, since the weather was cooperating. Hailey was still jealous but seemed happy to mostly ignore Callie. Hearing more about Seb and Faith's week with Braydon and Jayna reassured me that Mitchell was handling the overtime goal as well as could be expected. What we all needed after that was to get on the ice and put it behind us, but training camp didn't start till September.

"How did that watch thing go?" Hunts asked as he helped himself to more rice. Faith had made a stir-fry, something I could eat while still training. Faith was also working out in preparation for the new hockey season in the fall.

I shrugged. "Fine. Pretty well as expected."

Callie looked at me, questioning. I hadn't mentioned the shoot to her, had I?

"What was this one?" Faith asked, nudging Hailey's plate back in front of her. "You have to eat it all, Hailey."

"New watch line they've called Playmaker."

Faith laughed. "How can you show off a watch when you're in hockey gear?"

"That doesn't appear to be the kind of playmaking they were going for."

She rolled her eyes. "So who did they pair you up with for this one?"

"Do you know a model called Monique?"

Her brows creased. Then she pulled out her phone. "She must be new."

"I think so. They made her stretch out on a piano. A baby grand."

Faith was tapping on her phone. "And what were you doing?"

"Holding a glass of whiskey while staring out the window, thinking important playmaking thoughts."

She snorted. "Is this her?"

She held the phone out, with an array of photos of Monique. Callie narrowed her eyes at the phone before dropping her attention back to her plate. I wished Faith hadn't done that.

"That's her."

"Was she nice?"

"Seemed very nice."

"Did you go out with her?"

I shook my head, still a little confused by how I'd behaved that day.

"Oh, is she with someone?" It would drive Faith nuts if I pointed out to her that she was assuming Monique would have said yes.

"I hope not. Since she wanted to have dinner."

"Just dinner, I'm sure."

I smirked. "What can I say? Even your daughter wants to marry me."

"But you didn't—"

Hunter interrupted his wife. "He said he didn't go out with her. We don't have to pry."

Faith's eyes widened, looking at her husband. Hunter looked at Callie and then back. I did not need Hunter and Faith thinking there was something going on between Callie and me. I glanced over at her, concerned that they'd make her uncomfortable. Or else they'd watch us, twist everything I did to fit that narrative, ask questions I had no answer to.

Fortunately, Hailey decided she'd been overlooked long enough and called my name. I helped her finish her veggies and the awkward moment passed.

* * *

I helped Faith clean up while Hunter took Hailey for a bath, and Callie, at our insistence, stayed out enjoying the weather. Faith had been studying me and Callie for the rest of the dinner, so I expected an inquisition.

"So this is the woman you're teaching to play golf."

"Again, yes."

"And she's a lawyer."

"She's still a lawyer." I shook out a bowl before dropping it in the drying rack.

"And you hate lawyers."

"I hate most of them. I will admit to some lawyers being acceptable people, despite their chosen occupation."

"I assume she's one of these exceptions."

I rinsed off some cutlery. "Obviously." Sometimes I forgot that was Callie's job.

"But why are you doing this?" She shook her head. "If there's nothing going on between you, why go to the effort?"

I pulled the plug on the sink and snatched the tea towel from her to wipe my hands. It wasn't that there wasn't something between us, just that we weren't doing anything about it. Or had I been wrong, thinking I saw appreciation in her glances sometimes, when she didn't have her bristles up?

"I didn't say I wasn't attracted to her, I said I wasn't dating her. We have an arrangement. I teach her to get through her company golf tournament successfully, and she goes to my sister's wedding with me."

"That's bullshit. You could get any number of women to go to the wedding with you. Or go on your own and seduce the bridal party."

I leaned my hip on the counter. "I have no interest in seducing anyone at my sister's wedding." Not anyone who my family would have invited. "And it might not be as easy to find someone as you think. For a lot of reasons I don't want to go alone, and I'm careful about who I take with me. Partly because asking someone to a wedding can give rise to certain expectations." I glanced toward the balcony, where the one woman who wouldn't was sitting.

Faith snorted. "And you're sure Callie won't get any expectations."

"Not even if you put them on a platter with her name on them."

* * *

It hadn't been a perfect evening. Hailey was still jealous of Callie. I never brought dates over to Hunter's place, so her jealousy was amusing. I wasn't sure how much longer Kook would be able to maintain his popularity with the kid, but I'd enjoy it while I could.

Callie had been quiet, but I thought she'd mostly been comfortable. She appeared sincere when she thanked Faith and Seb for inviting her over. Callie had fit into our group surprisingly well. I hadn't felt like the odd person out while my two best friends were all couple-y.

We were halfway to her place when Callie broke the silence.

"Your friends think you didn't hook up with that model because of me."

I shot her a glance. I'd picked up on that but hadn't realized Callie had as well. "Does that bother you?"

She shrugged. "That's not the reason, is it?"

"You made it perfectly clear when I first met you that sex was not on the table. I listened. You don't feel like I'm pushing you for that, do you?"

From the corner of my eye, I saw her turn her head to look at me. "No, not at all. But..." She didn't complete the sentence.

"I understand that you don't want to muddy the waters with the arrangement we have. And we have become friends, I think. But you are an attractive woman, and I haven't missed that."

"Really?" She sounded shocked.

I wished there was more light so I could see her expression better. "Why would I lie?"

She was silent for a moment. "Thank you. Um, you're also attractive."

I held in a smile. I was confident in how I looked, and

spent a good portion of my time keeping my body in shape. But it was nice to hear she appreciated the effort. "By the way, when do you have time to go shopping?"

"Shopping?"

"The dress for the wedding. There are a couple of other events we can't avoid. Family dinner when we arrive, the rehearsal dinner, and the wedding itself."

"Fuck. Golf clothing won't cut it, will it? My suits for work won't either."

"Men will be in suits. Women will not."

She let out a long sigh, like she was expecting suicide drills rather than a shopping trip. "Okay, let's check our schedules."

Callie might be dreading this, but it would be one of the highlights of my summer. She was going to enjoy this, and I would prove to her how attractive and sexy she was.

* * *

*C*ALLIE

I HAD a lot of reasons to be grateful to Cooper. I was getting pretty good at golf after our trips to Briarwood and the driving range. I wasn't getting holes in one or even making par, but the balls were going in the right direction, I knew what I was doing, and I could eat dinner in the clubhouse without having to mentally go through the list of things to do and not do. There had been a couple of surprises: I hadn't expected that I would enjoy myself. It was a beautiful place. I'd been busy enough that taking time to stop and smell the roses—or in this case, the grass—wasn't something on my to-do list. The people...well, mostly they were the kind I felt uncomfortable around. People who'd grown up with things and knowing how to act in any situation. That was not me.

And Cooper and I had become more than just acquaintances who could attend a family event together. We'd become actual friends. I had few enough of those that I valued him.

But after that dinner with Faith and Seb Hunter, and the talk in the car on our way home after, I was too aware of Cooper as a man. For just a moment, the thought that he'd turned down that model because of me had thrilled me. Despite what I'd said the night I met him—that I wouldn't have sex with him—I hadn't thought he was interested. Not with the opportunities he had. But what he'd said in the car... He didn't appear to have any red hair or big boob fetish, and other than that, what did I really have to offer other than my brain?

Now, I had to focus to keep from noticing how broad his shoulders were, and the grace of his movements. Men and women watched and admired him. And I was no fucking better. It was like I'd eaten Eve's apple, and suddenly Cooper was a sexy man who thought I was attractive.

Today we were going dress shopping, and if anything could calm down my libido, that would do it. Darcy warned me not to fuss about the cost. I promised only to be reasonable. I wouldn't put it past Cooper to come up with something more expensive than the private golf lessons I'd wanted to win at the charity thing. If I was spending a fortune on a dress, I needed it to be something I could get value from in future as well.

I went down to meet him full of good intentions. But fuck, he was driving the Ferrari. Did he do Ferrari ads? They could just take photos of him sitting there, white shirt showing off his blue eyes and bright smile. I almost tripped, missing the step staring at him.

This was why he got paid money to be photographed. I couldn't let myself be sidetracked by blond hair and dimples. I drew in a breath and got myself under control. At least the sports car meant we weren't going to have too much crap to put in it later.

I'd debated for too long about what to wear, hoping to catch that look of approval when he saw me. When I put on the country club clothing, I felt good, but outside of those outfits I'd become self-conscious, even at work. I'd done some online shopping, found tops and things that were in the same colors as that country club stuff, so I thought I was getting better? I'd received two compliments on my clothes at work, which was definitely a first.

Ugh. Why couldn't I just study a textbook for this?

Anyway, I went with one of the sports dresses just to make life simple. But I was on edge. There was no golfing to distract us, and I felt unsettled.

Cooper smiled as I opened the door and slid down into the seat, watching my hemline carefully. "Good morning, Callie. You look lovely."

I almost smiled. *Gah!* He was just pleased that he'd managed to fix how I dressed. "I finally met your high standards?"

He raised his eyebrows. "Maybe I've been too critical."

"Maybe?"

He frowned, studying me and not moving the car. "Think of it this way—if new tax legislation was coming out that would affect how someone set up their corporation, wouldn't you say something about it if that topic came up in conversation?"

"No."

"No?" His eyebrows were getting a workout.

"If I give advice and they mess it up and make it worse, they'll blame me. Also, if I give it out for free, people will ask for more."

He laughed. "Well, I don't get paid to dress people, but I have a good eye. And it's a simple thing that can help."

Remember Callie, it's not personal. Just his weird pet project to dress people up. "It's also an expensive thing."

He signaled and slid out into traffic. "If it's too much, I'm happy to pay."

No. We had to keep our boundaries. "I can handle it. It's an investment, right?"

He nodded in approval. "It is. Especially at your firm. Why did you want to work for them? I would have expected you to be more comfortable in a less...maybe stuffy office?"

"They're the best."

"And that's important?"

He didn't understand, because he'd grown up with money. "If I'm partner, I'm invested in the firm, so I want to be sure it's secure. That it's stable and has a good reputation and will be around for a long time."

"And being partner is important to you?"

"If you're partner, they have a hard time getting rid of you." I stopped, because that was a little more honest than I had intended to be.

"Like having a no-movement clause in a hockey contract."

I appreciated that Cooper didn't make a big deal out of what I'd revealed. "What's that?" I was curious. This was a legal issue after all.

"A no-movement clause covers being traded to another team, and also being sent down to the farm team. It means they keep you on their NHL roster."

"Are they common?"

He shook his head. "An organization has to have a lot of confidence in the player to offer that."

I considered. "You have one?"

He smirked. "I do."

"Because you want to stay in Toronto?"

He shrugged. "I wouldn't necessarily be averse to moving, in the right circumstances. But this gives me control. And the team offered it, as an enticement."

Thinking of Seb and Faith and Hailey, it was more of an enticement than he admitted. "How many years do you have left on your contract?"

"Three years. At that point, I might rein in my agent to ask less on the next contract, so that I could finish my career here. Not many players spend their whole career with one team, so maybe..."

That wasn't information Cooper would trust to just anyone. I could only imagine the kind of contract negotiations his agent and the team would go through. "I won't share that with anyone."

"I didn't think you would."

But he'd given me something, after I'd revealed something, and I wanted to hug that thought tightly to my chest. That kind of honesty was more dangerous than his handsome face or fit body. It enticed reciprocal confessions and I did my best to keep my life private. I'd already told him I grew up in foster care. Hearing my story made people pity me, look at me differently. I didn't want that, especially from him.

I was relieved when we pulled into a lane off Bloor Street and stopped behind a shop, in a stall marked *Reserved*. I gave him the side-eye. "Is this one of your sponsors?"

"Nope."

He managed to get out of the car and come around to my side before I'd climbed out of the passenger seat. The damned car was too low. He held my hand as he helped me up. The back door of the shop opened, and another beautiful, put-together woman stood in the doorway. *Déjà vu.*

"Mr. Cooper?"

"Just Cooper, please." He used his charming smile and I tried not to frown. He could smile at whoever he wanted to.

"This way, please. And you must be Ms. Smith?"

I sighed. Bad enough that I was expecting to spend a lot of money to get criticized and feel awkward and dense. I didn't need to be the third wheel in a flirtation while I suffered through clothes shopping. But Cooper looked so pleased to have this chance to use me as his Barbie doll.

I forced a smile and said, "Yep. That's me."

Chapter 19

Dressed me up like a doll

CALLIE

FOR MOST PEOPLE, trying on beautiful clothes was not an issue. My figure and coloring always made clothes more challenging. But this wasn't just finding a pretty dress. There were layers of clothing, starting from the skin up. I'd worn the best bra and underwear I had, but I could feel the saleswoman's disapproval as we tried on yet something else.

The first thing was to find the dress—*the* dress. I'd have spent less time shopping for my own wedding dress if I ever lost my mind enough to consider marriage. But Cooper wanted to impress his family, so he was fussy. I was getting used to his magic now, how something he picked out would transform how I looked in ways I couldn't really figure out. Part of it was color, but there were infinite variations in a color, and some were magic and some were not.

Everything I tried on looked good, but not quite right. I wasn't sure whether to be relieved or dread another session. And then we found it. Despite the cost and the lack of practical usage, I loved the dress. It was green, but nothing like the dress I'd worn to the charity event. It was low cut for me, but in a classy way, and made me look...like the woman some part inside me had always wanted to look like. I coveted that dress as soon as I tried it on. I could fit in anywhere like this. Like I belonged. I didn't even mind the smug look on Cooper's face.

And it broke me. The saleswoman brought in lingerie that suited the dress, and I caved. With "the dress" out of the way, I tried on something for the family dinner, and the rehearsal, and the two of them dressed me up like a doll. The three dresses, more lingerie, shoes and purses were added on and I just let them. Something in the back of my brain balked at the idea of how much this would cost, but I muttered *investment* and shoved the thought down.

When we finally left the shop, I was tired but surprisingly happy after hours spent in a store. Not because there hadn't been any flirting, but because I was done. Definitely that. Cooper held open the car door for me.

"What about the clothes?" We hadn't brought out any bags with us. I only had my purse, where my credit card was almost too hot to touch after that trip. There were some tailoring adjustments to be made, but I was strangely reluctant to leave the items behind.

"They'll send them over."

"To your place or mine?" All the information they had on me was my credit card and that didn't come with an address.

"Yours. I gave them the address for the delivery."

Once Cooper was in the car, I frowned and asked, "How did they know my size and everything?"

He shrugged. "I told them."

Right. Like he had for that sportswear store that was his sponsor. "Well, thank you."

His eyebrows rose. "You're welcome. I thought you'd fight this a lot harder."

"Darcy told me not to be difficult. I'm sure I can wear these things again. And..." I swallowed and admitted the truth. "I like them."

A smile crossed his face, like I'd given him a gift by making that admission. He was always attractive, but this did something else. Something that was dangerous for my mental well-being and the limits I'd imposed on our relationship.

I was way too invested. It was a good thing we were almost finished with our arrangement. Just over a month. I could be sensible for a few weeks.

* * *

Cooper

I was having second thoughts about inviting Callie to the wedding.

The social circle my family was part of was Briarwood on steroids. I'd thought about how a tax lawyer would impress my family and mess with their assumptions about me. Someone from their world, with the stupid jock. It didn't matter that I made more money than any of them. Had been more successful. Since I hadn't toed the family line, they adjusted their qualifications to protect their own world view.

Making sure my underwear ads were posted where they couldn't miss seeing them had been petty, but I enjoyed imagining their reactions when asked about it. I refused to be ashamed of my choices.

Family get-togethers included a lot of subtle hostility. Growing up I'd learned how to handle that kind of battle. But had I made a mistake? Would this hurt Callie? The thought of something Pierce or my father said wounding her upset me more than anything they threw at me.

But she'd never back out now. She needed to think she was bringing something to our arrangement. I'd deal with this protective streak by keeping close to her and interceding as necessary. I'd introduce her as a friend, but there would be assumptions that we were more than that.

Our increased workouts helped keep me from obsessing over this upcoming trip. A couple more guys, like Oppy and Deek, had come back to town, so our on-ice training was pushing our fitness levels. Darcy joined us when we went to the driving range, and I spent evenings with the guys, maintaining those team bonds, checking their mental condition as well.

That was my job. Not worrying about a lawyer meeting my family.

Callie had gotten her clothes back from the tailors last week. We were flying out on Thursday. She had reluctantly agreed that I could pay for the flights because this was my event. I didn't tell her we were flying first class since my tight-fisted lawyer wouldn't have sprung for that. I grinned as I pictured her reaction when we boarded. I wasn't a small man, and since I had the money, I paid for comfort. There was also a reasonable chance that no one in first class would tell me how my team had messed up that last game in the Cup final, but someone in economy undoubtedly would. Call me a snob, but I had experience to back me up.

I picked her up in a limo—I didn't want to leave any of my cars in airport parking.

She walked out of her building in a dress, one of the outfits from my sponsor. It flattered her body, emphasizing her hourglass figure and making her hair glow. She looked cool and composed, her hair pulled back in a French twist, with discreet makeup. She had no jewelry beyond a couple of studs in her ears, and I had an urge to get her something. My mom and my sister wouldn't be vulgar, but they'd have a substantial investment in jewels on. I wanted Callie to look just as valued.

I mentally shook myself. Like Callie would let me buy her jewelry. And I didn't do that—buy things for my dates. Or friends.

The driver opened the door to let her in, then took her luggage to the trunk. I was about to tell her how good she looked when she cut me off.

"Don't say it."

I laughed. Such a Callie way to greet someone. "Don't say what?"

She rolled her eyes. "You want to gloat about these clothes."

It wasn't just the clothes. It was the whole look. "I was going to say you looked good."

"I knew it. I feel like a Stepford wife."

I couldn't imagine anyone less like a Stepford wife. "Are you uncomfortable?"

She squirmed. "Not exactly."

"I'm sorry, what was that?"

"I'm not saying it again."

"But I didn't hear."

She gave me a sharp-edged smile. "I said, how different

is it flying commercial as opposed to flying on your team jet?"

"I don't think that's what you said."

She shrugged. I let it go. She'd said it, I heard it, that would do.

"It's a bit more of a hassle with lineups and security, but I thought you'd be freaked out if I chartered a private jet for this."

Her eyes rounded. "You wouldn't."

"I *didn't*."

"Is your family all rich?"

"Rich is relative. They don't normally charter a private jet, but they could if they needed to."

"This is going to be an interesting trip." It didn't sound like she meant that in a good way. She was at least partly prepared.

When I steered her to first class to check in, she gave me some side-eye but otherwise didn't react. I was disappointed, but part of what I liked about Callie was the way she could surprise me.

Security was the usual pain. I had a trusted traveler card, but Callie did not, so I stayed with her. For passengers flying from Toronto to the US, there was Customs in Toronto, so we cleared through before boarding—the agent recognized me and that helped smooth things.

Fans also recognized me. Some wanted selfies, some to tell me I'd fucked up the finals, but we eventually found a corner in a bar to wait for our flight to be called.

Callie looked around at the other travelers, frowning at a guy staring at me. "People continually tell you how to do your job."

"Yep."

"You're a lot more patient than I would be."

I laughed. "I can only imagine what you'd do if someone tried to correct your tax opinions."

Her brow furrowed. "Why pay me if they don't trust me to do the work properly?"

"People don't think they know tax, but they do hockey."

"Does it bother you?"

"I don't get endorsement deals because I'm a private person." The publicity was another way to annoy my family, so I was patient with the public.

"But talking about how you lost at the end. That must be tough, rehashing it all the time."

I looked over her shoulder at the planes sitting on the tarmac. "It's shitty. But the only way to get over it is to start playing again and win it all this time."

"How do you not blow up at people blaming you for it?"

"I did make the pass Minnesota intercepted. And if I acted like an asshole, people wouldn't want to buy the products I endorse, and I'd lose out. So, it's worthwhile to be nice."

She narrowed her eyes. "It's more than that though."

I focused on her again. "I am one of the luckiest people on the planet, to get to do what I love and be paid and celebrated for it. I refuse to whine about something so many people wish they had."

Callie fidgeted with the glass in front of her. "If I did something, like yell at one of these people bothering you, would it reflect badly on you?"

Why was I so happy that she was worried about harming my reputation? "Don't worry about this. You're not going to go off on anyone, and we're just catching a flight. You've handled Benson, and the people at Briarwood, so you can handle this."

She cocked her head. "I think that's our flight they're calling."

She grabbed her carry-on and we headed for our gate. There were no hockey fans nearby, or if they were, they didn't speak to us. We got to board first and settled in our priority seats. I held back a grin at the way Callie touched the goodies on offer and eyed the amount of space we had. The flight attendant in first class widened her eyes when she saw me, but she didn't say anything.

Once we were in the air and had been offered beverages, Callie turned to me. "So, prepare me for your family."

"You'll have a lot in common. They're almost all lawyers. My sister is an investment analyst, and she's marrying a lawyer."

She glanced out the window then turned back. "Why didn't you become a lawyer too?"

"I'm a dumb jock."

"Bullshit."

I raised my brows. "I play hockey for a living, and I pose in my underwear."

"I have no idea how much intelligence is required to pose in your underwear, but you have to use your brain to play hockey."

"Believe me, not everyone who plays hockey is a member of Mensa."

"Neither is every lawyer, based on some of the shit I'm given to review. But your team practices plays and studies other teams and players, don't they? Maybe everyone isn't a genius, but you're smart."

It felt good to hear her say that, because a lot of people saw my face, my body and my career and assumed I wasn't intelligent. "Why do you think I'm smart?"

She rolled her eyes. "Are you fishing for compliments?"

"Not really. My family will challenge your opinion."

"I deal with intelligent people and morons and all the variations in between. I can tell the difference."

"They're well entrenched in their beliefs. Your opinion alone won't impress them."

"Maybe you should show them your portfolio."

It took me a minute to respond. How did— "How do you know about my portfolio?"

She rolled her eyes. "I don't know any details, but I know you have one. You play hockey for millions of dollars, have those endorsements you were talking about, pay way too much for clothes, have stupid expensive cars and a penthouse condo."

"I could be spending everything I have on that."

"But you aren't, because you're not an idiot."

I laughed. She might not have proved her point in logic, but she was right. I did have a healthy portfolio and could support myself in the lifestyle I enjoyed for the rest of my life. I played hockey now because I loved it. I loved having a team, fans, money and driving my family crazy. Why would I stop?

"You didn't tell me why you didn't become a lawyer."

"Does it offend you that I didn't pursue your profession?"

She rolled her eyes. "Look at all those fancy words from the dumb jock. No, I'm just curious why, considering your background."

Who knew what the fuck my family would say if it came up? I should explain, prepare her. "Spite had a big part in it, especially after the incident with Vicky. My family thought I was wasting my time with hockey, and I didn't want to live my life in their shadow."

She was still frowning.

"Not a good enough reason for you?"

"Just thinking."

"That I was petty?"

"That you either had enough privilege growing up that you could take that kind of gamble, or a passionate drive to play so you were willing to risk screwing up your future."

I took a sip of my drink while I worked through what she'd said. "Both. I grew up with a lot of privilege, and I had a safety net. But also, to make it to the pros you have to love doing it. It's too damned hard to do it as a hobby."

Callie had that crease between her brows as she processed the information I'd given her. "Let me see if I understand the dynamics for this visit. Your family is going to put you down while you flaunt your success in their faces."

It didn't sound flattering when she distilled it down like that. "Are you sorry you agreed?"

She shook her head. "Now I understand why I'm the perfect plus-one."

I watched her expression, checking if she was pissed. "Does that bother you?"

"You told me your brother was like Benson. Assuming that's correct, I'll enjoy helping you flaunt."

"Benson only wishes he could be an asshole on my brother's level."

She pursed her lips. "Do they follow hockey? Because your team lost the finals. Will that be something they use against you?"

"They'll try."

"And what will you do?"

"Pretend I don't care about losing as long as I get paid."

"They believe that?"

They certainly did. Time for a subject change. "You

said you were in foster care. What happened to your family?"

Her expression closed up. "I don't have one."

"You sprang up out of—what was it, some guy's head? Or a seashell?"

She rolled her eyes. "No. I have no idea who my father was. Neither did my mother. She was an addict. I bounced in and out of care till I was ten. She'd come back, swear she'd gotten clean and that she loved me and wanted me back. It never lasted."

"And when you were ten?"

"She stopped coming back."

Shit. I thought my family was fucked. Callie stared out the window, lips pressed tightly together. Things about Callie made a lot more sense now.

Chapter 20

He needed a slapping

CALLIE

COOPER HAD RENTED a Lexus at the airport to drive us. He'd also booked us a suite at a nearby hotel. Because of the wedding, apparently there wasn't a lot of room at the family home. I was more comfortable with the idea of staying in a hotel than a private house anyway.

Of course, my idea of a hotel room differed from his. He'd gotten the penthouse, which included a huge seating area with a piano, of all the absurd things, as well as two entire primary bedrooms with their own bathrooms. There was a kitchen that I had no intention of using, and a view over the city. Everything was in muted beige and brown, luxurious and comfortable.

It made me itchy. The contrast with my place was vast.

"Why don't you freshen up? We'll go and meet everyone at the house for dinner."

Right. Time to shower and put on expensive clothing. "I won't be long."

I was a little self-conscious, sharing space this closely with Cooper. I'd expected two separate rooms, not this. This was like my living arrangement with Darcy, and I didn't think of Darcy the way I did Cooper. Darcy was, for all intents and purposes, my brother.

I did not feel brotherly around Cooper. My feelings for him were veering into dangerously intimate territory, without that platonic shield. I'd seen him without his layer of charm, and he'd learned things about me that I didn't share. He was attractive, but more than that, he was good. Trustworthy. Kind. And tempting. But he had wanted a date who wouldn't get ideas, so it was a good thing I couldn't be interested in anything like that.

He was also very particular. I might have invested in appropriate lingerie and clothes for the wedding events, but I'd brought an old T-shirt and sleep shorts to wear at night. I'd need to be sure I was done for the day before I changed into those. Mr. Fussy would not approve.

There were expensive hair and bath products in the shower, and thick towels that actually absorbed. I took a long shower, enjoying the water pressure and heat, before getting ready for my performance. I hoped I could pull it off. Cooper was fulfilling his side of the bargain, so now it was up to me.

He was waiting when I came out of my room, staring out the windows at the view of the city before turning to greet me, wearing a lightweight gray suit, with a blue shirt that brought out his eyes. That was what he'd done to me—I noticed those things now.

"Gorgeous, Callie."

I glanced down, as if I didn't know what I was wearing. "You chose well."

The dress was in a buttery yellow. It was sleeveless,

with wide straps that gave lots of support and kept the dress from looking too formal. A high neckline, not exposing cleavage or too many freckles. It flared from under my bust, and draped in a way that made me look taller and slimmer. I was wearing tan slingbacks with a matching purse. My hair was up in a French twist, and I used a stronger lipstick shade than I usually wore.

I was pretty shocked myself at how poised and elegant I looked.

"Um, you look good as well. Will everyone be dressed like this?"

"You'll fit right in."

My shoulders relaxed. He understood what I really wanted to know.

"Shall we?"

I drew in a breath. "Ready as I'll ever be."

I'D BEEN PREPARED for a pretty nice house when we went to his family's home, but this was nice on a different level. The house was set back from the street with a tall stone wall. It was three stories high and even had a circle driveway at the front door. Red brick, looking New England, Mayflower, Waspy and rich. Cooper had definitely grown up with privilege. The driveway was full of cars, and there was a valet to take our rental. I was pretty sure the valet was just for this dinner party, but this was the kind of place that made you wonder. The door was standing open, and I followed Cooper up the front stairs and through the doorway.

It led to a large hallway where about twenty people

were gathered with drinks and murmured conversation. These were Cooper's family and the groom's family. I examined them as we paused in the doorway. They were a gorgeous group, all attractive, white, and well off. There were beautiful paintings on the wall, an expensive-looking carpet on the floor, and gleaming wood paneling, but some of the foster homes I'd been in seemed welcoming in comparison. I was damned glad I was wearing Cooper-approved clothes, because these people took dressing seriously. More than at our corporate events at the firm.

A tall, elegant man with perfectly graying dark hair crossed to greet us. "Whit. Glad you could make it in time."

I'd forgotten who Whit was until Cooper spoke. "I wouldn't miss it for the world. Father, this is Calliope Smith, my plus-one for the weekend. Callie, this is my father, Preston Cooper."

A beautiful and graceful woman followed him over. She had perfectly blonde hair, up in a twist like mine, and a dress even I could see was both expensive and flattering. Her eyes were the same color as Cooper's. She had blue stones in her earrings and necklace—sapphires, maybe? Matching the sleek lines of her blue dress.

Cooper continued. "My mother, Kendall."

Damn, she looked young. Her smile barely moved her face, so I leaned into my judgy side and decided she'd had work done.

More perfectly groomed people gathered before us. Cooper continued his introductions, looking stiffer with each one. "This is my brother, Pierce. The bride is my sister Tinsley, and her fiancé, Easton Yates."

Cooper's brother looked like a poor man's Cooper, and that must have chafed him. Not quite as tall or as blond or as fit or good-looking. His sister had his father's darker coloring but her mother's perfect features. Her fiancé looked like a model from a preppy college catalog, one of the "successful alumni" shots. I was never going to remember all these ridiculous names.

"Nice to meet you—may I call you Callie?"

"Of course, sir," I agreed as I shook Preston's hand.

He gripped it just a little too tightly. *Used to demonstrating dominance through greeting rituals.* "Call me Preston. We aren't formal here."

I kept my snort inside. *Not formal, my ass.* We were dressed like we were going to a photo shoot, and everyone was standing stiffly in place.

"So, what do you do, Callie?" There was just a touch of patronizing in his tone. I'd heard it often enough and could recognize it easily. "Whit hasn't told us much about you."

I stood a little straighter. Time to impress them. "I'm a tax attorney with Anderson, Krys and Chan. I'm not sure if you're familiar with them—they're located in Toronto."

His eyebrows shot up. "I am familiar with the firm. Whit must have told you we're lawyers as well. We've worked with them from time to time."

I nodded.

"How long have you worked there?"

There was something in his tone. It was polite, but skeptical. Like Cooper had coached me on how to impress his family by throwing names around but I wasn't actually the person I was claiming to be.

"Since I finished law school."

"And where did you go to school?"

I took a sip of sparkling water, letting the tension build before I answered. "Oh, I've stayed in Toronto my whole life. I graduated from U of T, University of Toronto."

U of T was the top law school in Canada. It wasn't Yale or Harvard or Oxford, but I hadn't had the money or connections to even apply at those places. U of T was still ranked in the top twenty schools globally.

"That's not a bad school. We have always attended Harvard, but we recognize that's not the be-all and end-all."

I kept my expression smoothly polite. *Nice way to exclude your nonconformist child.*

"Is Cargill still teaching there?"

Again, checking the details to see if I was who I claimed to be. "He retired a couple of years ago, I believe. I'm sure a lot of students were relieved. He was demanding, but if you made it through his class, you knew your stuff."

His face relaxed. I'd passed that test.

"So, a tax attorney. I don't think we've come across your name in any of our dealings up there."

"Lorne Peters has dealt with more of our clients based in the US."

A flash in his eyes. Yeah, he knew Lorne. Lorne was fifty and an avid golfer. Tansy Gordon did most of the work for him, but he was certainly well connected.

"Why did you choose to specialize in that field?"

"It was a challenge." Yeah, that sounded like I found other parts of the legal world too easy, and I was okay giving that impression to this man. "And as long as there are taxes, I'll have a job."

He laughed and I smiled as well, but it wasn't a joke. Without money or connections, I had to make myself necessary.

"Very admirable. But I mustn't monopolize you."

Cooper's mother took over the conversation, as if this was a practiced routine. "Lovely to meet you, Callie. Such a"—the slightest of pauses before she continued—"pretty name."

I was not going to volunteer that my flaky mother had called me Calliope because she thought it was *such* a pretty name.

"How did you meet Whit?"

Still freaked me out to hear anyone call him Whit. I shot a glance at where he was speaking to his sister. *So* not a Whit. "At a charity event for the children's hospital in Toronto."

She nodded. "Are you involved with that charity?"

I shook my head. I was lucky to have been asked to fill up a table. But no need to share that.

"And how long have you two been dating?"

I tilted my head. "We're just friends."

Her eyebrows moved slightly upward. *Botox?* "Oh?"

"We're both very busy at this point in our careers."

"Yes, I'm sure your work keeps you occupied. Whit, well..." She shook her head as she looked at her son. "It's the offseason, so he shouldn't have anything to do."

The woman had no idea of what her son's life was like. I'd picked up enough from our time together to know he kept busy with charity events and sponsorships when he wasn't working out and training. He wasn't spending his summer on the couch playing video games and eating chips.

I forced a polite smile. "I'm sure that made it easier to schedule the wedding, but he still spends an incredible amount of time with his training as well as sponsor and charity commitments."

"Of course." Her tone was dismissive, and I really needed to control this defensiveness. "You should talk to Pierce. You'd have so much in common."

I kept my smile, but since Pierce was already giving

major Benson vibes, I hoped there wouldn't be *too* much in common.

Everyone headed toward the dining room, probably following some signal I'd missed. Cooper kept close to me till we reached the table. There were name cards at each setting, and all the "couples" were split up. I was seated by Pierce for dinner. *Lucky me!*

Pierce was more polished than Benson, and much cleverer. He managed to disparage his brother oh so politely, and the insults were wrapped in supposed compliments.

I kept a smile on my face and talked as little as possible. My fingernails were digging half-moon shapes into my palms.

Cooper, seated by his father, grew more and more stiff. I'd seen him when fans or critics discussed his hockey team's loss, and this was different. His knuckles were white on his fork.

I wanted to either slap Preston upside his perfectly groomed head, or give him a Power Point presentation on just how admirable his son was.

"You must be quite the hockey fan." A voice in my ear brought me back from my violent thoughts.

I wasn't sure if Pierce was suggesting that I was only willing to slum it with a hockey player because of my supposed passion for the sport, or that a shared love of hockey was the only way to make Cooper's company palatable. Or both. Probably both. He needed a slapping as well.

I set down my fork, afraid I might use it on his smug face. "Actually, I'm not a fan of any sportsball."

"Really? I find it hard to picture you and Whit spending time together if you're not a hockey person."

I tilted my head. "I have friends who aren't lawyers, but we manage to enjoy ourselves without talking about law, or tax." Did this family only discuss business? The number of people who enjoyed discussing legal issues was pretty small. "I like to spend time when I'm not focused on my job."

I didn't have many friends who weren't connected to work. But Darcy counted, and he wasn't a lawyer, and we didn't talk about my job. His, yes, because funny things happened. Pretty sure Pierce wouldn't appreciate stories like that.

"I always thought Whit tended to run on and on about his sport. Which is bad enough. But when he does that modeling, like some sort of life studies class. Don't you find that a little...vulgar?"

He had no idea the kind of vulgar I'd grown up with. I narrowed my eyes. "The ads are very popular in Toronto. He has a lot of fans."

Pierce looked like he'd swallowed something sour. "He always wanted attention, and he found a way to get it."

Someone was jealous.

Pierce watched the groom's sister flirt with Cooper with that sour look on his face. "I just find it difficult to imagine the two of you together. What do you talk about?"

Cooper went on about clothing more than hockey, in my experience, but I wasn't going to tell him that since I didn't plan to announce my very different upbringing. Which left— "We've actually spent a lot of time discussing golf. We've been playing together."

Pierce's eyes lit up. "Oh, I love golf. When I can get the time away. Where have you been playing?"

Pierce didn't react to Briarwood, but he was happy to talk golf. Mostly *at* me rather than with me, but I was good with that. Conversations would be much the same at the tournament next month. Since I wasn't an expert in the subject, being able to listen and nod would earn some points, which was the whole reason for me to attend the event.

Fortunately, before Pierce could put me to sleep with a recap of his last round at some golf course in the area that should have impressed me, Preston rose to his feet at the end of the table to do a "welcome to the family" speech to his new son-in-law and family, and a recap of the activities that would follow for the next couple of days. There were some barbs, very cleverly disguised, that hit Cooper, and my hands fisted uselessly in my lap.

Not long after the dinner, Cooper managed to make excuses for us to leave, pleading travel fatigue. I did my best to look tired, and we said our goodbyes and went to get the rental from the valet.

He examined my face. "You survived?"

"Barely. And you?"

He shrugged. The valet stopped the car at the foot of the steps and got out to open my door. I was finally getting used to this.

It was a short trip to the hotel. Cooper pointed out some landmarks, but it was the polite version of him.

He'd said he'd wanted a date for the wedding who wouldn't expect too much from him. But what he really needed was an ally. He was so tense I wasn't sure he'd make it through the weekend without something snapping. It would serve his family right if he went off on them, but I was afraid he'd hurt himself instead.

Another valet at the hotel. It was a good thing I didn't travel by car often or I'd soon be standing around waiting for someone to open the door all the time.

We didn't speak on the way up in the elevator since we weren't alone for most of the trip. I had my own room key but let Cooper open the door, flicking on lights as he led the way to the sitting room.

"I didn't have a say in the seating arrangement, or I would have spared you Pierce."

He didn't need to worry about me. Pierce was smug and irritating, but Preston was a greater hazard. "Once I got him onto the topic of golf, things were fine."

His gaze sharpened. "And before?"

I shrugged. "Benson 2.0, like you said."

"What did he say? Did he try to put you down?"

"He managed to insult the both of us for spending time together. But he was more focused on your supposed flaws than mine."

His lips twisted. "Yeah, my family has a master's in that. I shouldn't have brought you."

Was I not holding up my end? Did my upbringing show through? "Why not?"

He frowned down at me. "Because this is shitty, and you don't deserve it."

My whole body softened when he said that. Someone caring that I had an unpleasant time didn't happen often. Especially when he was getting the brunt of it. "You don't deserve it either. It's just a few days. I'll be fine. But..."

He deserved consideration too. Something to offset his family and how they affected him. He'd done enough that I'd be successful at the company tournament in a few weeks. But for this wedding? My credentials as a tax attorney weren't sufficient. He might not have expressed it, but he needed someone to help him survive his nasty family.

Maybe it was the wine, or the food, which had both been excellent, but I wanted to take away all the poison his family spewed. Maybe it was something else, making me want to protect and comfort him. I wasn't going to think about that now.

Would this be a massive mistake?

His rigid posture, the bleakness in his eyes, inspired me take a chance. Awkward and clumsy.

"Want to fuck?"

Chapter 21

Flustered and off-balance

Cooper

She was blunt. So blunt. Why did I find that such a turn-on?

It was a shitty day and I felt like shit. Bad enough for me, but to inflict it on Callie? I never should have done it. But she surprised me again. Being insulted and looked down on didn't faze her. And then... *Want to fuck?*

I'd had a lot of women proposition me. Sometimes they weren't subtle at all—hand on my dick non-subtle, and we both knew what that was about. This was something totally different—her posture stiff and the words thrown out like a challenge.

We'd become close, friends and encroaching on more. Despite the platonic rule she'd set up, I'd never been able to ignore Callie's body. Something about her made me want to map those freckles, see if they were everywhere. Did she like someone playing with her tits? Was she ticklish? What

202

did she look like when she came? I wanted to see her lose that control she wrapped around herself.

But she'd never indicated she wanted to get physical. "Where's this coming from?" I shook my head. "I don't do pity sex. Or reluctant virgins."

"I'm not—" She broke off. "Sorry. I'm not reluctant, or a virgin. I'm interested."

"But you said no sex?"

"I know. It's not...it was never that I don't find you attractive. But..." She shrugged. "Selfishly, I didn't want to mess up our deal. And if you wanted someone, you have models like that watch ad woman—I'm not really your type."

"You have no idea what my type is."

She crossed her arms around her waist. "It's okay, you can say no. I just..."

"Just?"

"I think you need someone to take care of you. Not only to get off, but to be appreciated."

To be appreciated? How long since I'd been appreciated for something other than my face, or body, or wealth, or hockey skills? When had someone wanted to take care of me because they thought I'd had a rough day?

"Callie, I don't want you to feel obligated, or indebted, but you can appreciate me any time you want."

"Really?" She looked hopeful, unsure if I'd turn her down.

"Anytime." This shitty day was looking up. Way up.

Her brows lowered. "It's either that or I'm going to be slapping some of your relatives tomorrow."

I laughed, something I'd never have expected after an evening of my father's insults. "Sex would definitely be better than you taking on my family."

"Slapping them would feel good."

"Sex will feel better."

There it went, that stubborn chin lifting, but there was a smile fighting to come out. "Oh, you're that good you can make guarantees?"

I cocked my head. "I'm confident. Well, there could be mitigating factors."

"Mitigating factors?"

I grinned at her. "Being in a war zone—an active one. Serial killer on our heels. Gunshot or stab wound. Flu or pneumonia." I dropped the grin. "If you're asexual or in pain or mentally incapable of getting into sex? Then no, I couldn't make sure you came. But otherwise, all it takes is time and paying attention."

"Time?"

"I don't have other plans tonight."

I stared at her wide eyes and flushed cheeks. The arms around her waist had loosened. She might not know it yet, but we had already started. Before I touched her, I was going to seduce her with words.

She ran her teeth over her lush bottom lip. "And paying attention. Like, how?"

"Well, I use all the senses." I lowered my voice. "Like sound. Some people are good at vocalizing what they want, others you have to listen to the nonverbal sounds. Moaning, panting, catches in their breath—that all can tell you how they're feeling."

"But what if you're also panting and moaning?" Her voice was a little breathy, like she was imagining those sounds in context.

"I make sure my partner is doing that first."

She frowned. "Huh."

Had none of her partners made her pleasure a priority?

But I didn't want her to dwell on her past. "And sight. If it's not pitch black, and I do prefer some light, there are dilated pupils, flushed skin, hard nipples. Those are pretty good indicators. Shivers and twitches—the body has a lot of ways to indicate how it feels, if you're watching."

The flush from her cheeks was moving down her neck and chest. "Um, touch next?"

"That's also good. A wet pussy, for example." And there, a sudden intake of breath. Something about that had Callie getting into the game. "That one also covers smell and taste— at least I hope so."

My voice was rasping now, and I was getting hard just imagining *her* smell and taste. We were standing two meters apart, not touching, but this was already more intimate than most of the hookups I'd had.

"How did your partners pay attention, Callie?" I kept my voice low, soft. Seducing her with the tone.

She looked down. "With a hard dick and a guy yelling he's coming. It didn't normally take much time."

"Tonight is going to be different."

I reached for her hand and she let me thread our fingers together. I led the way to my room.

Callie paused in the doorway.

I turned. She was staring at the bed. "Want to sit, talk a bit first?"

She turned her attention to me. Then the chin went up again. "No."

She crossed to the couch at the side of the room. It was a lightweight wool, in a rich brown, comfortable to relax in. She ran her hands over the surface, then bent her arm up to grab the zipper at the back of the dress.

She frowned as she twisted, trying to get the zipper to cooperate.

"May I help?"

A frustrated growl. "Please."

This close, I could see the patterns of the freckles on her shoulders and neck. I clasped the pull of the zipper, pausing to make sure she was good with this. I slowly lowered it, exposing more of those freckles. I pressed closer, breath touching her skin, and goose bumps came up.

"May I kiss you?"

She shuddered and nodded. I pressed my lips to her neck, tasting sweat and skin, with a hint of something unique to Callie. I lowered the zipper, following with my lips as she relaxed into my caresses.

Her bra strap was yellow, matching the dress, wide to support her ample breasts. I whispered in her ear. "Can I take it all off?"

She nodded again, inhaling a shaky breath.

I finished lowering the zipper and brushed the straps off her shoulders. The dress pooled at her feet, leaving her in a matching set of undergarments. I ghosted my fingers up her spine, then reached for the hooks on her bra.

She tensed, and I paused.

"I should tell you, I'm okay giving oral, but anal is a hard no. Don't try to talk me into it, I've tried it and I'm not doing it again. Condoms are nonnegotiable. And I'm on birth control." The words rushed out of her.

"Good to know. I'm also strict about condoms. I won't push you on your boundaries."

Her shoulders relaxed.

I wanted her to stay relaxed, so I stepped back. I could remove the lingerie later. "My turn."

She twisted around, eyes wide. I slid off my jacket and tossed it on the couch.

"You can wait on the bed and watch if you want." I put

a teasing note in my voice and she pressed her lips together, fighting a smile.

"Sure." She turned and walked to the bed.

No, she fucking sashayed, those hips swinging, and I took an involuntary step after her.

She climbed on the bed, legs curled up beside her. She waved a hand. "Okay, take it off."

It didn't take long to get rid of the shirt and tie. Callie's eyes traced over my chest, so I flexed. The way her eyes widened made me want to do it again, to impress her.

I unbuckled my belt, sliding it slowly through the loops on my pants. She watched closely as I unzipped and let the pants fall. For once, I didn't care if they wrinkled. This was more important.

There was a little gasp, my cock pressing against my branded underwear. She looked amazing, pupils wide and a flush on her cheeks. She curled one finger to bring me over.

I watched her watch me as I took three steps to the bed. She kept still.

"I'm going to touch you now, okay?"

Her head moved up and down, but she didn't speak.

I started with her collarbone. My finger moved gently, delicately...a whisper of contact that startled a shiver from her. I traced from freckle to freckle, watching as her chest lifted on each breath before a trembling exhale. The freckles made a path to the strap of her bra, her skin like silk beneath my fingers.

Clear, creamy skin, with those tantalizing freckles that covered all of her body that I could see. Her bra didn't reveal much, but I traced over the top of the garment, pausing in the middle. I could see the faint raised bumps as her nipples hardened.

I followed the path of her bra around to her other strap,

and up toward her neck. A flush moved down her chest, adding a rosy tint to her skin. Had anyone done this to her before? Had she only had quick, negotiated encounters? If so, I was going to ruin her for assholes like that. After me, I wanted her to insist on being treated well.

But I didn't want to think about that, not now.

As my fingers neared the other side of her neck, I wrapped my hand around it and nudged her forward. Her eyes, which had closed, flashed open. I dipped down to kiss her.

* * *

CALLIE

I COULDN'T FOCUS, flustered and off-balance. Cooper wasn't keeping to the plan. There was a goal for these things —orgasms, preferably mutual. It wasn't that difficult to follow the road map. My breasts were always the main attraction, so guys would play with them, I'd go down on them, once in a while someone might go down on me, then penis in vagina and hope for the best.

Cooper wasn't taking the interstate, but back roads I'd never explored. He was revving me up like his fancy Ferrari and I couldn't even understand. How the hell had a finger on my neck and shoulder shot heat to my pussy? Like, why had no one told me this was an erogenous zone?

Then he brought me closer, and finally his lips neared mine for a kiss.

My brain scrambled to keep up. Okay, kissing. He was aroused, since what looked to be a good-sized dick was hard in those fancy underpants he was wearing. I braced for that kind of kiss. Hard, fast, possessive. Instead, he brushed my lips with his. Gentle, teasing, and nowhere near enough. I wanted more. I pressed toward him and he retreated, just enough to keep up those soft touches.

I melted, no defenses against tenderness.

He smiled and moved his lips to my cheeks. My temple. Down my nose. I couldn't help it, a whimper slipped out.

Then along my neck, pressing behind my ear. I almost levitated, only his hand on the back of my neck keeping me close. I shuddered, and needed more. I pulled away, sliding back across the bed. He followed me, grinning, dimples at maximum power. Breathing hard with flushed cheeks, but still, grinning.

No, not going to let him get away with that. He obviously had a shit ton of practice, and I wasn't in that league, but I had learned: people did to you what they wanted done to them. Cooper gave light kisses and touches around my head and neck, so let's see how he would respond to that.

I pressed one hand against his chest—skin and hard muscles hot beneath my hands, light enough that he could have easily resisted—and pushed him down on his back. Then I leaned my head down and rubbed my nose against the bottom of his chin. He shifted, breath in my ear, so I licked. From his neck up to his ear, and he groaned.

"Do that again."

I did, adding a gentle nip. His hand curled into my hair and I let my fingers explore.

It was an awesome chest. Muscled, lightly tanned. He probably never burned, lucky sod. My hands wandered, brushing over his nipples, chasing down his ribs while I kissed and licked my way over to his mouth.

This time there was no gentle brushing. This time his mouth was firm and his tongue pressed past my lips, dueling with mine. This kiss was heat and passion, like in the books Darcy read and I sometimes borrowed. I couldn't compare it to anything I'd experienced before. It was new and exciting and took me to greater heights of arousal. Alarms rang in the back of my brain, but for once my body was taking the lead.

His hands moved to my bra and released the catch. He slid the straps down as I pushed closer to him. I didn't realize how much I was hampering his progress until his hands framed my face and he gently broke the kiss.

I leaned back. He hadn't touched my breasts or my ass or any expected areas, and I was already wet and wanting. My previous lovers had been missing some essential skills.

"Holy fuck." His eyes were glued to my boobs, now free of the bra I'd been wearing, almost in his face.

I had big breasts. Developed early, and partly because of that, I had a kind of love/hate relationship with them. They were heavy, made running a challenge, and were often in the way. But at times like this? They were powerful. This man, a freaking gift of nature, was staring at them, amazed by them. Moved by them.

I knelt up, enjoying the power I felt as he stared at me, admiring and desiring. I reached my hands to my panties to slide them off, but Mr. Pro Athlete used his quick reflexes and rock-hard abs to sit up and put his hands over mine.

"I'm in charge of removing those." His whisper was in my ear, and a shiver ran over me. "Wait."

But first...he slid off the bed, removed what were undoubtedly extremely expensive underwear, and bent to the suitcase on the luggage stand, grabbing a condom. I barely noticed, staring at an incredibly fit ass.

He looked fantastic in those posters and billboards, but they were photos, right? Airbrushed, enhanced—no one could be that perfect. And he wasn't perfect, but I had no complaints. Damn, how did one man look that good?

He had the body, the face, the attitude. But what really made my breathing speed up was the look in his eyes when he turned back to me. Like I looked as good to him as he did to me. I was glad I'd bought these panties. He was not complaining about colors now.

His eyes ran over my body, my skin tingling in response as if he'd touched me. "Where do I want to start?"

I wanted him everywhere. But as his eyes lingered on my boobs, I knew his answer. It was the boobs. Always the boobs. I cupped them in my hands and his eyes flared. "Maybe this is where?" I reached my thumbs to touch my nipples, already embarrassingly erect.

He groaned and then crawled on the bed. I waited for his hands on my breasts, but he surprised me. He reached over for another kiss. The only part of our bodies that met were our lips, but I was burning, everywhere.

I gasped when he pulled his lips away. He gently nudged me to lie down, and then resumed kissing me, over my chin, my neck, and down, finally to my breasts.

Oh my god...

Chapter 22

Another part of the time and space continuum

Cooper

Those tits were amazing. Pink tips over gently freckled skin. Generously sized, and I wanted to do so much with them. My hands, my mouth. I wanted to fuck my cock between them and cover them with my come.

But not now. I gathered the shreds of my control. My goal was for Callie to come undone, not think I was an animal. I kissed her, moving from her mouth to her neck. And then, when I was no longer reacting like a horny teenager, I flicked my tongue over her nipple.

She quivered, a moan sounding in her throat. Someone liked that. I wanted more of those sounds.

I used my tongue, my fingers, and finally my mouth. She tasted exquisite. I could have spent hours tasting her, playing with her breasts and listening to her sounds. She twisted underneath me, pulling me close with her hands in my hair, and then pushing me away when the sensations got too much. My cock was hard as a rock but I ignored it, keeping all my attention on her.

There was more to Callie than tits, as incredible as they were. I nuzzled between them and worked my way down her body. Her pubic hair was bright red, beckoning to me, and that pussy was my goal. If I wanted to see her really lose it, eating her out should do it.

I fucked my tongue into her belly button to gauge her response, then suddenly she shoved me off and onto my back. *Note to self: avoid her belly button in future.*

But in a moment, she'd grabbed the condom and straddled my hips.

Her hair was a mess, her head thrashing while I feasted on her breasts. Her skin was flushed, from her cheeks down over her chest. Her eyes were focused on me, pupils wide. She looked debauched and beautiful. I wanted to memorize her looking this way.

She tore the condom wrapper open and my cock twitched.

"I don't want to complain, but I was planning to go down on you."

She shook her head. "I want you in me, now."

I reached for the condom but she brushed my hands aside. I tightened my abs, working on my control as the feeling of her hands on my cock, smoothing the condom down, sent fire through my blood. She lifted onto her knees, grabbed me in one hand and slid down. Her tight warmth enveloped my dick and I groaned. Callie whined, dropping her hands to my pecs and shoving herself up again. Those gorgeous breasts were almost in my face, moving as she rose and fell, hips rolling.

The sight of her above me, face flushed, body shivering with pleasure, was doing things to me. My athlete stamina couldn't match this. I wasn't going to last. Her pussy was tight and hugged me perfectly, stimulating every nerve. But I wanted to see her go first. I spit on my thumb and moved it to her clit. I started with a gentle touch, and she quivered. A little harder and she whispered *fuck* as her body tightened and gripped me.

Her head dropped and I kept up the pressure. Something like a scream ripped from her throat as she came. She collapsed on my chest and I gripped her tightly, switching our positions while my cock stayed inside her. Once she was whimpering beneath me, limp with pleasure, I finally released my control and snapped my hips, chasing my orgasm. It crashed over me like a tsunami.

"Fuck, Callie, fucking fuck."

I was wrecked, but I managed to pull out and roll beside her before my limbs gave out.

* * *

IT TOOK a few minutes to come back to myself. I could hear Callie, the sound of her panting breaths mingling with mine. When I looked over, her eyes were closed, her hair spread over the pillow. I liked that image. There was so much passion behind that prickly exterior.

There was still a pink flush over her face and upper body. Her chest rising up and down and those glorious tits. *Incredible.* She was incredible. I wanted to wrap her in my arms and hold her till we could do this again.

I finally pulled myself to a sitting position on the side of the bed, checking that my legs were going to function. I didn't want to leave her, but I had a condom to deal with. I looked back and her eyes were still shut. I went to the bathroom and chucked the rubber.

I washed my hands, saw my reflection in the mirror. There was the same flushed skin on my neck and chest as Callie. My beard had started to grow in a five o'clock shadow. That would have left marks on Callie, which my hindbrain was pleased to consider. My hair was a mess. I took a moment to straighten it out, the pink on my skin fading.

I'd marked Callie, but she hadn't marked me. Until the end, she'd still held on to some of her control, keeping me out. I threw some water on my face and swallowed a few mouthfuls, then returned to the bedroom.

Callie was back in her bra and underwear. She was folding her dress in her arms. Anger and disappointment shot through me.

I leaned against the door frame of the en suite. "Leaving?"

She fussed with her dress. "I'll get back to my room. We've got another day of your family tomorrow."

Something clenched inside. "There's no rush."

"I need to wash off this makeup, and my stuff is in the other room."

But I want to sleep with you in my bed. I couldn't let those words out. I didn't even know where they came from. I always slept alone, and normally I was the one taking off after sex.

Maybe that was it, the reason for the disappointment. Pride, or ego or something, because she was leaving first. My family always fucked with my head, and she was probably right. Better not to complicate this. "Sleep well. Rehearsal dinner tomorrow with a new bunch of assholes added to the mix."

She stood for a moment, frowning at me. Had my tone

been off? I had to get myself together before more family interactions tomorrow.

She drew in a long breath. "Right. And um...you were right."

"About?"

Her cheeks turned red. "It was good. It was really good. So, like, five-star review."

She fled then, while I stared after her.

* * *

CALLIE

FIVE-STAR REVIEW.

I was so...stupid at this kind of thing. But I had to get away. Best sex of my life, bar none, but now my head was messed up and I almost felt like crying. I definitely didn't want to wait for the suggestion that I should leave, since I might have burst into tears, which would have been incredibly embarrassing.

I needed to talk to someone I trusted. So I stripped out of my pretty underwear and showered. Once I was in my shorts and T-shirt, ready to sleep, I called Darcy. There was no answer the first couple of rings. I'd checked his schedule so he wasn't working. Maybe he'd gone to sleep early?

"Callie? That you?"

"Yeah, it's me."

"How was— Put me on video. I need to see you."

I checked that I was decent, as decent as the old clothes could be, and switched to video.

"Callie, are you okay?"

"Sure."

He shook his head. "No, that's not your okay face."

"I have an okay face?"

He nodded fervently. "Yeah, your 'I don't give a fuck and you can't touch me' face."

I blinked at him. "That's not what I look like now?"

He cocked his head and studied me. "No, I think that's a more 'what the fuck have I done' face."

I sighed. "It's actually 'I just fucked and now I'm fucked' face."

Darcy's brows drew together. "Seriously, Callie, are you okay?"

I dropped on my bed. "Not really sure right now."

He was on our couch. "Should we talk?"

I hated talking about my feelings. But my thoughts were jumbled and a strange urge to cry kept coming over me. I had to face Cooper in the morning and get through more time with his family, so talking was what I needed.

"Yeah."

"What happened?"

"Cooper and I..."

His eyes bugged out. "You and the hockey hottie... hooked up?"

"We did."

He dropped his head back. "Give me a moment. That's awesome. No, wait, did he hurt you?"

I shook my head.

"Was it good?"

Good didn't begin to cover it. I nodded.

"I don't suppose you'd give me details?" He leaned forward, batting his eyes at me. Darcy was cute, and he was excellent at puppy-dog eyes, but I was charm-immune.

"I'm not giving you a play-by-play, no."

He sighed. "At least tell me about his cock. It was nice, right? Did they augment for those billboards?"

"New rule. We do not discuss details of any private parts that have been inside me."

Darcy's jaw dropped. "But parts of Cooper have been in you?"

"That's the definition of hooking up, isn't it?"

He ignored that comment. "And it was good. How good? Like, yeah, I came, it was fine? Or yeah, I entered another part of the time and space continuum it was so good?"

He was exaggerating, but not by much. "Closer to the second."

Darcy fanned his face. Suddenly he frowned. "And he asked you to leave after that?"

"We're sharing a suite, so it wasn't really leaving. And I was the one who said I had to go."

He narrowed his eyes, looking for who knew what in my expression. "Did he make you feel like you needed to?"

I shook my head. "He was...I think he wanted to do it again. Maybe even have me stay the night. But I could be wrong." He'd been upset to find me almost dressed when he came out of the bathroom. Better for him to regret my leaving than my staying.

"But you left."

I shrugged.

"So, why are you fucked, Callie? Do you like him?"

Did I like him? He was attractive. Considerate. Kind. Whole layers below the public Cooper people saw. But I didn't "like" people. "Not the way you're thinking." I didn't, did I?

"Then what is it?"

"It was...it was the best sex of my life. He took his time.

Paid attention, as he called it. I didn't even recognize myself."

"Holy shit."

"What?"

"That must have been spectacular. I'm envious."

"But this wasn't supposed to be about sex." Sex that made me feel this way—it could lead to feelings, and that wasn't allowed.

"So you two did the deed, you came incredibly hard, and you took off like a bat out of hell after."

I opened my mouth to protest, but he had the essentials there.

"If he offers another incredible orgasm, you can say no. But don't say no just because you're scared, sweetie."

"I'm not scared."

"Aren't you?"

I swallowed. "If I was scared, then wouldn't it be a sign that there was danger, and I should avoid it?"

"Well, yeah. If this was 50,000 BC and we lived in caves and there might be a saber-toothed tiger around." Darcy waved his hand at the screen, and yeah, there was a notable shortage of tigers and caves. "You've worked so hard to make something of yourself, to feel safe. Maybe you've done too much of that."

Darcy knew me better than anyone else. We'd both had too little security growing up. Had I gone too far to the opposite extreme in the interests of being safe? Far enough that it was going to hurt me?

"You're saying I should have sex with Cooper as an acceptable risk?"

He choked. "How much risk is there? You used protection, right?"

"Of course." No accidental pregnancies.

"Will it harm your career or your chances of making partner?"

"No, not when the firm does charity work with the hockey team."

"Will the sex ruin you for anyone else?"

I rolled my eyes at him.

"Will you get hurt?"

I narrowed my eyes. "Are you asking if I'll fall in love with him?"

"Callie, despite what you think, that wouldn't be the worst thing. Especially if he falls in love with you."

"Not gonna happen." Cooper was not falling in love with me, and I wouldn't let myself fall in love with him. With anyone.

Darcy laid his head on the couch. "It's your life. But maybe consider if this might be a gift. You've earned a reward. Treat yourself to some hot sexy times while you learn how to be a country club zombie. And you know, if you meet any of his teammates who aren't strictly straight..."

I doubted any hockey players were out, but if I found one, I'd definitely introduce him to Darcy. He had emerged from the same hellish background I had, but it hadn't made him hard and prickly like me. He hadn't closed himself off to a relationship. I didn't know how he could consider a risk like that, but he did.

"You might be right. I'll think about it."

"And give me details?"

"Never."

Chapter 23

Lose control

CALLIE

I DIDN'T HAVE to cross swords with Pierce at the rehearsal. Since I wasn't in the wedding party, I just sat in the back of the church while they went through the complicated movements that made up the wedding service. My gaze lingered on Cooper, noticing the stiffness of his posture and the superficiality of his smiles. I couldn't hear what his relatives said to him, but I could see how they ate away at his confidence.

Fuckers.

Sitting there through endless repeats, I considered the whole exercise. I doubted I'd ever get married. That would involve a level of trust I'd never imagined happening. If I did, it wasn't going to be like this. Too much stress.

A man sat down in the pew beside me. I turned a startled glance and recognized Remington Winthrop. Just what I needed—more assholes.

"Do I know you?" He leaned back, one ankle crossed over the other knee, perfectly at ease.

"I met you at Briarwood in Toronto. I was golfing with Cooper."

He raised a brow. "Cooper? Oh, Whit."

I didn't reply. They could argue over names if they wanted.

"That's right, I remember now. So you're here with Whit for the wedding? You his girlfriend?" His eyes dropped to my chest, then my legs, and finally back up.

"We're friends." Last night notwithstanding.

"What's your name again? And how did you meet Whit?"

I could challenge his right to interrogate me, but I didn't want to embarrass Cooper. "Callie Smith. I met him at a charity dinner my firm was involved with."

His eyebrow rose. "What firm is that?"

"Anderson, Krys and Chan."

Both eyebrows were rushing for his hairline. Just like the Cooper family, he'd heard of the firm, which made sense if he was doing business in Toronto.

"Paralegal?"

Right. Because I had big boobs. None of the paralegals had been invited to the dinner. "Tax attorney."

His brows couldn't get any higher, but they tried. "Really? That's impressive."

The easy explanation for this chauvinism was that the idea of a female lawyer disconcerted him, but I was sure the real reason was because I was with Cooper. "It does seem to surprise everyone I meet here. I should have brought my diploma. Or a pay stub."

He laughed. "We're just more surprised that you're with Cooper, if you're that smart."

"Why?"

Winthrop tugged on his ankle. "He's a hockey player."

"Apparently they have hockey players at Harvard. I don't think stupidity is required to play the sport."

"But it helps," he said with another laugh.

I didn't join him.

He smirked. "Oh, is that it? You want to become Mrs. Cooper? He must be bringing in the cash—maybe you'd like to do something a little easier than tax for the rest of your life?"

I imagined slapping his ridiculous face, and it was incredibly satisfying. It had been years since I'd had those urges. This wedding was bringing them out. But again, I let the insult go. I couldn't imagine it helping Cooper, and I kept my eye on the prize. I didn't need to antagonize these people who knew the firm I worked for. They might have influence. "I enjoy my work, and I'm not looking for anyone to support me. But since personal questions are so popular, what about you? Looking to marry someone with a lot of money and spend your time on the golf course?"

He didn't fall for the diversion. "You're protective of him."

"I said he was a friend. I don't call many people that, and I don't take friendship lightly."

"Maybe you should open up to the possibilities of more friendships. They might benefit you." His eyes were on my breasts again and I knew exactly what kind of friendship he was talking about.

"I keep business and my personal life separate. My friends aren't part of my work life, and my colleagues aren't friends. It helps to keep the lines clear."

He reached into his pocket and pulled out a business

card, holding it out to me. "If you change your mind, here's how to contact me."

I really didn't want to take his card, but it would only antagonize him to refuse. I didn't get one of my cards out though. I didn't want this man to reach out to me, even for tax advice. I had Benson in my day-to-day life and that was more than enough.

The dinner after the rehearsal was more of the same. I wasn't sitting with Cooper, again, but neither was I with Pierce or Winthrop so I called it a win. I made laborious conversation with a brother of the groom, a guy who only became animated when he could talk about sailing, and noticed the tension in Cooper's jaw as he was talked at by... an uncle? Cousin? Some stuffy relation. Like last night.

On the way back to the hotel, I made a suggestion. "Perhaps sex would help you relax?"

He flashed a glance at me. "I'm happy with a repeat, but thought I'd have to convince you. I got through my family's bullshit by making up a pitch."

I shrugged. "Good thing you weren't a disappointment last night."

He laughed, and some of that tension left his expression.

We were quiet again on the way up to the suite. When we got there, I happily slid my feet out of the expensive shoes and sighed.

"Want a drink?" Cooper asked.

"Water would be great."

Cooper walked into the kitchen and grabbed a couple of water bottles from the fridge. He passed me one, taking one for himself. Then he leaned over the island and studied me. "Want to hear the sales pitch?"

"Sure. Pitch me."

"You don't like losing control. Now, good sex kind of demands losing it, but what if we do this in a way that you have control over me?"

I was intrigued. "How did you imagine that taking place?"

His lips curved up in a dirty grin. "Oh, I imagined a lot of possibilities."

I shivered, because now I was coming up with some porn-worthy ideas of my own.

"I narrowed it down to something within the bounds of practicality."

I didn't put Cooper and sex together in any way that was practical, but I was definitely interested.

"I don't have any handcuffs or ropes—" He straightened. "But I could sacrifice a tie or two to the cause."

It took me a minute. "You mean, to tie you up?"

He held up his hand. "Don't get too excited there. I'm not leaving myself completely at your mercy. But if my hands were tied up, and I lay on the bed while you ran the show...would that give you enough control to enjoy yourself without regretting anything later?"

I sucked in a breath. The man saw too much of me. The wise course would be to stop this before he learned any more. But while we were here, in a different country, teaming up against his family, I could pretend this was an anomaly. Not part of my regular life. And thinking of it, that incredible body laid out on his bed, naked, hands tied and me in control? Too damned bad if it was risky, I wanted it. Enough that my hands were trembling with desire. I wanted it and I was going to take it. "Let's go."

Unfortunately, he didn't move. "That's a yes?"

"Yes. It's a yes."

"And you're not going to regret it? Because that's hell on a man's ego."

I blinked at him. That was the second time he mentioned my regretting it. Once could be a throwaway, but not twice. Did he think I had regrets?

He shrugged and stood up. "Okay, bedroom."

"Wait."

His body froze, eyes meeting mine before skittering over my shoulder. "Changed your mind?"

I shook my head. "No. But so you know, I don't regret last night."

Now he met my gaze. "You sure?"

"I hate the thought of stroking your ego. It's already incredibly inflated. But last time was good. Very good. Top ten good." Best ever, but I had to save some of myself with this man. "I don't regret how much I enjoyed myself, but it scares me."

His confidence was back, and his gaze on me was too perceptive. "What are you afraid of, Callie, if you lose control in my bed?"

A shiver ran down my spine. Something about the way he said those words—*lose control in my bed*—made a part inside me push to the surface, want to show him how out of control I could be. I was familiar with that part, and it led to bad decisions. I reined it in. "Of doing something incredibly stupid."

"What stupid thing could you do? Aside from whips and shackles, I'm pretty open when it comes to sex."

I twisted my lips. "Yeah, well sometimes sex gets mixed up with feelings. I won't risk that."

My life had derailed, almost ruining my future, when I thought men fucking me meant they cared for me. My stupid heart opened to them, desperate for affection. I'd learned that they were using me, and I wouldn't allow that again.

His eyes narrowed. "Do you...want a relationship?"

I snorted. "Please. I'm not that stupid. Neither of us wants that." *Talk about ego.* "I mixed up sex and love when I was young. I won't do it again. But I haven't let my control go like last night in a long time. It could be a problem."

He nodded slowly. "Are you afraid you can't control yourself if we do this again?"

"Maybe last time was a fluke. I've been on my own for too long."

That got to him. "I promise, Callie, that wasn't a fluke. And cards on the table, I'd like to continue having sex with you while this chemistry thing works. How about we agree to call a halt if either of us starts to feel like this might be more?"

Did he say *we* because he was being tactful? Was he worried about developing feelings? Not likely. People didn't fall for me. In any case, some amazing sex was my treat. An indulgence for a brief time. If it started to get out of hand, if feelings got involved, we'd end it. "And this doesn't affect our agreement?"

A strange look crossed his face but I couldn't read it. He held up two fingers. "I swear."

"So, can we get to where I tie you up and use you?"

The familiar confident expression was back on his face. "I'll do the tying. But yeah, we can see if this works for you."

"Go get your ties, then. We've got work to do."

Chapter 24

We'll sacrifice these

I FOLLOWED him to his bedroom.

He pulled the tie from around his neck and inspected it. "This might not be recoverable when we're done, but I'm not sure I want to wear it again anyway." He picked up his tie from the previous day. "Okay, we'll sacrifice these."

"Take off your shirt."

Amusement crossed his face, and one side of his mouth tilted up. "Bossy, are we?"

I grabbed the ties from his hand. "You said I could be in control."

"I did. I also said I was doing the tying."

"Get your shirt off and then you can tie yourself up. I want you naked." I was nervous, but if I was calling the shots? It helped the nerves.

He unbuttoned his dress shirt slowly, watching me the whole time. He threw it toward the chair. "Happy?"

I was, as much by his doing what I asked as by the chest now exposed to my view. I passed him a tie.

He held it in his hand. "Do you want me to remove anything else?"

"Not yet."

He smiled a little wider. "This is going to be very interesting."

"And still you aren't tied up."

"Yes, ma'am."

He made some kind of complicated knot that bound the two bits of fabric—I was betting on them being silk—and wrapped one end around one wrist. A bit more maneuvering, and he had both wrists tied together in front of him.

I stood up. He was still watching me with that little grin when I turned him, then shoved him so he fell on his back on the bed. His arms jerked, moving instinctively to protect his fall, but the knots he'd made were good. His wrists stayed together. He ended up in a clumsy sprawl across his mattress.

I climbed onto the bed while he lay back, hands shackled, eyes on me. I tugged on his feet and brought his legs up. Then I rolled him over till he was mostly in the middle of the oversized bed. His feet were hanging off the foot, but I'd probably need his help to drag his body up toward the headboard, and that would erode the impression of being in control. Good enough. It might make pulling the rest of his clothes off a little easier.

"Hands over your head."

His eyebrows rode up but he did as I asked. I took a moment to appreciate the objective beauty of his fit body, and then moved to his waistband.

"Having fun?" he asked.

I paused, my hands on the button of his pants. "I didn't ask you to talk."

The eyebrows stayed high, but I felt his dick twitch. It was getting hard, so I didn't worry that I was crossing any kind of line or upsetting him. Maybe Mr. Hockey didn't get bossed around very often. This might be good for him.

I pulled down the zipper and tugged. He didn't lift his ass to help, and when I glared at him I got an unhelpful smirk. He was going to make me ask. Instead, I pinched his ass cheek and he flinched away. Giving me the opportunity to yank the clothing over his ass.

Score one for me. His dick was pressing up in his underwear, so he liked what I was doing.

I grabbed the waistband of his briefs and he tensed, expecting another pinch. But I had more than one way to skin this cat. I pulled on the fabric until it started to stress, and he lifted his ass the tiniest amount, but enough that I was able to pull them over his dick and down his legs. Yeah, he didn't want me to rip them—they probably cost a fortune, unless that was something else he didn't pay for. I shook my head. *Not the time.*

I slid off and went to the foot of the bed. His feet hanging over the edge made it easy to remove the last of his clothing. I stood in place for a minute and stared at him. Took my time enjoying the view. This was something I'd never had before. A naked man, mine to play with. A gorgeous, incredibly fit hockey player. I was still dressed, and it gave me the illusion of power. I shivered again and his erection twitched. This was working for him too.

Now, what did I want to do next?

I wanted him to lose it. Lose that confident shell he projected and make him forget his disapproving family. I could go right for his dick. But he'd expect that, and I wasn't ready to move things along that quickly. There were other places that had sensitive nerves. Some I'd discovered last night. Now I could hunt for them as long as I wished.

I didn't want to bother with clothes later, so I undid the zip on my dress and pulled it off. When my face was no longer hidden in the fabric, I found his gaze focused on my body.

I was wearing more of the lacy lingerie I'd bought for this trip. I wasn't sure how often I'd wear it. The salesclerk swore it would support my breasts, but it wasn't one of my usual bras and I kept waiting for a strap to break, or a boob to pop out of the cups, shallower than I was used to.

Right now, it was worth the expense. Cooper's irises were almost completely blotted out by his pupils, and he swallowed and licked his lips. *Excellent.* Now that his sense of sight was fully engaged, I was going to work on touch. I slid a knee onto the big bed, beside Cooper's hip.

"Are you sure you don't want to take off more clothes?" His voice was raspy, and his eyes were stuck on my cleavage.

"Nah, I'm good."

His arms jerked but he forced them back over his head. "You're going to kill me, aren't you?"

I bent down, the lace over my breasts touching his ribs and bicep as I whispered in his ear, "I'm going to take your control away."

His body shuddered, but he stayed in place. I ran my tongue up over his ear and he shuddered again. Then I gently bit his earlobe.

"Fuck!"

"Not yet," I whispered. And I got to work.

I used my mouth, my hands, even my hair and boobs to touch every inch of glorious skin stretched over his frame. I took time, touching the places that seemed to drive him crazy. I watched the goose bumps on his skin, and how his body twitched. I listened to the moans that escaped his mouth. I felt when his abdomen tensed so much that I worried he might harm himself. But the nonstop cursing assured me he was doing okay.

I finally worked my way down to his hips, tasting, licking, sucking, biting, lightly scratching. When I bypassed his dick, only my hair brushing over it as I headed for his thick thighs, he began to plead.

"Come on. Bring that pussy up here and I'll make you feel so good."

He was still coherent. I kept going.

He had sensitive skin behind his knees, and ticklish feet. As I headed back up his body his hips thrust and the begging became a little messier.

"Please. Callie, come on. Please—oh fuck!"

That was when I swallowed him down. Being the girl with big boobs and no self-esteem in high school had given me the reputation of being easy. I'd been willing to do a lot to feel important to someone. It wasn't the ideal reason for it, but I knew how to give a stellar blow job. I had no gag reflex and could deep throat with the best of them.

I pulled in a breath, and then pushed his dick down into my throat. I held him there for a moment and swallowed.

"Fuck— Shit— No, I'm gonna— Don't stop—"

I pulled back and his hips thrust up, following my mouth. There was drool running down my chin, and I wiped it off with one hand while I watched his face.

He blinked his eyes open. "Jesus fuck, Callie. That was incredible. But you do that again and I'll come."

I smiled smugly. "That's not what I want, Cooper."

His chest was lifting and falling, sweat gathering

between his pecs and over his ribs and face. "Your mouth is lethal."

I'd been complimented on my oral skills before. But I wanted my own pleasure out of this, and that meant getting his dick inside me.

I reached back and undid my bra, sliding down the straps and letting it fall onto the bed. He drew in a long breath. I slid to the side and stood, taking off the panties, enjoying his gaze.

I squatted by his luggage while I searched for the condoms we needed. Then I returned to the bed, my hips swinging, enjoying his appreciation.

I sat across his thighs with the packet in my hand and carefully ripped it open. His dick in front of me was rock-hard, flushed, and leaking. I ran my hand down it, feeling the velvety soft skin over the hard column. He hissed, so I did it again, slower. Then I carefully pushed the condom over him.

"If you don't want lube, the offer to eat you out is still on the table."

I didn't need lube. Playing with him, imagining what I would do to him, had already gotten me wet. With his cheeks flushed, hair damp and sweaty, eyes slitted open to watch me, he looked hotter than he did in those fucking billboards.

"I don't need it." I pushed up on my knees and crawled forward, breasts hanging over his body.

"Oh, fuck, Callie."

Instead of grabbing his dick and filling myself with it, I copied his move of the night before, and leaned down and kissed him. He opened, his tongue searching my mouth, and his shoulders jerked as his arms lifted then settled back down. I gripped his hair in my hands, messing it up, pulling it, taking the pleasure I wanted from him. It was too good.

I pulled back and caught my breath. "Okay, I'm going to ride you now. I don't want you to come till I do."

He blinked at me. "Don't know if I can promise that."

"Try. Try hard. Show me your stamina."

I reached for his dick, held it firm and then slowly slid down.

I was ready, wet and aroused, but i\he was big, and the pressure was a lot. When I was finally fully seated, I took a long breath and rolled my hips, pleasuring myself. He started swearing again.

I braced my hands on his broad chest and lifted myself. Up, and then down, letting that dick fill me up and rub me inside with warm, firm pressure. I shuddered.

I straightened, lifting my hands and holding my breasts. I let my fingers flick my nipples as I lifted and dropped, pleasure spiking from my breasts to my pussy, goose bumps rising on my skin. I moaned, close to losing control myself. Watching the man beneath me, tendons tight and muscles clenched to keep himself in position. Another roll of my hips, and he snapped.

I'd done it. His control was gone. Frantically, he tugged his hands out of the knot on his tie and grabbed my waist. Those powerful arms lifted me up and over onto my back. Then he gripped my wrists, holding my hands down to the bed. He notched himself between my thighs and pressed in. He wasn't gentle, and he wasn't careful. He was a man pushed to his limits and he pounded into me. The waves of pleasure rippled over my body and I met him thrust for thrust, demanding everything he could give me.

"Close," I panted.

He gripped both wrists in one hand and moved the

other to my clit. It didn't take long before I screamed as my orgasm rushed over me, racking my body with shudders. I was vaguely aware of Cooper shouting something, and then he collapsed on top of me.

Every cell in my body was relaxed, sated with pleasure. Cooper now had his name on the top two sexual experiences of my life. I couldn't even remember what the third would have been.

I closed my eyes, letting the aftershocks ripple through as something warm inside made me want to purr. Right now, there was nothing more I wanted.

Chapter 25

The final performance

COOPER

THAT HAD BEEN...SOMETHING.

I'd never given up control like that before. There were too many risks. I was the captain of the team, the face of several products, and I carefully managed my brand. People wanted things from me. A piece of my hair, my clothes, even my sperm. I had rules to protect myself and I was never too vulnerable.

I trusted Callie. She was about as far from a jersey chaser as I could get. She didn't want photos, or stories about how she banged the hockey player. She didn't want my possessions or my celebrity. All she wanted was golf lessons and orgasms.

I was relaxed in a way I couldn't remember after I'd fucked someone. She'd taken over and I hadn't been responsible for her pleasure. She'd focused on me, not so I'd want to fuck her again, but because she wanted to drive me crazy. All I'd had to do was lie back and take it...until it had

236

become too much. Damn, I was surprised how much I liked it.

I also liked a lax and sated Callie lying flat on my bed after screaming, she'd come so hard. I wouldn't tease her about that because my own throat was a little scratchy and I'd made some noises I wasn't proud of. Would totally do it again though.

I turned to watch her. Callie's eyes blinked open, staring blankly at the ceiling. "Did that work for you?" I asked.

A grin crossed her face, something softer and less guarded than I'd seen before. "It'll do."

I propped myself up on one elbow. "If you have any complaints, maybe you want to speak to the woman who was in charge."

She looked up at me. "Someone else took over at the end there."

Was she upset about that? "Sorry." Her smile widened, something a little bit dirty in it. I was on board.

"I said I wanted you to lose control. And you did." She shrugged and my eyes fell to those incredible tits.

I pulled my gaze back up to her face. She was still soft and open, a side few got to see, and it softened something in me. "I've never done that."

That frown between her brows. "No?"

"I don't trust a lot of people to not take advantage."

Her eyes widened and then she nodded. "Something we have in common. People suck."

I snorted. "Yeah, some of them do."

I felt the tension returning to her body. She was putting her armor back on.

"Do you want to stay?" If that armor was coming on so she'd be ready for me to kick her out, I wanted her to know she didn't need it yet.

"Are you sure?"

"Trust me, I don't offer that often." It had been a long time.

Her lips twitched as she considered. I stole another look at her body, still uncovered in the bed. She didn't have any hang-ups about being nude. Freckles covered as much of her creamy skin as I could see, and her pussy was covered by red hair. I needed to get a lot more personal with that. I hadn't tasted her yet.

I wanted her to stay.

"I'd like to have that delectable body close by for another round."

Amusement flashed in her eyes. "You up for that?"

"I will be."

She stayed the night. I'd thought it would be hard to sleep with someone sharing the bed again, but the sex must have worn me out because I slept like a baby.

I woke her up with my mouth on her pussy, and it was everything I'd hoped.

I was actually in a good mood when we left for the wedding.

* * *

THIS WAS THE FINAL PERFORMANCE. I stood at the front of the church, with my brother and some buddies of the groom's, dressed up in tuxes while we waited for the bridal party to come down the aisle. I mostly ignored Pierce's whispered comments. Much better to remember last night.

The church was packed. The huge stone building was filled with flowers, so that the air was thick with their scent. There was an arch of white blooms over the doorway where the bridal party would appear, and matching bouquets on the end of every pew, as well as almost filling the altar area around us. The white was a backdrop for the well-dressed people in the pews, highlighting the tuxes and vivid colors of the women's dresses. I spotted Callie easily—that bright hair was a beacon where the sun fell through a window and lit her up.

She hadn't been willing to wear a fascinator, which a lot of the women here were showing off, but her hair alone made her stand out. The dress was gorgeous and hugged her body just right. After the last two nights, it gave me ideas that I couldn't do anything about, not with the eyes of several hundred people on me.

The music started, everyone stirred, and the bridal procession began. I kept the proper interested expression on my face but I wasn't paying attention to the bridesmaids coming down the aisle. I focused on Callie. She was sitting on her own, but it didn't seem to bother her. She watched the women walking oh so slowly down the aisle, but I'd bet my Ferrari that she wasn't planning her own wedding. She was probably taking notes in case she was invited to something similar by someone in her firm.

Her glance swung forward and our eyes met. She rolled hers and I had to fight to keep from laughing.

Then came the bride, my father leading her to the front of the church. Dad was in an immaculate tux, and Tinsley looked breathtaking in her simple but perfectly fitting gown. She wasn't wearing the traditional veil, so her face was visible. Both she and my father looked confident, pleased with themselves, and proud. I compared it to Faith and Seb's wedding, when she'd looked like the world revolved around him. And though Hunts would deny it to his dying day, he'd had tears in his eyes.

If I ever— My smile dropped as I reined in those

thoughts. I was never. Not getting married, not exposing some poor woman to a lifetime connection to my family, not giving my brother a weapon against me.

You can't be cheated on if you don't have someone who's yours.

My eyes swung to Callie again. Yeah, she'd been exposed to enough this weekend. It was a good thing we had set up boundaries, because she was much too appealing.

* * *

THE RECEPTION DRAGGED on as well. I made polite talk to people I hadn't seen since my parents' anniversary party two years ago. They were all friends of my family or the groom's. The more interesting friends I'd made on my own were not invited. Before the evening was turned over to the band, I was able to catch up with Callie for a couple of moments. We'd finished the dinner and the first dance with the couple and the parents and family. My responsibilities weren't over yet, but I could see the light at the end of the tunnel.

"How are you surviving?" I asked.

She looked around the reception hall, flowers and candles on every surface, well-modulated voices filling the room. "Your family likes ceremony, don't they?"

"They live on it."

"I can see you fitting in here. I mean, obviously you do, but at the same time this doesn't seem like you at all."

"Not sure fitting in is much of a compliment."

A smile crossed her face. "I meant that you know all the unwritten rules. You know how to dress and dance and how to use the utensils properly. Which wines are right, and how to talk to people."

Callie placed a higher value on those things than I did, because she didn't have them. "Are you having an okay time? Are people bothering you?"

She shrugged. "I'm all right. I'm quiet and following what everyone else does."

"Have you danced?"

She shook her head. "I've been very carefully avoiding anyone who looks like they want to ask me."

I'd never asked if Callie danced. "Not a dancer?"

"I don't think what we did back in high school would be called dancing here."

I held back a grin. "So, no cotillions?"

Her eyes widened. "That's a real thing?"

I let my smile escape. "Real enough. Come on, dance with me before I have to take a turn with my mother's friends."

"What kind of dance?"

I held out my hand. "This is a slow one. I'll take care of you."

For once, that idea didn't chase her away. She hesitated but put her hand in mine.

I knew her hand. It had touched every part of my body, and those memories sent goose bumps over my skin. I hid the effect she had on me by pulling her in close and moving to the music, leading her gently and covering any missteps.

There weren't many. Whatever kind of dancing she'd done in the past, she was able to follow my lead. We didn't speak. I noticed eyes watching us but I didn't care. I spent less and less time with this family I'd been born into. I had a full, happy life in Toronto. Over the years, it had become obvious that no amount of success I had would be enough for my father and brother to admit they'd been wrong. This visit with Callie had made the contrast clear. She was the only one here worth a damn. And these people, with their focus on appearances, were not worth the bother.

The song wrapped up and something more up-tempo started. I wanted to end the dance with a kiss, but instead I pulled back. "I have about another hour of social obligations, then we can go back to the hotel."

Her cheeks flushed. From the warmth of the room? The dancing? The promise of what we would do when we got away? Whatever—there was something about her tonight. But I didn't want her to face any more of my family's ire, so I stepped back and let her go.

My mother found me, asked me to dance with the groom's grandmother. I put on the polite smile required and did my duty. After the grandmother, the wife of one of Pierce's friends asked me to dance. I held out a hand, counting down the dances in my head till I could say my duty was done.

"So, you're the hockey player." She moved a little closer. "I've noticed your billboards."

I saw where this was going. I made a little more room between us. "My sponsor will be happy to hear that."

She wiggled closer again. "You know, I read that people get very horny at weddings." She giggled.

"Family drama and an open bar—makes perfect sense."

She giggled again. "This might be a little forward, but..." Some more squirming, and suddenly a hotel room card was in her hand. She felt her way down my chest and slid it into my jacket pocket. "Room 2241."

"You're wearing a wedding ring."

She shrugged. "We understand each other."

"That's nice, but I don't do wives." Her cheeks flushed. Whether at the blunt response or the rejection, I wasn't sure. "And I may model underwear, but I'm not actually a prostitute."

Her body stiffened. "You don't have to be crude."

"And you don't need to treat me like an idiot because I'm a professional athlete. I know Pierce and his friends have plans tonight, but they won't understand their wives slumming."

Her cheeks were bright red now. "Like anyone would take you seriously. We all know you couldn't handle it so you left to do this hockey thing."

"Intelligence isn't measured by the university someone attends."

Her nose moved up. "I think I'm done with this dance."

I released my arms, relieved to do so. "Then please, let's move off the floor." I reached my hand into my front pocket and pulled out the key card. "You should take this back."

I didn't think her face could get redder, but she snatched the card, looking around the room in case someone was watching. Several people were. She turned and walked off, doing her best to look offended, as if I'd made a pass at her.

I had reached my limit. I looked around for Callie, ready to call this event done.

Chapter 26

If we were friends

CALLIE

I FOUND a quiet corner and watched. The protocols people followed here were strange to me, but when I wasn't sure what I should do, a quiet corner never did me wrong.

It was research, anyway. Cooper's family had more money than any of the partners at my firm, but if I understood how people behaved here, it would help me when, hopefully, I had to attend the wedding of a partner or their kid. From here, I could see who was close to the bride and groom, and who wasn't. I could tell that at some of the tables people were talking business, while at others, things were more relaxed, and people laughed.

Cooper was dancing with some woman older than his parents. Possibly a relation, or a connection to the family firm. I'd learned a lot from him. I'd also learned a lot about him. He was smiling out there but it wasn't a real smile. The dimples were out, and he was charming people, but I'd seen those real smiles, and they were different.

I frowned. What was I supposed to do with that knowledge?

"Not dancing, Callie? I saw you up there with Cooper—did he trample your feet?"

Pierce. The asshole Benson aspired to be. He shared so many features with Cooper, and yet they didn't work right. Even if they looked the same, I could never confuse them. Pierce was one of the blessed people. Wealthy, healthy, attractive, and intelligent. If he knew my story, my whole story, the way he looked at me would change. Now that I'd met Pierce, it was obvious how Benson's attitude had prompted Cooper to help me with my golfing problem.

I shook my head in response to his question.

Pierce sat down beside me. I shot him a glance from the corner of my eye. He had an angle—Pierce would always have an angle. Was he looking for information on Cooper? He wouldn't get it from me.

"We haven't seen that much of you, Callie. Whit has kept you busy."

"It's a wedding. It's kept everyone busy."

We had not been fucking nonstop the way Pierce implied with his knowing look. Damn it, this was why Cooper's ideas about dressing to look good didn't always work. I preferred to look boring, not like someone's fuck buddy. And damn Pierce for making me feel like that. Especially in this dress, which I loved.

"Still, I'd like to get to know you."

I held in a shudder of revulsion. "There isn't much to know about me. We went through the basics the first night." I didn't want to talk about my least favorite subject, namely me.

Pierce leaned back. "Tax law is a challenging specialty."

It was. Again, something I'd already been asked about, and not something that merited a long discussion.

Pierce kept talking, but his eyes were on Cooper. "And with the work that involves, I expect you'd like to be a partner someday."

I narrowed my eyes. Was he fucking with me? Did his firm have influence with mine, even though I hadn't seen any connections? Could this deal with Cooper have any negative consequences at the firm?

"I'm just guessing. You're smart, ambitious, beautiful..." He let that trail off.

I was smart, very smart, and I had ambitions, but not to take over the world. I just wanted to ensure my life was as safe as I could make it. I was *not* beautiful. Pierce thought flattery about my appearance would numb some of my brain cells.

"We do business with your firm, could maybe put in a word." He waited, a little smile on his face, as if he expected me to jump all over that.

"You're going to recommend me as partner material, someone you've only known for days."

He shrugged. "It's called networking. You need connections if you want to get somewhere, and a chat at a wedding can have more impact than any CV."

This was the way it worked for the privileged. The rest of us? SOL. I hated that.

"Are you telling me that being Cooper's date to his sister's wedding is going to get me on the fast track to partner?" Might as well lay it all out. He'd probably lie about it, but at least I'd be able to watch his reactions, get a feel for how much shit he was shoveling.

"No, Whit burned any bridges with the family when he had his picture plastered around the city in his underwear.

Bringing you to this wedding is the smartest thing he's done in years. If you want to make your mark as an attorney, he's not going to help you. But I could."

What the hell kind of word was he going to put in, when he'd never seen any of my work?

He looked over the room. "If we were friends."

Every hair on my body stood up when he said that. It wasn't just the words. More than what he said was how he'd said it—the tone. It wasn't the first time I'd heard it. Back in high school, a teacher had offered me help on a test, if we were "friends." I knew what kind of friends he meant. Sure, back then I'd had a reputation, one I'd earned, but I'd only bartered sex for affection. Not for grades. This wasn't a real offer, obviously. Pierce thought I was stupid enough to sleep with him and hope that got me a recommendation. "Being friendly is definitely going to get me a legitimate job offer." My voice was flat.

The fucker grinned at me. "I've got a room upstairs—we could work out the details. See which brother can better help your future. Even if you're not interested in making partner, we could have some fun together. Helen just gave Whit her room key, so he's going to be busy."

I'd been watching Cooper too. But I'd seen him return the plastic card. I had no idea if Pierce had, but he thought I'd sleep with him because I was upset Cooper might sleep with someone else. Like I'd want to strike back at Cooper by fucking his brother.

Maybe that was the tactic he'd used on Cooper's high school girlfriend.

Pierce put his hand on my thigh. High on my thigh. I picked it up and dropped it back on his own leg. "Find a way to fuck with Cooper without using me."

I stood up and left.

* * *

I WAS ALMOST at the reception entrance, ready to catch my own cab, when Cooper caught up to me.

"I saw Pierce corner you, and then you left. Are you okay?"

Somehow, despite happening often enough, those propositions never failed to upset me. Make me think somehow I'd asked for the advance, even though logically I knew I hadn't.

"He said he could help me make partner and invited me to his room upstairs."

Cooper swore long and proficiently. "That's it. I've had it. Let's get out of here."

"Don't you need to stay till the end? You're one of the groomsmen."

"I don't fucking care."

"Whittaker!"

His father stalked out of the ballroom, his mother following as usual. Behind them, Pierce smirked as if he'd accomplished something. Maybe this was what he'd wanted.

"We're leaving," Cooper said flatly.

"No, you are not. You have obligations to this family, and you will fulfill them before you take off with your—"

"Be very careful how you finish that sentence, Father, because I'm better with my fists than either you or Pierce."

His father drew himself up. "You've embarrassed this family sufficiently. You will apologize."

Cooper shook his head. Pierce's mouth fell open.

"I have no obligation to be insulted for choosing my own career, one where I'm valued and wealthier than any of you.

I don't have to be reprimanded for prioritizing people based on something other than their social standing and wealth. And I definitely don't need to apologize for removing my date from an event where she has to deal with sleazy propositions from my jealous brother."

"Whittaker Zane Cooper. That is more than enough. We'll discuss this later, including your accusation, but you will do as you're asked right now."

"I've done that for the last time. Come on, Callie."

He gripped my elbow in his large hand, steering me away from his family. I expected some yelling, but no, not these people. Cooper walked us out without a look back, but his hand was vibrating with tension as we left.

* * *

We were quiet on the way back to the hotel. We were in a cab, since this was expected to be a drinking occasion, and I didn't want to say anything publicly. Was he okay? Had he broken with his family, or was this part of their dynamic? If Cooper wanted to brush them off, it was probably good for him.

Back in the room, I removed my sandals with a sigh of relief. I was used to flats at work, and I had no intention of wearing heels regularly.

"Tired?" Cooper asked.

I turned to check his expression. His gaze lifted from my feet, over my body, and ended on my face. There was heat there. I knew exactly what he was asking.

He didn't want to talk. He wanted to do what we'd done the last couple of nights and wash the memory of them away. The smart thing would be to say I was tired. This weekend—dealing with his family, sleeping with him—was threatening the barriers I kept up for safety. Feelings were stirring. But there was something around the slight down-turn of his mouth, the lines around his eyes... His family had hurt him, drained the confidence that was a core part of his identity.

I wasn't going to do that to him tonight.

I shook my head and he led me to his room. He framed my face in those big, callused hands and kissed me, gently, then with growing passion. I leaned in and let him lead.

He removed my clothing, carefully, with soft kisses on the newly exposed skin. He took off his tux before I could help, and placed me on his bed as if he was posing me. And then he took me apart, with his hands and mouth, until I cried out as I came.

He wrapped his arms around me and fell asleep while I stared at the wall, thoughts and feelings whirling in my brain.

* * *

THE NEXT MORNING on the way to the airport, Cooper got a phone call. He barely spoke, but I imagined, from the way his jaw tensed and his fingers tightened on the steering wheel, that it was someone in his family.

Just before we arrived at the airport car rental kiosk, Cooper broke in.

"Pierce, after what you did, with Vicky and then with Callie last night? You have no moral high ground. You never did. I don't give a flying fuck what you think about me or my life or anything else. I'm done. Remove me from the family tree or whatever the fuck you want." He hung up the call and turned into the lot.

He didn't look like he wanted to talk. What he did want, and indulged as soon as we were on the plane, was to drink. I couldn't blame him. I'd only been exposed to the Coopers for a weekend, and I'd have thrown back a few drinks if it wasn't morning and one of us needed to be sober.

It was a Sunday morning flight and the plane was only half full. Based on my experiences this summer, the people who would normally fill up first class were out on the golf links. The only other couple up here with us were immersed in a movie.

The flight attendant was keeping her distance, since every time she came near Cooper he asked for more alcohol. I had my e-reader out, but I wasn't reading. The quiet gave me time to think, and it confirmed the conclusions I'd reached last night.

I wanted to ignore it, for just a bit longer, and enjoy this little bubble out of my usual life. But I always faced things head-on, and this urge to push a harsh truth aside meant I had to take steps now. Cooper was staring at the seat back in front of him, glass of whiskey in his hand. His fourth or fifth? "Cooper."

He turned to me. His eyes were slightly unfocused and his mouth a little loose.

"We're done."

He blinked at me, brows lowering. "What?"

"Our deal. It's done."

"Your tournament isn't for another three weeks. We should still get some time in at Briarwood. This part, the wedding, it was the worst and it's over."

I shook my head. "We have to stop now."

He tried to clear his brain from whatever amount of alcohol he'd consumed. "Callie, I'm not in any condition to work this through right now, but let me get home, sleep this off, get my head straight again."

I had to tell him.

"Cooper—this was supposed to be fun, right? Just fun. No feelings. The problem is that I'm starting to get feelings, and we said that's when this ends. I can survive the golf tournament. You've survived your sister's wedding. Our deal is done."

There. I'd said it. It was out there.

I stole a look at Cooper. I wasn't sure what I expected. I knew he wasn't going to say he was in love with me and throw his arms around me. That wasn't what I wanted. I had a plan, and romantic feelings were not part of it.

Just last night, I'd said no to Cooper's brother. I didn't want a position that I got by fucking someone, true. If I'd been smart, I might have been able to manipulate the situation with Pierce to get what I wanted without sleeping with the asshole. But I hadn't considered that. I'd only thought about Cooper. I couldn't run my life that way.

Cooper was staring at me like I'd sprouted horns. "What?"

"You heard me."

"But...we were having fun. I'm an asshole, really. You'll get over this. It was just the wedding stuff."

I didn't need someone to explain my feelings to me. "I don't lie to myself. I meant what I said. Thank you for your help, and I hope this weekend was enough to repay you. I have work to do, and you start back with hockey. This is the right time."

The announcement of our arrival and imminent landing came through the cabin. I took my e-reader, which I hadn't used, and slid it into my briefcase. I kept my phone handy, ready to pick up any messages or emails that had arrived while we were flying.

Cooper ran a hand through his hair. "We should talk about this. Not now, obviously, but I need to think."

I sighed. Why couldn't he just accept this? "Cooper, really, it's okay. I don't want feelings. Not like that. I can't see you anymore."

He had both hands in his hair now. "Damn it, why did I drink so much?"

"Because you had a shitty time, and you needed to get out of your head. It's fine."

And I might be doing the same thing shortly. Drinking and ice cream and reminding myself of what was really important, and I should be fine, right? I didn't want romance, or a relationship. Cooper was totally the wrong guy for that if I did. I just needed some time away from him, away from the orgasms he was so good at, and I'd be back to my normal self. Except that I'd be great at the country club, and better dressed than I'd been before.

This wedding had been a horrible experience for the most part, and I was angry with his family. I'd wanted to make him feel better, so I'd crossed that line and had sex with him. It wasn't his fault what I was feeling. That was all on me, not him.

"Hey." I touched his arm and he looked up at me, eyes focusing a little better. "You know I'm not good at faking things. I really, really appreciate how you've helped me. I enjoyed our time together. But it needs to end now. You don't want me to get clingy and emotional."

"I have a hard time picturing that."

Me too. "So, we'll say goodbye, and it's all good. I promise I'm fine. Totally."

"Fine."

I nodded.

His lips pinched. "Well then, what else matters?"

My jaw dropped, but he put in his earphones and ignored me.

Damn it if I didn't feel hurt, and that was the problem. Feelings sucked.

Chapter 27

Just wedding or sex hormones

COOPER

I WAS REASONABLY SOBER when I got to Seb's place. Callie had vanished from the airport as soon as she got her luggage, and made her own way home while I was getting my brain working well enough to identify my own bag. I texted, asking her to let me know she got home okay. She didn't respond.

By habit, I was quiet when I helped myself into Faith and Hunter's place. I'd known them in college, and I knew they grabbed sexy times whenever they could work it around Hailey. But Faith was at a camp with Braydon and Jayna for the week again, so Hunter would be home with my goddaughter.

Hailey must have been napping, because I didn't hear anything about Kook when I came around the corner. Hunter was on the couch with the TV on, but he was only half awake. Apparently, parenting was murder on your sleep, and Hunter was doing it solo this week. I'd promised to help out once I got back from the wedding. I'd thought Callie would help too. *Welp.*

Hunter blinked at me and the bag I was rolling in behind me. I'd come straight here from the airport, avoiding my place. I wasn't in a mood to be on my own.

"Are you moving in, Coop?" He sat up. "To help with Hailey?" He sounded awfully pleased about that.

"I came straight from the airport. I could crash for a couple of days, but rookie camp is gonna start."

He slumped back down. "Any help is appreciated. It's like when Faith is gone, Hailey doubles her energy."

"Beer?"

He checked the time and shrugged. I pulled a couple out of the fridge. I walked over to the couch and sat beside him, passing over a can.

"How was the wedding?"

I shrugged. "Big. Expensive. Over."

"And your family?"

I took a swallow of the beer, the cool liquid refreshing in my throat. "The same as ever. I told them to fuck off. We'll see how that plays out."

"Sorry."

Hunter didn't know everything about my family, but he'd been to visit and he knew enough. I didn't share with anyone about my brother and my ex, and fuck why I'd told Callie. Pierce had figured out she was my soft spot and gone after her. Exactly why I didn't want to have a soft spot. Thinking of Callie made me swallow more beer.

As if my thoughts had conjured her in his brain, Hunts asked, "Where's Callie?"

"Probably at her place." When his eyebrows shot up, I broke the news. "We're over. Whatever the fuck you want to call what we were doing, it's done."

His forehead furrowed. "Why? I thought you two were getting along."

I smiled, but there was no humor in it. "She's had enough. She can handle the club and the golf tournament. And with the wedding over, she's done."

Hunter sat up. "What the hell? Why?"

I couldn't answer that.

"Wait, did she end it?"

My gut burned, but I nodded and drained the last of the beer.

"Why? What did you do?"

I hadn't done anything, had I? "Apparently she's getting feelings, so she's bailing."

Hunter was wide-awake now. "What?"

My beer was empty and I wanted another. But I was too damned wiped to get up off the couch. I didn't want to move, ever again.

"Did you tell her you have feelings too?"

Hunter had to be more exhausted than I'd thought. How long had Faith been gone? "No."

"Then go tell her!"

"I'm not going to lie to her, Hunts." Not like it would work anyway.

"Oh don't be an idiot. You have feelings."

I sighed. I leaned my head against the back of the couch, staring at the ceiling. "Sure, I liked her. But not what you're talking about." I'd blocked anything like that years ago.

"Are you stupid? I've been with you a long time. This woman—she was different."

She was. But that wasn't a path I wanted to follow. "Hunts, it was going to end sometime. Might as well be now."

"Why did it have to end?"

"What did you think would happen? We'd get married and have babies and live happily ever after?"

"What's wrong with that?"

"Nothing. It's great—for the right people."

"You don't think you're the right people?"

I shook my head. "I know I'm not. It's like...pool."

"Huh?"

"I can whip your ass in pool. Every time. Right?"

"This isn't—"

I kept going, not letting him interrupt. "But beer pong. Faith is a beer pong savant. I'd never play a game with her, thinking I could win. I'd play for fun but I wouldn't wager on it."

"So you're saying love is beer pong." He was looking at me like I was nuts, but that was it.

"Hunts, what you have with Faith is great. It's special. It totally works for the two of you. But that's not how it is for everyone. Your parents, Faith's parents...there are a lot of fuckups out there. I'm just focusing my energy on the games I can win."

"Yeah?" His voice was skeptical.

"Yeah."

"You can talk a good game all you want, but you know what I think?"

I didn't and I didn't want to.

"I think you've already bet on this, and you're gonna regret not going for it."

I shook my head. This was something I might regret getting into, but not getting out of.

Then he smirked. The fucker smirked at me.

"Oh, this is going to be fun to watch."

* * *

CALLIE

DARCY WASN'T HOME when I got there, which was a relief. I needed some time before he found out he wouldn't be seeing his new bestie, the hockey hottie. Or would he? At the driving range, Cooper had wanted to try some little hole-in-the-wall restaurant Darcy knew. Would Cooper still want to do that? If he did, would Darcy think he had to choose between the two of us?

That wasn't fair. Darcy was a Cooper fan and that was fine. I just didn't want to hear about him now. Not right away. Not till these feelings were under control. Which shouldn't take too long. They didn't take long to start, so logically they would end just as quickly.

But damn, I hadn't slipped like this in a long, long time. There was an ache in my chest. When I started to write down my plans for the week, keeping busy, I wanted to text Cooper and ask him to forget everything I said on the plane. Check out the messages he'd sent after, and find out what he was thinking.

Yeah, I'd caught feelings. And indulging them would only encourage them. Feed them so they grew. No, the way to get rid of them was to starve them. Beat them down. Refuse to let them see the light of day.

I opened up a CRA ruling, one that would require my whole mind to comprehend. I'd just focus on that till my mind gave up, and I could go to sleep without thinking about anyone.

Darcy texted that he was going out with friends after work. I assured him I was fine.

I did finally go to bed, but my mind insisted on probing at memories of Cooper. It was a relief to finally fall asleep.

* * *

I woke up late, feeling groggy. I'd scheduled the day off work, unsure if there'd be a delay in traveling and not wanting to set up meetings I might have to cancel. I could catch up on emails here at the condo, since I didn't have a lot else to do. I'd be ready to go once I was in the office tomorrow.

I started the coffee and opened my laptop. Work was good. I did my job, people were happy I did, and they paid me money. Work didn't make my chest compress, as if breathing was painful. It didn't keep me up at night and make my eyes itchy.

Damn Cooper.

No, this was on me. I was the one who started feeling things. I didn't have the experience I needed or the brains to remember that soft touches and tender kisses didn't mean affection. I wasn't used to them, and they'd messed me up. *Lesson learned.*

While I was moping, my laptop open in front of me and not reading a damned word, Darcy stumbled out of his room. He was in boxers and a rumpled tee, hair tilted to the left in a leaning tower kind of way.

He rubbed his eyes. "What are you doing here?" His voice was puzzled.

The question hit me hard. Did Darcy think I was leaving him behind, spending too much time on Cooper? How did I let myself do that? I'd never wanted to be wrapped up in a lover and forget my friend. A friend who'd stuck.

"You have someone here? In your room? I can go back to mine."

Darcy walked up behind me, picking up on my panic. Stupid emotions, all over the place.

He wrapped his arms around me. "No, it's just me. But I thought you'd be with Cooper."

I couldn't help stiffening when he said Cooper's name.

Darcy pulled back. "What's up, Callie?"

I swallowed. Might as well start spreading the news. "I won't be spending time with Cooper anymore."

Darcy's eyes widened. He wrapped himself around me again. "What happened? Something at the wedding? Do I need to hurt him?"

The thought of Darcy hurting Cooper was laughable. Cooper was a lot bigger, and so much fitter. I appreciated the offer, though I'd never accept it.

I appreciated it so much I broke down in tears.

Fuck.

I sobbed on him for way too long, but he just held me and let me get it out. Get those feelings out. Which was good. I needed them gone. Gone, over, and forgotten.

"I'm s-sorry," I finally hiccupped. "I don't know why I did that. It was stupid."

Darcy dragged me over to the couch. "No, it's not stupid. Sit down and tell me what happened."

I sniffed. "Sex. And then I got feelings. Romantic feelings. We had an agreement we weren't going to do that. So I told him we had to stop this...whatever. He had his wedding date and I'm ready for the golf tournament, so it was time to end things anyway Do you think maybe it was just wedding or sex hormones or something?"

Darcy rubbed my back. "I haven't seen you cry since you were twelve. Sorry, Cal, but I think that's more than wedding hormones and orgasms."

I'd known it but hoped anyway. "I told him on the flight back."

His hand stilled. "And what did he say?"

Despite my overall weepy miasma, I had to smile a little bit. "He said he was an asshole and I'd get over it."

Darcy leaned against me. "He didn't want to stop being with you."

I closed my eyes. I had enough problems with my own hopes, let alone dealing with Darcy's. "He's not an asshole. But Darcy, I don't want this. *Feelings*. And not with Cooper."

"Do you want it with anyone?"

I was twitchy, talking about this. "I don't know. I like things simple. Easy."

"Controlled," Darcy responded.

I nodded. Years of chaos growing up, and yeah, I wanted calm. Order. *Control*. I'd worked hard to get to where I was. And Cooper—well, damn it, I'd cried. I couldn't risk more.

"What if he has feelings too? You two just...worked, I thought."

"Come on, Darce. I'm not the woman who organizes charity events and watches hockey games and whatever else his girlfriend would need to do. I have a job, a really demanding job, and it's important to me. I'm not good at peopling. I'd bore people talking about tax. I can't even pick out the right clothes." Cooper could do his Cooper thing. Be charming and smile and no one but Faith and Seb would know what he was like under all that. Which was what Cooper wanted as well.

But we'd been a little too honest with each other. Exposed things we didn't want exposed. He'd got past the protection I put up to make sure my life would be under control, and I needed to get that set up again. I'd had a good life before Cooper decided he hated my dress and took me on as a project. I'd learned from him, and I'd use the knowledge he gave me. About golf and country clubs and how to put on a better outer layer to impress people.

I'd learned other, less welcome lessons. That part of me still wanted to be loved. I had Darcy, and if he found someone to love him—and god, I hoped he did—I would be what Cooper was with Faith and Seb. It was a good life, and a safe one.

I gathered myself together. Time to start that life. "Wanna go out for breakfast? My treat."

Darcy grabbed my chin so I had to face him.

"What? Are my eyes all red?" My nose probably was too.

"Just want you to know that this is his loss."

I snorted.

"No, really. You are an awesome person, and when you let someone in, you do anything for them. I'm privileged to be one of those people."

Now my eyes were watering up again. "Darcy, don't you dare get me crying again. Let's get some food and you can tell me what's up with you."

He pulled me in for another hug and I gripped him tightly.

Whatever my life was like, I couldn't imagine it without Darcy. And I would do anything for him.

Chapter 28

Romance and hearts and feelings

Cooper

I spent two days with Hunter and Hailey, and it was exhausting.

Hunter was right: Hailey went nonstop. I had to leave for workouts and a couple of team meetings, and when I got back to their condo, Hailey would launch herself at me like a rocket. I'd suspect Hunter had been keeping her calm till then, but he always looked wiped out.

Then Faith got home, and Hailey only wanted her mom. Which was totally as it should be. I finally went back to my place. It was my home, and where I spent my off-ice time. I liked being at my place.

It was quiet. I should have been happy, after Hailey time, but it was too quiet.

Callie was right. Neither of us were interested in a relationship based on romantic feelings. Sure, we'd grown close. Shared things, gotten to know each other. Too well. When you added sex to that—things did get confusing. Knowing she was feeling something... I couldn't lead her on. Maybe my ego was too big. I wasn't used to someone telling me no. That would be why I was so unsettled, still dwelling on this.

Fuck that. I'd been told no in the past and it had hurt. But it had been a long time, and I'd never let myself get in a situation again where hearing no was going to devastate me. I didn't want to tell Callie I was finished with her, so I should be happy she took the initiative, but this was totally messing with my head.

Fortunately, rookie camp started and I had that to keep me busy and wear me out. Guys were returning to Toronto and I needed to check in with them, see if they were ready mentally and physically for the upcoming season. After the way the last one ended, we'd done what Coach said and kept that feeling, that horrible failure feeling, and we were using it to drive us forward this season. As captain, I had to lead. Take blame for that loss and propel us into something better. And the only thing better was the Cup.

I was in good shape, as were most of the team. If you wanted to play at this level, you couldn't slack off all summer and hope to keep up in training camp. But those first practices were brutal, and I added some extra cardio and weights, just to make sure I was at my peak. There were younger guys coming up all the time, and I was turning thirty this year. That was old in hockey years. Someday I wouldn't be the best, but I made sure that day was as far in the future as possible.

I hung out with my teammates. Did a photo shoot for a sponsor. And at the end of every day came home to my quiet condo and thought about Callie. It was...not me.

Callie had changed me. I finally had to admit what that meant. Those damned feelings she'd talked about.

When I couldn't take it anymore and we had a day off practice, I asked Hunter to go for a run.

We stretched, then started a slow pace to get to the waterfront pathway. It was early in the morning, and most of the few people around were doing the same as we were.

I set a fast but steady pace. Hunter trained with Faith when he could and made use of our team facility, so he was still fit. Once we were warmed up and getting into a groove, he spoke.

"What's up, Coop?"

If I'd just wanted the exercise, we could have run on treadmills at the practice facility. Not a lot of privacy though. I'd asked to run outside for a reason.

"It's Callie."

"Huh," he grunted. "I thought there was no Callie anymore."

There wasn't supposed to be. Anyone else, I'd been able to say goodbye and it was over. "Yeah, well my brain hasn't gotten the message."

This was when he could start saying he'd told me, whatever. But since he was a nicer guy than I was, he didn't. "What's your brain doing, then?"

I shook my head. "It keeps thinking about her. I want to tell her stuff." I might as well say it. "I miss her."

We ran without talking for a few hundred meters. We passed a woman running with a stroller, baby inside, and two men who tried to speed up to match us when we went by them, but they fell back.

"So you want to see her again."

"Apparently."

Hunter turned his head. "This means you have feelings for her."

"Fuck. I know. But why?"

Hunter laughed. "Why do you have feelings?"

"I'm not a robot. Of course I have feelings. Just not *these* feelings. Why can't I forget her? If someone doesn't want me, someone else will. So why can't I just let her go? What has she done to me?"

Hunter didn't speak and I turned to see why. He was frowning, sweat showing on his T-shirt.

"What?"

He shrugged. I turned forward again.

"She got to you, Cooper. She got under that top layer you show most people."

"I didn't want her to." Hell if I wanted anyone there.

"I know. But she's not like anyone you've known before."

That was true, but I didn't think that really explained anything. "So, this is just because she's different? Will it go away?"

"No, it's like...is she impressed that you're a hockey player? Or make a lot of money?"

Callie, who didn't care about any kind of sportsball and had come up with conversational tricks to distract people from that. The woman who'd been adamant about paying her way and not being obligated to me. "Nope."

Then his meaning hit me. "You're saying the only reason women like me is because of my money and reputation?" That hurt. I looked good. I was well educated, could talk about a wide range of subjects, and I dressed better than most of the people I met. I had more than money and fame.

"Not all women. But some. Others just think you're good-looking."

This was not doing my ego any good.

Hunter continued. "Callie doesn't care about that, or that you can charm people."

"Obviously I didn't charm her."

"But that's good."

"How?"

Hunter stopped, so I slowed and turned to face him.

"I think she got to know the real Cooper, the one hidden below the charm. She liked him. And it scared her, and it scares you."

I felt something gripping my chest, and it wasn't a shortage of breath.

"You've got strong feelings for her. Now you have to decide if you're going to do something about it or ignore them and keep on the way you have been. If you can still be happy that way now."

I lifted my shirt to wipe sweat off my forehead. I heard a gasp and saw the wide eyes of a pair of women runners coming the other way. I dropped the shirt and nodded at Hunter to keep running. He rolled his eyes but got back on our pace.

When we were a good distance away from anyone else, I said, "I *want* to ignore these feelings. But I've been trying to get over her and it's not working."

He grinned. "Then I guess you need to do something about it."

I let that thought settle in my brain. That meant naming this feeling, and getting involved with Callie, who could rip up my world if I let her in. But it also meant that I'd have someone, someone like Faith was for Hunter. Only *my* someone. Someone to be with when I wasn't on for fans or the media. Someone who would ignore my bullshit and see the real me. And who might just like it enough to stay.

But Callie was spooked. She'd already decided not to

risk anything when she realized she had picked up these feelings.

To be fair, I hadn't let her know that I had skin in the game. I'd been spooked as well. Would that be enough to convince her to risk it? I didn't know the odds on that. But hell, seeing her again would—just the thought of it was warming me up inside, where I'd been feeling cold. And empty.

So far, I'd succeeded in almost every goal I'd set. I'd made it in the NHL. I'd accumulated a lot of money. I'd been a success my family couldn't ignore, winning any competition they thought we were in.

I could do this. I just had to figure out a plan.

I turned to the guy beside me. He owed me when it came to romance and hearts and feelings; he and Faith had struggled back in school, and I'd played a part in getting them to at least speak to each other.

"Okay, Hunter. How am I going to get my girl?"

* * *

CALLIE

"Do you need to rent clubs?" Leonie asked as I passed her desk. "And you're staying for the meal, correct?"

Right, the tournament. I would need clubs, since I didn't have the ones Cooper had brought to Briarwood for me. I'd done my best to shove anything related to Cooper and golf to the back of my mind. The stupid golf tournament was this weekend though, so I wasn't exactly successful.

"Yes, I will need clubs, and I am staying for the meal."

Otherwise, the time with Cooper would be just a useless heartache.

Leonie nodded and beckoned me closer. I frowned, but leaned over her desk.

"I asked around and I think I know what the problem with Benson is."

I'd almost forgotten Benson, having bigger things to worry about. "Okay, what is it?"

"Apparently, there's been talk among the partners lately that they need to be more diverse. If you look at the photos on the website, they're almost all white men. They need women and POC."

They should also diversify based on sexual preferences and abilities, but those wouldn't immediately show up on the partner page. "Benson thinks I'll get partner because I'm a woman?"

"Unless he can show that you're not very good."

"But there are other women associates."

Leonie smiled, a smug expression on her face. "None doing as good work as you. Tax is a difficult specialty."

"Thank you for letting me know." And when I got back to myself, I could deal with Benson. Once I wasn't hung up on Cooper.

I worked longer hours, trying to maintain my usual volume of work and because time without work was time where memories haunted me. But when I slept I had no control over the dreams I had. Dreams that made facing reality every morning that much harder. It had to stop.

It was a relief when tournament day arrived. Maybe this would finally give me a chance to end the stupid thoughts. Benson was waiting with a checklist by the doors of the bus the firm had hired to take us to Briarwood. He narrowed his eyes when I showed up. I was wearing the same skort and shirt I'd worn the first time I'd been to Briarwood. They looked newish, but not brand-new, like I had them in my closet ready for an event like this. They were perfect for Briarwood. I had the same dress to change into for dinner.

"Did you manage to get some golf lessons in?" he asked.

"Yes." I wasn't going to engage with him any more than necessary.

"I hope you don't hold us up on the greens."

I smiled, showing teeth. "I hope so too."

He would have liked to keep needling me, but more people appeared and I was free to board.

The vehicle was nothing like the city transit buses I was familiar with. This one had tinted windows and individual seats. There weren't twenty people wedged in the aisles, and no one in the back was playing music through their headphones loud enough to be heard by the driver. People looked at each other and spoke.

I sat down beside Eva, a woman from family law who I knew slightly. "Do you mind if I join you?"

"Not at all. You look nice."

"Thank you."

If I'd been left on my own to dress, I'd have looked like some of the others on the bus, whose clothes were too new, or too old, too fancy or too plain. Things I wouldn't have noticed BC—Before Cooper. I didn't have the best sense of style or color, but some of those pants? Hurt my eyes.

I didn't have to worry whether I fit in or looked good. And I wasn't worried about breaking an unwritten rule. If Benson wanted to keep glaring at me, he was welcome, but he wasn't going to find anything to complain about. He might have thought today was the day he'd torpedo my partner chances, but he was wrong.

Everyone was punctual, and there wasn't a lot of traffic

on a Saturday morning so we made good time. We soon were turning into the drive of the club. Eva sucked in her breath when she first saw the gleaming white split-rail fences surrounding lush green grass. It was impressive. Beautiful. And for once, I was at ease in that kind of place. Her eyes widened, and she swallowed. I'd probably looked the same the first time I came with Cooper.

I had to stop thinking about Cooper.

"Have you been here before?" She shook her head. "I've been a few times, so let me know if you have questions."

Her brows went up, but she didn't tell me I was a liar or ask for details to prove it.

We'd been sitting in the back of the bus, so we were among the last people to exit. Our group gathered in a rough circle as everyone stepped away from the vehicle, waiting to be instructed what to do next. I saw two of the partners walking this way, ready to get us organized and out on the greens. That should be it, right? Or did they do a speech or something first?

I took a long, calming breath and then almost choked when I saw Cooper across the parking lot. Seeing him in person hit me like someone whacked a golf club into my stomach. He was behind Mr. Anderson and Mr. Chan who had stopped to talk to us.

I didn't hear the initial greeting from Mr. Anderson to the group. I hadn't seen Cooper for almost three weeks, and I drank in the sight of him. He was taller than anyone else, and I swear the stupid sun was making a halo around him. He was wearing golf pants I could remember—I remembered too much about him—and a blue shirt that was obviously the perfect shade. His bright blue eyes under his hat were looking right at me. For a moment, everyone else faded away.

I blinked. Cooper was looking at me, and so were his teammates who I hadn't even noticed at first. I forced my gaze to move on from Cooper and recognized Seb Hunter and Ducky and JJ. They were a little flushed and sweaty, so they'd probably just finished a round.

Cooper knew this was the day of our tournament. He didn't even like golfing that much. So why be here, why now? I wiped my sweaty palms on my skirt. At least if they were done, he wouldn't be around for the rest of the day and I might be able to breathe again.

People around me began to recognize Cooper and his buddies. Heads turned his way, and even Mr. Anderson stopped speaking to look. Cooper smiled at me, and my knees wanted to fold.

"Hey, Callie! You ready to knock 'em dead out there?" His voice carried to our whole group.

Those heads swiveled back toward me. I fought to stay still, not throw myself at him. I had to swallow before I could speak. "I didn't expect to see you here." Or really, ever again.

"Did I forget to tell you we were playing a round?"

Oh yeah, he'd forgotten that all right. He'd also forgotten that we weren't friends anymore. He didn't have to tell me things, and I was better off not knowing what he was doing.

He crossed to stand in front of me and held out a bag of clubs. The ones I'd used when he brought me here. "You left your clubs in the Bentley. Watch out for that spot on the fourth green. Hunts got caught up there, like you did last time."

I felt the eyes of everyone in our group on me. "Okay. I will."

What else was I supposed to say? That the last time was

four weeks ago? That despite what he was implying, I wasn't part of this place? That we weren't a couple? That I was confused and gut hurt and so glad to see him and totally lost?

He looked around, as if he'd just noticed that this whole group of people were watching us. "Sorry to interrupt. I'll get the highlights later."

The four of them wandered into the clubhouse. Everyone stared at me.

I'd spent my whole time at this law firm, at school, trying not to do anything wrong. My focus had been on not making any mistakes. I'd hoped if I never messed up, then I'd succeed. Cooper didn't do that. He didn't fade into the background. He worked and trained to make things happen, putting himself forward as someone who succeeded, not just someone who didn't fail. And he was doing that for me now.

How was I supposed to get over him?

Mr. Chan noticed me, for the first time in months. Not because I'd done something wrong or right. But because, thanks to Cooper, I looked like someone who mattered. Someone who knew successful people and came to fancy clubs and played golf with them.

"I didn't know you golfed, Callie."

Heaven forbid he thought I was good and then found out how bad I was. "I don't, not really. I've only played a handful of times."

He put a hand on my shoulder. "I'm sure you'll do us proud out there." He smiled.

He saw me as an asset, more than just a brain with taxes. He was noticing me as partner material.

And that was thanks to Cooper. How was I supposed to repay him for that?

Chapter 29

Cooper's glitter

CALLIE

COOPER HAD SPARKLED glitter on me and everyone wanted some of it. I'd expected to take my turns on the course, making polite conversation as necessary. Instead, people wanted my opinion on their swing, or club choice, or other things I had no knowledge of. I insisted I didn't know much, but they watched and tried to emulate me. Well, until it became obvious I really didn't know how to golf well. But they still wanted to talk to me

No, they wanted to talk to the woman who knew #57, Cooper. I was only popular by proxy. I was sure they hoped that somehow they'd be part of Cooper's exalted orbit if they were part of mine. I didn't have an orbit, but they wanted to be part of it anyway.

The partners were playing with important clients, while we lowly non-partners were grouped together. But when we finished the last hole, Mr. Chan came over to ask how I'd done.

"Maybe Cooper is better teaching hockey," he joked.

Obviously Cooper would be better at anything hockey related, but I knew enough to just smile and nod. I swear, the more I tried to downplay the Cooper thing, the more people wanted to be in on it. I was tempted to say we'd broken up, but it was hard to break up when we hadn't been dating. Cooper had given a very different impression this morning. That hadn't been by accident.

Mr. Anderson stopped by the table to thank me for the heads-up about the fourth green, even though I hadn't been the one to mention it.

"We've been overlooking your potential, Calliope. I'll ask my assistant to set up a meeting to discuss your future. I think you can be an asset to the firm."

That was...promising. But it didn't thrill me the way I'd expected.

I just wanted to get away from it all. I needed to think, and that wasn't going to happen with all these people trying to grab some of Cooper's glitter. It was kind of sweet to see how much it chafed Benson's ass though.

* * *

Cooper

Can we talk?

I needed an ally, someone else who might be willing to take a risk for me, and for the possibility of Callie and me. Someone with access to Callie anytime. If he'd talk to me, and I could convince him it would be good for Callie, maybe Darcy would help.

About?

Callie.

Why?

What was I willing to share?

Because I miss her.

It was the truth, and if Darcy was going to help me, I had to open up to him.

The country club had been a good start. Her job was important. I'd wanted Callie to see that professionally I was an asset, not a liability. Now she needed to know that she wasn't alone when it came to these uncomfortable emotions.

She didn't answer texts, calls or emails. She didn't do social media, so I couldn't get to her that way either. I knew where she worked, and where she lived. With my position on the Blaze I knew I'd be allowed into Anderson, Krys and Chan. But she might be with a client, or I'd be interrupting her work, and possibly have an audience while I spilled my guts.

I'd already gotten into her condo building, so I could do that again...but it didn't feel right. That was her space. Using my reputation to force access she didn't want to give wouldn't help.

Okay.

I could almost taste the hesitation in his response.

Since Darcy was working evenings this week, and I didn't want to wait, we met just after the Top Shelf opened in the afternoon. I'd finished training camp for the day, and this was a window of time before he started his shift. Also, since fans were discouraged from bothering players here, it was an opportunity to meet in public with reasonable privacy.

I was waiting inside at the bar when Darcy arrived. He looked around with wide eyes. I waved him over. "What would you like? I've got a tab."

"Um, just a Coke."

"Sure?"

"Yeah, I get into less trouble at work if I'm sober."

Right, he wasn't drinking alcohol before his job. I asked for some sparkling water, needing my own wits sharp. Once we had our drinks, I led the way over to a table in the back where the team usually met after games. The place was empty, but I didn't want to be overheard.

Darcy sat on a chair and looked around. It was a big bar, two stories, with golden woodwork and brass trim. At his hour, there was little noise other than music playing in the background. Most of the staff were either busy behind the large bar or setting up tables on the second floor.

"Never been here before?"

He shook his head. "I've heard about it. It's nice."

A silence fell. The clock was ticking, and I didn't ask Darcy to meet me to talk about the bar. Time to lay it on the line. "Callie tells you everything, right?"

He nodded.

"After the wedding, she told me we'd met the terms of our agreement. But since she was developing feelings, she wanted to stop seeing me."

He nodded slowly. "She's hurting. She doesn't let many people get close. You know about what it was like for her, growing up?"

"She grew up in foster care."

Darcy nodded. "That's where we met, when she was about ten. That's when they gave up on her mother. No one sticks around for her. Except me. So, I'm sorry if you miss her, but I'm not going to help you see her again."

"I'm going to stick around too."

Darcy raised his brows.

"I don't date. I have what I thought were ironclad

reasons, so it took me a little time to figure this out after Callie cut me off. But she's not the only one with feelings, and I didn't welcome them either."

"So why are we here?"

"Because being without her hurts. I'm not sleeping well and I'm losing focus. Every time my phone buzzes, I hope it's her. I want to know how that damned golf tournament went and if I helped or not. I want to see that little crease she gets between her eyebrows when she's thinking and rub it away with my finger. I want to take her apart in my bed and see her, without her guard up, looking happy and relaxed. I want to hear her growl when I ask her something before she's had coffee. I want...I want a lot, and I want it all with her."

Darcy's jaw had dropped while I spoke, and now he closed his mouth and swallowed. "Really?"

"Really. If I had to choose between her and the Cup... well, I only get to keep the Cup for a day. I want her for all the days."

A smile crossed Darcy's face. Finally, a glimmer of hope and I could breathe easier. These were things Callie should hear first, but she wasn't listening.

"Wow. That's...incredible." He stared at me, spinning the glass on the table. "What do you want me to do?"

"I wondered..." Darcy raised an eyebrow. "Could you take her someplace? Someplace public, so she's not threatened, but where I have a chance to meet you so I can make my case."

He took a swallow of his drink, then ran his finger up and down the side of the glass. "Without telling her in advance."

"She won't come otherwise."

Darcy's hands were now on his lap. He stared at the

table. I wanted to push, convince him he should do this. But he had to decide this was worth doing on his own. If he said no, I would find some other way. Maybe the office after all?

"I think I can do that. But I need time to consider everything first. If this goes sideways, I'm risking the most important relationship in my life."

"You can blame it all on me if it goes wrong. You have my number. If you decide you will, just let me know when and where. Preferably when I'm not playing." Preseason games were coming up, and as captain, it would look bad if I skipped a game. That I was even considering it told how twisted up I was.

Darcy nodded. "I think— I think I can do it." He met my gaze. "But only because I believe this is good for her."

"I'm glad she has you, someone to look after her. To be on her side. I want to be that too."

"Don't hurt her."

I flinched. "I'd like to make sure she's never hurt again."

He bit his lip. "Okay, I'll let you know. But I gotta get to work now."

"Thank you for talking to me. And if you decide to help me, I owe you. Anything."

Darcy met my gaze. "No, you won't owe me. If I do it, it's for her."

* * *

CALLIE

I WAS OFF MY GAME. I was definitely off, or I'd have noticed Darcy was up to something. And I wouldn't have been thinking in sports analogies. When I entered the restaurant where I was supposed to meet him for dinner, I was completely blindsided to see Cooper sitting in the booth across from him.

I could have turned around and walked out. I could also have stomped over and told them off. What I did was drink in the sight of Cooper for long seconds. I missed him. I'd thought these feelings would diminish. I thought they *had* started to diminish, but one glimpse of him and my insides caved. And then began to spread warmth as I soaked in his body, his face, and mostly, his eyes. They were shadowed, as if he'd been having difficult nights as well since I'd last seen him. But they were blazing, focused on me.

This wasn't good. Not for my recovery, not for my mental health.

Darcy stood up and walked toward me. I switched my focus to him.

"I don't blame you if you're angry with me. Cooper talked to me and convinced me that he had something you needed to hear. I think you should listen to him, but if you really don't want to, we'll walk away."

I heard something like a growl from where Cooper was sitting, but I concentrated on Darcy's words. Now that I was over the first shock, and had soaked up some Cooper, I was angry. It had been *my* decision, *my* choice, to end what was going on between us. Cooper was pushing my friend. Pushing me through my friend.

Rubbing up against that was the trust I had in Darcy. He wouldn't have set this up if Cooper was playing some kind of game. Darcy might admire Cooper as a hockey player, but he would put me first, wouldn't he?

Mixed in with the anger and doubts, I was curious about what Cooper was up to. I'd refused to read or listen to his messages, since only a Cooper blackout would get me

over these feelings. Part of me wanted to spend any additional minutes with him that I could. That part of me was
dangerous. But that part also fed on dreams that had no
basis in reality. It would be better to hear what he had to
say, and deal with it, rather than imagining things that the
dangerous part of me wanted to twist into hope.

I did my best to look like I was in control and not an
emotional mess. I hated being vulnerable like this, which
was why I'd put an end to this thing with Cooper as soon as
I realized feelings were happening.

"I'll listen," I told Darcy. "But you stay." Nothing too
painful was going to happen with Darcy here.

Darcy returned to his seat. They'd been here long
enough that they each had been served a drink. Cooper
started to slide over, but I sat beside Darcy. It was harder
than it should have been to meet Cooper's gaze again.

Cooper relaxed, which made me nervous. I had to calm
down, use my brain. Not everything was a zero-sum game.
The fact that Cooper thought this was good for him didn't
mean it was bad for me. I reined in my racing thoughts the
best I could and waited for him to speak.

"It's good to see you again, Callie. I appreciate you
listening."

I nodded. It was easier to keep a nod from revealing
anything than it was with words.

His glance went to Darcy, and then to the cup of coffee
in front of him. He finally looked at me again.

"You wanted to end this, between me and you, because
we'd promised no feelings. I understand. But you're not the
only one who came down with feelings, so I think we should
open the discussion again."

I blinked. It took a moment for those words to process. I
wasn't the only one who came down with feelings?

Oh. I took another look at Cooper. I'd already noticed that he looked tired, with shadows under the blue eyes and lines bracketing his mouth. But now I let myself see the warmth in his expression, the softness around that mouth. I wasn't an expert on reading faces, but the best I could figure, he was telling the truth. I was more than an arrangement, more than benefits. He wanted...to do something with feelings. Something where we both had feelings. Dating, relationship, romantic involvement.

Oh, hell no.

The panic crept up my body, paralyzing my throat, making it impossible to do more than pull in air and keep myself upright. I didn't want a relationship. I didn't want to weave someone's life into mine. I wanted to be in control of my life, not defenseless when they pulled away. I wasn't giving up my security, my safety, for the chance to have it all blown up when someone else changed the rules or the end game again and left me behind.

Images of my mother, my foster families, the boys who'd promised everything in high school flooded my brain. It felt like the entire world had been frozen with my panic.

Both Darcy and Cooper were watching me, waiting for a response. My control must have been holding, since neither of them were reacting, arguing to change my mind. I drew in a long breath. I fought back the panic and thought past my knee-jerk reaction.

I was not being attacked. I didn't need to fight. But I also didn't need to agree. Cooper might have had an epiphany but that was not my problem.

I held up my hand and tested my voice. "Give me a minute." They exchanged glances and waited.

I knew Cooper. Not well enough to have seen this coming, but I did know a lot about him. He was determined and worked hard for what he wanted. The reason he had his position in the hockey world was because of that. I couldn't leave him an opening, or he'd keep pushing. He hadn't let anyone in since he was in high school and I didn't want to hurt him. But I needed to make sure he knew this wasn't happening. *Ever.*

A tendril of anger unfurled in my chest. He thought he just had to say he was up for dating or whatever and I'd agree? Until he wanted to move on again? I hadn't done a lot of relationships, but I was pretty sure breaking up got harder the longer the relationship went on. I'd suffered enough. I wanted it over. I wanted to be me again.

The anger let me speak and let my brain control what I said. "I appreciate that you told me that, Cooper. But you misunderstood."

His face lost expression. His lips tightened.

"I didn't want to stop our arrangement because only I had feelings. It was because feelings were involved at all. I don't want that."

I prepared to leave, but his hand shot out, holding my arm. I felt the jolt run through my body as his skin touched mine.

"Why?"

I vibrated with the need to get out of there. I already felt the urge to cry working its way through my nervous system. And I couldn't, not now. "I need something I can count on. Something that lasts. Not feelings. Not promises."

He took his hand back. I wanted to feel it again so desperately I almost grabbed for it, so I knew I was doing the right thing.

"Something you can count on."

I stood, more quickly than gracefully. "Yes."

"Like your career. Your bank account. Your place."

I was surprised he caught on so quickly. "Exactly. Relationships don't last. Feelings can't be held to a contract. I'm fine on my own, so I don't need to gamble. Goodbye, Cooper."

And damn it, my voice trembled as I said that. But I turned and walked away, as quickly as I could without looking like I was running.

Chapter 30

There's always a later

COOPER

SHIT. Fuck. Fucking shit. Shitty fuck.

I'd been too confident. Sure that if Callie knew I wanted more, wanted a real relationship, that we were golden. I'd have her. That meeting had been a hard check to my ego.

Worse to my heart. I had some excellent old scotch, and it was tempting to indulge and make that pain go away for a while. But we were into preseason games at the end of September. After the devastating end to last season, it was my job to lead us all the way this time. Jeopardizing that for my teammates would be selfish and immature.

The first couple of weeks of training camp were always brutal, running drills, finding out who'd worked out over the summer and who'd slacked off. This year, not many had. Even our new guy, Daniel Astrom, known as Fitch, was keeping up, despite being on the wrong side of thirty and therefore old in hockey terms. We were all determined that this year we were winning.

Things were a little easier in the preseason, but at least burning through the workout Coach gave us had pushed thoughts of Callie to the side.

Maybe it was just as well not to have distractions this year. *Focus on winning and nothing else.*

Except JJ had to nudge me when practice ended, since my mind had gone back to Callie.

In the locker room after, I shook off my personal black cloud and put on my captain hat. I checked how the new guy was doing. Being traded could fuck you up and make you unsure of your standing.

"You're married?" I didn't know if the rumors I'd heard were true.

"Divorced. Almost—waiting on the final paperwork." He pulled on a T-shirt. "I'm looking for a place for just me. Don't want to buy anything right now."

"How do you feel about a roommate?"

"You have a spare bedroom you're offering?"

I shook my head. "Not me. Ducky likes to have someone. He's a social guy, so if you want to get out and see the city and meet people, he'd make sure you have the opportunity."

Fitch—I didn't know the history of his nickname—frowned at the floor. "I'm not sure about a roommate who's ten years younger than I am."

"That's your call. You won't find anyone easier to get along with though."

"I'll think about it. You sure he wants a roomie?"

"I'll double check with him, but pretty sure. He's in a nice building, pool and gym, not far from the arena."

Fitch raised his brows. "Are you suggesting this so I can keep an eye on him, or so he can keep an eye on me?"

"The former, if anything. He's a good kid, but he's a little too trusting."

Daniel looked over to where Ducky was laughing at something Crash had said. "Women?"

"He hooks up, but so far no women problems."

"Give him time."

And there came Callie back into my thoughts. Maybe Fitch and I should start a club. JJ would be a founding member too.

At lunch, where I checked that Ducky would be happy to have another roommate, and saw him talking with Fitch, JJ pulled me aside.

"Got a minute?"

"Sure." If JJ needed to talk, I was available.

We sat at an empty table in a corner of the room.

He stared at me, and then nodded before speaking. "You okay? Something seems off."

I'd done my best to cover up, but JJ was a quiet guy who watched people. He knew me well, and if anyone other than Hunts was to know if I was in trouble, it was JJ. "I'm dealing with something. I'll try not to let it affect my play."

"Fuck. That's not what I'm asking about. You helped me after I came here, and if you need anything, ask. I know you want to be our fearless captain for the rest of the team, but you're human."

I sighed. He was right. I should give him some idea of what my problem was, in case it did bleed out on the ice. And if I was going to tell anyone on the team, it was JJ. "It's Callie."

"Thought maybe that was it. You're not just friends."

"We were. Then we were friends with benefits, and

288

then, after the wedding, she said we were done because she was getting feelings."

JJ frowned. "Why's that a problem? You obviously have some pretty strong feelings for her too."

"You'd think that would solve the problem, wouldn't you?"

A soft smile crossed his face. "So, she doesn't want to get serious about a hockey player?"

"She doesn't want to get serious about anyone."

"Ever?"

"I won't tell her story, since that's private. I'll just say that she's only had one person stick with her, and she's not willing to risk trusting someone else."

"Who's that person?"

"Her roommate. He's gay, so it's not romantic. More like siblings, which neither of them have. They only have each other."

"How does he feel about you?"

"I think he likes me. He helped me talk to her so I could tell her I wanted to date. Take the feelings and run with them. As you can probably tell, that didn't fly. I hope Callie wasn't too angry with him."

JJ rested his chin on his fists, elbows propped on the table. He stared over my shoulder. Despite myself, I wondered if he had some insight, something that could change my current situation.

"So she doesn't think you'll stay, and won't risk anything unless you can prove you will."

"I guess that's it."

"You need a way to prove you're going to stick around."

"And how do I do that? Propose?"

His mouth turned down. "Marriages don't always last."

Fuck. His ex had cheated on him and left him, in a

public, messy way. "Sorry, didn't mean to bring up the past."

He shrugged. "It's okay. It's the reaction I get from everyone now that's more frustrating than my feelings about Sharleen."

"It was a shitty thing she did."

"It was, and there's nothing that can change that. But maybe we can do something for you. Is there anything your girl would consider proof? What makes her feel secure? What does she trust in?"

Could I get her the partnership she wanted? But no, she wanted to earn it, because then it was hers and couldn't be taken away.

An idea formed in my head. Her idea of security. That was her deepest need. If I wanted her to give us a chance, she had to feel secure about me. To get her to trust me, maybe I needed to show her I trusted her first.

* * *

CALLIE

FEELINGS SUCKED. So badly.

I'd made the right call breaking off...whatever it was Cooper and I had. Because I was all up in my feelings. If we'd kept going—ugh. This was horrible enough now.

I was not a little sad. I was *wake up in the morning and cry* sad. *Not want to get out of bed* sad. I'd wondered if maybe this was something different—clinical depression or something like that. But the way I'd responded to seeing Cooper again? The excitement I felt every time my phone pinged, only to be disappointed when it wasn't him, despite never reading or responding to any of his previous messages? Yeah, this was all about the stupid feelings.

I dragged myself out to the kitchen for coffee and groaned. A huge bouquet of yellow roses had arrived a couple of days ago. The note said Cooper was keeping his promise—when he'd gotten my address from the charity. He'd said he would send flowers when I didn't expect it, and I definitely hadn't expected these. They were a constant, irritating, beautiful and aromatic reminder I didn't need, but they were too beautiful to throw away. They wouldn't last forever though. So symbolic.

I hadn't slept well, again. Thankfully, Darcy was on an early shift and already had the caffeine burbling.

"Thanks," I mumbled, pretending not to see the concern on his face.

"You okay?"

I swallowed a mouthful of coffee, slightly burning my taste buds, but shrugged. "Yeah, just had a hard time getting to sleep."

He frowned. "When did you last have an easy time falling asleep?"

I shook my head. We both knew the answer to that. In Connecticut, when I'd slept with Cooper. But I'd lived for years without the man, and I'd get tired enough to start sleeping again without him around.

"I've got passes for a VIP screening. Want to go see a movie this weekend?"

"I should work." My focus at the office had been off, and I needed to catch up.

"Callie, you have to do something other than go to the office and mope all the time. Come out for drinks, or watch a movie, or *something*. It's not healthy to be like this." His hand swept up and down, indicating me.

I looked down. I was wearing the shorts and T-shirt I normally slept in, with an open robe over top. If Darcy had a guest over, I'd tie up the robe. "What?"

"You're losing weight."

"Isn't that a good thing?"

"Not universally, no. And you've worn that same T-shirt for two weeks now."

Had I?

"You've got circles under your eyes, your face is pale, and even your hair is, like, muted somehow."

That wasn't possible, was it? I grabbed a strand, looked at the red between my fingers. Was it less bright? "Thanks for the pep talk."

"You're miserable. And you don't have to be."

I held up my hand. "Don't say it."

"You know I'm right."

"I'd be more miserable later."

"You don't know that there'd be a later."

I turned for my bedroom. "There's always a later."

* * *

I RUBBED my hands over my eyes, trying to improve my concentration. I was at the office physically. But mentally? I'd been reading the same document for half an hour, and it wasn't sinking in. A notification popped up on the screen.

A new client, Mr. Whittaker, was scheduled to meet me in the small boardroom at eleven o'clock. Wait, had I missed that before?

I messaged reception.

What is this Whittaker meeting about?

. . .

NEW CLIENT, transferring assets, worried about tax consequences.

FOR WHITTAKER'S SAKE, I hoped this wasn't too complicated. I was going to have to take some kind of sleeping aid tonight, because I couldn't function like this.

I grabbed a notepad and pen and my laptop to make my way to the boardroom. I stopped to get another cup of coffee at the break room. My client deserved my best, not the half-assed performance I'd been giving lately.

Darcy's face popped into my head. Was I inflicting misery on myself needlessly? Should I have given Cooper a chance?

I blinked my roommate's image away. This was not the time. Instead, I walked briskly down the hallway to the reserved room. I was early, the way I preferred. After setting everything down on the table, I opened my laptop and pulled up my cheat sheet—notes I'd made previously to remind myself of the major issues to consider for asset transfers. I didn't know if my client was planning to transfer to his family, or a trust, or a foundation of some type, and those kinds of details were important to work out his best plan going forward.

Wait, had I seen a headline about a change to trust rules recently? I started a search just before I heard footsteps indicating someone was headed this way.

I looked up with my polite smile, only for my mouth to drop open when I realized Cooper was the man following the receptionist. The connections finally tweaked in my brain—*Whittaker* Cooper.

I stood up, glaring at the man. "What the— What are you doing here?"

The receptionist smiled warmly at him and I wanted to shove her out of the room. "This is your appointment, Mr. Whittaker." She raised an eyebrow at me, so she knew who he was.

Damned golf tournament and damned hockey player.

"Thank you, Elena. You can go now."

She left slowly, casting a glance back at Cooper as she went. He, however, was looking at me.

For a moment, I just enjoyed seeing him again. Blond hair, blue eyes looking tired and wary, perfectly fitting suit and a polite smile. I wanted to walk over and wrap him in a hug and assure him everything would be okay. And that thought finally snapped me out of my stupor.

"Please sit down, Mr. Whittaker."

I indicated a seat at the other side of the table from my computer, but he chose the chair beside me. I hesitated, and then sat down, much too close and much too aware of him. I told my nerves to calm down. The walls on the side of the room facing the hallway were glass. Nothing untoward was going to happen.

Once we were seated, and I glared at the unnecessary passersby who wanted to look at the famous hockey player, I turned my attention to Cooper. "Why are you here?"

"I wanted your advice on some tax issues. I didn't use my full name when I booked the appointment."

So I wouldn't turn it down.

"Because I didn't want to distract any of the hockey fans here."

With anyone else, I'd have considered his ego was inflated, but another person slowed down to stare as they passed by the glass wall. "You have lawyers. And accountants." Good ones too.

He nodded. "But they're fighting me on this."

What the hell was he planning to do?

He pulled some papers out of the envelope he'd brought with him and set them on the table. "This is what I want." He slid the documents over to me.

I wasn't stupid—he had a plan here that didn't involve his finances. But I couldn't resist looking at whatever was on those papers. This was my thing, and I was curious.

First was a list of assets. His condo, his cars, his investments. I wanted to show his asshole brother and father this, let them know just how smart their stupid jock was with his money. But I shouldn't be reading this. "This is very personal data."

He shrugged. "Client privilege, right? And I trust you."

He could, because I was honest and wouldn't do anything with this information. But he should be more cautious. I shot him a look. He hadn't amassed this much wealth by being stupid. There was something else...

And the next page revealed it. He wanted to transfer everything to a trust...that I would be a trustee and beneficiary of. I closed my eyes and rubbed my lids. If I was hallucinating things now, I definitely had to get more sleep. I opened them and reread the document.

"What the fuck—" I had to lower my voice. Telling a client, even someone who wasn't really a client, *what the fuck* wouldn't fly with the partners. "What are you doing here? This is...it's a conflict of interest and it's stupid and the tax consequences— What is this really about?"

No smirk on his face. He took a long breath, moving his shoulders to release tension. "I heard what you said at the restaurant. You're afraid of relationships. In your experience no one stays. I want to show you I will."

I looked down at his papers. "By...buying me?"

His head jerked sideways. "No, that's not it."

I honestly had no idea what it was. "Explain."

"You want to earn things so they can't be taken away."

I nodded. How had I earned this? If he said sex...

"You need security, financial security, because you trust that."

I drew in a breath, almost flinching at the accuracy of that statement.

"I want you to trust me. So first, I'm trusting you. I want you to have access to anything I have, at any time, so you can make decisions without worrying about money. Whether it's becoming partner here, or going out on your own, or doing nothing, this should be enough for you to be secure."

I nodded, my lips pressed tightly together.

"I trust that if you commit to us, to a relationship, that you'll stay. I trust you enough that I can share anything I have with you. Right now, all this money, the perfect condo, my cars—I'm miserable. I want you more than any of this. It's not doing me any good. So, have it."

I couldn't, and I wouldn't. I tried to find words.

Cooper, meanwhile, continued his speech. "I want to promise I'll never leave you—get a notary to stamp it—but no one can guarantee they'll live forever."

I jerked. "Wait, what are you talking about? Who said anything about forever?"

"Me. That's what this is for." He nudged his paperwork. "It's trust. With a trust. If you can have everything I've valued, then maybe you will trust that I'll stay, as long as I'm able." He paused, scanning my face.

No clue what he saw there, because my brain? Had mostly shut down.

"My manager, my accountant and my lawyer all told me

I'm crazy and won't touch this. You tell me the best way to do this for tax purposes and I can make them do it."

I shook my head because no way was I going to take over his portfolio, or his home or his cars. He stood, papers lying on the table. I looked up at him, still confused.

"Callie, this is how much I'm in. You're worth more to me than any of this stuff. I'll risk it all. I just want you to risk giving us a chance."

He ran a finger over my chin, closing my mouth that had fallen open again, and walked out.

Chapter 31

A fucking ugly green dress

CALLIE

I GOT nothing done for the rest of the day. It was Cooper's fault.

Everyone who could think of a question for me stopped by to ask it and then mention Cooper. I seized the excuse he had given that it was a tax issue. Mr. Anderson even came by, curious as to whether this meant Cooper might become a client. He almost promised a partnership if that happened.

Cooper would do it if I asked him to. The documents he'd left with me proved it. But I didn't want to earn my place by using him, so I told Mr. Anderson no and ignored his look of disappointment. Years of hard work, and it was someone I could be dating that had tipped the scales in my favor.

Leonie gleefully told me that Benson's department was getting a new female lawyer they'd poached from another firm, and rumors were that she'd been promised partnership consideration. Would that be more competition for me as well as him? I should care, but I smiled and thanked her and stared uselessly at my computer screen for the rest of the day.

For once, I left right on time. I'd texted Darcy, told him we needed to talk, immediately.

I ordered pizza as soon as I got to the condo and changed into sweats. Then I paced until Darcy arrived with the pizza in hand—he'd met the delivery guy in the lobby.

He frowned when I made another lap around the living room. "Okay, what's the 911?"

"Cooper."

He set the pizza down. "Give me a minute. I have to get out of this shirt. It's covered in popcorn butter. Don't ask."

While I waited for him, I opened the pizza boxes, got plates, and found a bottle of wine.

Darcy returned with wet hair and his own sweats on. He grabbed a plate. "Okay, spill."

I passed him a glass of wine, settling on the couch with my own piece. "Cooper came to the office. He may not be mentally competent." That would explain what he'd done today.

Darcy did a spit take with his wine, spraying over his T-shirt. "Damn, I just cleaned up. What did Cooper do? Serenade you with a boom box? Buy you an expensive painting?" Darcy did love a rom-com.

I explained the less exciting reality of Cooper's visit.

This time, Darcy choked on his pizza. "OMG! He's in love with you!"

I frowned. "He didn't say that."

"Callie, he's giving you everything he owns to show he trusts you."

"But he didn't *say* it. He didn't say the word."

"He's saying it in a different way. And damn it, Callie, it's the way you understand. If he said 'I love you,' would you believe him?"

I chewed on my bottom lip. I'd had people say it before. My mom, each time she'd rescued me from foster care, only to drop me off later. Boyfriends, or guys I'd thought were boyfriends but were only using me.

Darcy said it, but it was his being there, all the time, that told me he lived it. And Cooper...

"I have to think."

Darcy enfolded me in a hug. "I know, sweetie. But do more than that. Feel. Figure out how you feel about this guy. Because he's making a grand gesture, and you could really hurt him. I totally understand why you don't want a relationship, but that doesn't mean you don't *need* it. If you're willing to go all in, then this is your chance. But don't go in only halfway."

I leaned back, eyes annoyingly damp. "I don't know, Darce. You're right, I don't want to hurt him. But if he left too..."

"He's showing you he won't."

"But how can he know that? People love to make promises but they don't keep them. And for this...well..." I looked down at the faded, stretched-out gray T-shirt I had on, long enough to mostly hide my figure. "There's no way I'm enough."

Darcy grabbed my chin. "You damned well are enough, Callie."

I whispered through a mouth that couldn't move thanks to his grip. "I'm scared."

"Oh, sweetie, I know. How brave can you be?"

I didn't know.

** * **

THANKFULLY THE NEXT day was Friday, because I needed the weekend to work out my thoughts. I got through the day at work, somehow, and came home to an empty condo. Darcy was working closing, so he'd be gone till after midnight.

A list. That should help. A list of pros and cons. I grabbed a pen and a piece of paper and sat at the table with a glass of wine and dragged a line down the middle of the sheet.

Pros on the left, cons on the right.

The cons came easy. Risk of getting hurt. Risk of hurting him. Sudden public exposure—I could only imagine pictures of me showing up with Cooper at things like that charity dinner in the papers. Conflicts from two demanding careers. Kids. Did he want kids? Did I? His popularity, my lack of hockey interest, his family.

Time for the pros. Sex. Money. I wanted to stand on my own, but even though I had no intention of keeping his assets, having a wealthy partner did mean there was a buffer, a big one, between me and living in dingy motel rooms and eating ramen. Never wanted to repeat that.

The con list was winning. Were there more pros?

I'd never have to worry if I'd chosen the right outfit, if I was with Mr. It's Not Hard to Look Good. I could get better at golf, so I'd be able to do well at the annual tournament. I might eat out more, with someone to go with and who had a budget that could handle meals. Darcy's schedule was all over the place, and even with the minimal rent I charged him, his budget was tight.

Maybe I could learn how to drive.

I was filling up the pro side with frivolous issues to try to even out the cons. Which told me I already knew the answer. I was just scared. The pen fell from my hand.

I drew in a breath. I wanted this. Enough to do it. My breathing grew shallow, and I dropped my head into my hands. I wasn't just scared, I was terrified.

* * *

I spent the rest of the night watching some of Darcy's rom-coms. Assuring myself that people with different backgrounds and circumstances could make a go of it. Trying to lose myself in the stories so I wouldn't start panicking again. I was still there when Darcy came home.

"You okay, Callie?"

I was almost vibrating in my seat. "No. I'm not."

Darcy crossed the room and dropped on the couch beside me. "What's wrong?"

I huffed a nervous breath. "I made a decision."

He cocked his head. "It's a little concerning that I can't tell what you decided based on the way you're acting."

I nodded. "I know. Maybe I'm wrong. Maybe I should say no."

He put his hand on his chest. "You decided...yes?"

"I made a list but I kept pushing things to the pro side so I must want it but I'm freaking out. Seriously. That must mean it's the wrong decision, right?"

Darcy put his hands on my shoulders. "Breathe, Callie. Take some deep breaths."

I focused on him and drew in several long breaths, expelling them slowly. "Okay, thanks."

"I think this freak-out isn't because you made the wrong

decision. I think it proves it's the right one. Because you're pushing out of your comfort zone, and it's scary, but it's good."

"It's going to be so far out of my zone. I never planned on anyone like him."

"Did you call him?"

I shook my head. "I needed to sit on it first. Do my freaking out."

"Are you sure this is what you want?"

"I have no idea how we can possibly work. We both have challenging careers, we've never discussed children, I'm a fashion disaster and it's his, I don't know, love language."

"And yet?"

I bit my lip. "I've never felt like this about anyone before. I want to be with him, and not just because of the sex. I'll even watch hockey if he wants. I think..." Another long breath. "I must love him."

The words felt awkward and yet, a relief.

Darcy's grin split his face. "I'm so happy for you, Callie."

"His goddaughter calls him Kook."

Darcy fell back on the cushions. "I'm swooning here."

I dropped back with him. "It's too late to call him now. He's training and doing, like, practice games."

Darcy rolled his eyes. "You have a lot to learn. And after he went to your office, you need to do something a little better than sending him a text.

"Like what?"

"Hmmm. Let me think."

* * *

Kim Findlay

"YOU DON'T HAVE to do this," I said.

I hadn't heard from Callie, and the days had moved on leaden skates. Hunts had dragged me out to the Top Shelf for a guy's night. Pretty sure it was as much about getting away from Hailey for a bit as anything else. He looked way too happy for bro-consoling-bro time.

He shrugged. "You'd do the same for me."

I would. I had, back in college, and again when he and Faith were doing long-distance for the first year after we graduated. I'd helped him plan out the proposal he'd put together for her when she came home that Christmas. Since that year, they'd been together, and he hadn't needed cheering up for anything Faith-related. When he'd had to retire, I'd been there for him. So, he owed me.

"No news is good news, right?" He held up his glass and I touched mine to his.

He was right. Callie hadn't said no. But she hadn't said yes, and I was afraid the longer she spent in her own head, without me there in person to tip the scales in my favor, the likelier she was to run. I had to give her space though. I'd pushed all I could.

I'd expected Hunts to invite some of the team to come out with us. If his plan was to distract me or cheer me up, him sitting across from me without speaking wasn't really working. Instead of talking, he was preoccupied, staring past me toward the door and the bar.

Which, now that I thought of it, was sketchy as hell. I was about to ask him what was up when an expression crossed his face—it lit up like when Faith appeared. Was that his plan? I turned around, but what caught my eye wasn't Faith.

It was a green dress. A fucking ugly green dress. With shocking red hair above it.

The noise around me faded, like the volume of the music and conversations had been dialed down. Everything around that green dress was muted, forming a flat frame around Callie. The blood in my veins slowed, and my entire body was cold and frozen in place.

She walked toward our table, biting her lip. She was nervous, but she was here. Fuck, she'd decided. And suddenly I didn't want to know. I'd rather live in a limbo where she hadn't yet said no.

"I'm heading out," Hunts said. He passed by Callie and she smiled at him.

The sound and colors rushed back in. This was a setup. Hunts had brought me here on purpose, and he knew Callie was coming. That meant *she'd* set this up. She'd set it up, and worn the fucking ugly green dress, and there she was, standing by the table, waiting for me to do something other than stare at her.

Shit. My mouth was hanging open. Was I drooling?

"Cooper?"

I snapped back to something like my normal self. "Callie— Sit down. You look..."

She smirked. "I look?"

"Beautiful. Fucking beautiful."

She frowned down at her dress. "Really?"

"Absolutely. You can wear that every day of your life as long as I can see you in it."

She bit her lip again. "I think that's more convincing than trying to give me all your worldly possessions. You know, that you plan to stick around."

Calling her beautiful in that dress was all I'd needed to do? *Shit.* But she still looked hesitant. She was questioning if I'd stay around. "Oh, I do. And you damned well better be saying yes if you're here in that dress."

She drew in a long shaky breath. "Yeah. That's why I'm here. I'm in."

Chapter 32

My body couldn't contain it

COOPER

I DRAGGED Callie out of the bar and to my condo. We needed some privacy, someplace that wasn't the favorite hangout of the professional teams in town. I didn't want anyone to listen in on the talk we were due for.

But we didn't speak on the way. I drove the Bentley down into the parking spot beside the Ferrari and didn't even check if my baby was all right. We rode up to my condo in silence, the air vibrating between us. I was in some weird space where things were about to exceed my expectations or crash to the ground, and saying one word might break the spell and she'd be gone.

When the doors finally slid open into my foyer, I couldn't help reaching for her. I pulled her close, weaving my hands into her hair so she couldn't vanish. I pressed my lips to hers and she kissed me back just as hungrily. Then there was no more hesitation.

We shed clothes as we kissed our way to my bedroom,

barely breaking contact. We made it to my bed and I laid her down carefully. The green dress was gone, but it didn't matter, just that she was here.

I kissed every freckle on her skin, teasing her breasts, eating her pussy till she was writhing and wet. She passed me a condom, watching with heated eyes as I covered myself. When I was finally sheathed in her body, I paused to stare down at her.

This time, I didn't worry about her leaving or when I'd see her again. This time, we were doing this for real, together.

She wrapped her legs around me. "Please."

I gave her what she wanted. And when I finally spent, my head buried in her neck, I whispered, "I love you."

When we recovered from the first round, her head was on my shoulder, my arms keeping her tightly beside me, and we finally talked.

"So this is my new condo?" she teased. "I should take a tour."

"Move in anytime."

"You're not giving me all your assets."

I wouldn't have to. One of these days, once she'd grown comfortable with us together, I'd give her a ring. Make those promises to stay, forever. Life was full of change, and nothing was guaranteed, but I couldn't imagine ever choosing to walk away from this woman. "Sure? You could learn to drive the Bentley."

She shook her head. "People can get strange about money. I don't want to make that an issue."

But presents... Christmas was coming in about three months. And when was her birthday?

She poked me with a finger. "I don't know what you're thinking, but I'm sure I won't like it."

She'd argue about it, but there was no way I wasn't going to enjoy treating my partner. Lover. Girlfriend. "But you're doing this. Giving us a chance. Dating, being together."

She let out a long sigh. "Yeah. I am. And I should say this to you..."

"Not if you don't want to. Not if you don't mean it."

"I never say things I don't mean. At least, not intentionally. I do love you, Cooper, but I'm not sure I'm any good at it."

"I'm not sure either. But I'm sure I'm gonna try."

"I don't want to hurt you. I never want to do that, but I will. I don't know how to say the right things, and when I'm upset I block everyone out. It's how I've had to deal with things all my life."

"I can be patient. I keep people out too."

She drew in a shaky breath. "But what I feel for you is bigger than anything I can remember. So I'll try. You'll have to give me chances, but I will try."

"That's all I ask."

I drew her close, breathed in her scent. She wrapped herself around me, dropping kisses on my neck, which led to more kissing and...

After a second round, she finally took the tour of the condo. I watched her as she wandered through the place, wearing one of my T-shirts. It had my name and number on it, so I'd never worn it, but I liked it on her. It marked her as mine.

I'd chosen neutral grays for the space, with red and yellow accents and black leather furniture in the great room. It reflected the team's colors, which had provided this space. I expected a comment from her on that, but she didn't say anything until she looked out the floor-to-ceiling windows, over the lake.

"I made some other decisions."

I crossed to her and wrapped my arms around her from behind. Whatever she wanted, I'd support her.

"I don't know how to do relationships, and I've been spending most of my time working, trying to be noticed as a potential partner. But after your visit, it was obvious I could make that goal by using you. And that felt wrong."

"They asked you to bring me in as a client?"

"Nothing that blunt, but I read between the lines. I remember you asking me why I chose that firm. Now I'm second-guessing whether Anderson, Krys and Chan is the right place for me after all."

I kept my arms around her and kissed her neck. This was a hell of a big thing for her.

"I'm going to scale back my hours to a more normal level for the next several months. While we do this relationship stuff. I'll see if that changes things at the firm. I'm not going to wait to live my life anymore. And if that's a problem for them, if the only way to make partner there is to work eighty-hour weeks, maybe it's not right for me after all. If they work with your family, well..."

"Whatever you want, I'm here. If I can help, I will."

She twisted in my arms so she was facing me. "I still want to make partner on my own. I appreciate your support, but I don't want to earn a position using you any more than I do using sex. But the partnership can wait, and maybe it won't happen. I'm damned good at my job, so I'll always have work if I want it. Have you seen the job openings for tax attorneys?"

I shook my head, but I could believe she'd kept an eye on that. She pressed up and kissed me, and what I was feeling inside was so big, it felt like my body couldn't contain it.

"You'll always be safe, Callie. You might not let me give you everything legally, but it's all yours. The stuff on paper, and..." I lifted her hand to the left side of my chest. "Everything else as well."

A corner of her mouth ticked up. "Maybe I should accept the Ferrari."

I growled and picked her up. This tour was over and we were going back to the bedroom.

Epilogue

A special kiss cam

CALLIE

THE AIR WAS COOL, smelling of ice. Did ice have a smell? I thought so. Excitement vibrated through the people in the arena, the crowd still a little sparse as the players spilled onto the ice for their warming up routine.

My first hockey game, and we were here early enough for warm-ups.

A couple of rows over, I saw one of the guys from the team—Ducky, who'd been at the driving range. He was sitting in the stands, not wearing his hockey uniform, with a woman sitting beside him. He waved, so I waved back.

"Why is one of the players sitting in the stands?" I asked Darcy. He was keeping me company on my first foray into live sportsball. He'd been fully Team Cooper since we started...dating? Two weeks ago. That sounded kind of high school. We were in a relationship. Where we were exclusive and had sex and where I agreed to come to the first hockey game of the season, wearing a Cooper 57 jersey.

One Cooper provided for me and signed. Conspicuously. Enough so that three people had already asked me about it. Darcy had a jersey too, but his didn't have the big autograph. When anyone asked about mine, he just giggled.

"Where?" Darcy asked.

"Up two rows and about ten seats over. Ducky."

Darcy craned his neck. "I read that he'd injured his knee. He must be sitting out."

"Is that his wife or girlfriend with him?"

"He's single! He was one of the ones I hoped was on Team Closeted."

"Maybe she's just a friend."

Darcy sighed. "Probably not. But you met him, right? We could ask him to sign my jersey?"

I'd rather do a tax audit, but I didn't say so. I owed Darcy. And I was saved from answering when the crowd started to make noise as the players appeared on the ice.

Darcy fixed his attention on the players. "Do you see him?"

I peered, and yes, I saw Cooper. I ignored Darcy and for the first time watched my...boyfriend skate.

He was fast. They were all fast. They whipped around in some pattern that made sense to them but none to me, fortunately not hitting each other. Still, once I spotted him, my eyes followed Cooper. He spoke to a lot of the guys as they paused to do...stuff. It was easy to see he was respected by his teammates. Sure, he was the captain, but that was just a title. The way he acted... He was really a team leader.

Then he skated over to the glass near our seats, looking up and finding us easily. He beckoned, and Darcy pushed me out of my seat to walk down to where Cooper waited. By now there were more people, and some had gathered by the glass. Mostly kids, all excited to be near him.

He smiled at them, let them take pictures, but waved at me again and they parted enough for me to get down to the glass, feeling incredibly self-conscious.

He made a spin motion. I rolled my eyes but turned around so he could see that yes, I was wearing the jersey he gave me and hadn't bought another one with someone else's name on it.

He held his hands up to the glass, making a funnel around his mouth. "Second intermission—stay in your seat."

I nodded, but was I going to be bored out of my mind by the second intermission? Darcy had refused to let me bring a book.

Everyone watched as I climbed up to my seat again, while Cooper went back to doing whatever stuff hockey players did before they all left the ice again.

The lights went down, and the players came back on. The visiting team first, from Ottawa, and then the Blaze. The arena was full by now and the crowd was loud for their favorites.

"And number 57, playing defense, your team captain, Cooper!"

Everyone cheered, including Darcy. I stood and applauded. I'd known Cooper was kind of a big deal. But here, now, with all these people screaming for him? He was *really* a big deal.

I didn't let people in. But I'd let in this guy who was bigger than life, and losing him would destroy me.

The national anthem was sung, the lights went up, and the game finally started.

I really didn't know the sport at all. I didn't realize the players got on the ice, played for a few minutes, and then sat down on the team bench for a while. That meant Cooper wasn't on the ice the whole time, but I watched him closely while he was.

They went so fast. And hit each other really hard. I flinched as some bulky Ottawa player smashed into Cooper. He shook it off, said something to the guy, and skated away again.

"Doesn't that hurt?" I asked Darcy. Some other guys were skating now so I didn't need to watch as obsessively.

"They wear pads, but yeah, it must. I hear they can get pretty bruised up in a game."

"What?"

He shook his head at me. "They're big boys and they play hard. And they get well paid for it. It's part of his life."

I apparently was missing essential information about being with an athlete. I hadn't seen Cooper with bruises when we were together, but it hadn't been hockey season. Would he be bruised up tonight? "They don't mind?"

He looked at the ice. "Apparently not."

Cooper jumped over the side back onto the ice along with some other players. He didn't look upset, just focused on the game.

Huh. Maybe I'd thought he'd be shooting glances at me. Nope. Totally into the game.

After the first period, Ottawa had scored, and the Blaze had not. Darcy asked if I wanted to stretch my legs during the intermission, maybe get something to drink. We went out to the mezzanine where there were vendors, and just like at the movie theaters, the prices were inflated. It rubbed me wrong, but I still bought us beer because Darcy was here to keep me company and I wanted to thank him. Though, based on the way he was absorbed in the game, he didn't mind being here at all.

We missed a couple of minutes of the second period by

the time we were back in our seats. Not long after we returned, Ottawa scored, and the mood of the crowd deflated. Even more after another goal.

I didn't have to know hockey to know this wasn't good.

Then, a few minutes later, Cooper was on the ice and something happened—it was kind of a blur, and there was a loud noise and everyone around us stood and cheered.

"What happened?"

"Watch the Jumbotron."

They replayed what ended up being a goal. They slowed it down so I could see it better.

"Cooper got the assist!" Darcy pointed out.

"Yay?"

Darcy nudged me. "Yes, yay."

Then the crowd got to me. I found myself groaning when someone was pushed into the boards by another player, and sighing when Ottawa scored. I booed loudly before I realized what I was doing.

Darcy laughed at me. I poked him. "Don't say anything."

The game was going again before everyone sat down.

Intermittently everything stopped. We were in another of the commercial breaks Darcy had explained to me in the first period.

He sighed. "Something is wrong with the team."

The guy sitting beside Darcy agreed with him.

Despite myself, I asked, "Why?"

"Ottawa was one of the lowest-ranked teams last season, and they didn't do much to improve over the summer. The Blaze aren't looking good against them. Maybe it's just a hangover from that loss in the finals, but I hope they shake it off."

Darcy's new friend nodded. "They had a short offseason. Maybe they haven't got what it takes. And losing, in overtime like that? Brutal."

Not long after, the players all cleared the ice and the second intermission started. There were a couple of fans out to play some kind of game. I'd have chanced getting through the ladies room if Cooper hadn't asked me to stay put. Darcy was talking with his new friend, and I didn't want to intrude on their conversation. An announcement distracted me from my complaining bladder.

"And now, a special kiss cam you won't want to miss."

The kiss cam had been going on all night. Darcy and I had debated what to do if they put it on us. My suggestion had been walking out, while he thought he should kiss my hand or pretend to make out with me. I'd vetoed both ideas, so fortunately it hadn't come up.

But suddenly the spotlight was on me. And before I could escape, someone was in the aisle by my seat.

I jerked my head around and forgot to breathe.

It was Cooper, bulked out with pads and skates, but no helmet. His hair was flat and sweaty and as messy as I'd ever seen it outside of when we'd been in bed together. He had a sexy grin on, dimples in full force, and his eyes were lit up— mischievous. He dropped to his knees and grabbed my chin with one hand.

"Ready to go public?"

All of my doubts pushed forward. "Are you sure? I'm not good at the hockey stuff."

"I'm sure. I'll handle my hockey, and you handle your law stuff. I just want you there while I do it."

I drew in a breath. "Okay, then."

He leaned over and pressed his lips to mine.

Those lips were lethal. His whole mouth was. I lost track of time and where we were till he pulled away.

His pupils were dilated and he was breathing fast. I was the same. The sounds of the arena around us rushed back in, loud and intrusive. Cheering? Why the hell would he kiss me like that here? I wanted to shove off his gear and—

"Someone will bring you down after, okay? So I can see you when I'm done here."

I nodded, a little short of the brainpower to make words. Then he was gone, and I realized we'd been on the kiss cam. Everyone in the building had seen that. We'd gone public, all right.

People commented around me until the start of the third period distracted them.

"Wow," Darcy breathed in my ear. "I'm swooning over here."

I let out a shaky breath.

I'd been claimed, publicly. And in return, I'd claimed Cooper as mine.

No one could predict the future. There were no guarantees. But for the first time, I was someone's priority. He wanted the world to know we were together.

It wouldn't be easy, I knew that. I sat up a little taller. A relationship would take work, and that was something I could do. I would work the hell out of this.

Cooper was on the ice again and I let a big smile escape. For once, I felt confident, saying in my head, *Mine.*

Bonus scene

Want to find out how Callie made her peace with Hailey? Join my newsletter for a bonus scene https://subscribepage.io/mf8ijZ

Next in the Toronto Blaze: Replay

Pre-order Book 3:
https://books2read.com/u/47JeYL

Katie

Staying up to watch one more episode of *Outlander* was a mistake. The hall light almost blinded me, dragging me out of Scotland and back to the condo. Madeline was home. I quickly hit pause and pulled out my headphones. Someone crashed into the wall, and I heard the sounds of kissing and moaning.

Shit. She'd brought someone home and here I was, sitting in the living room like a voyeur. If they took some time - another moan - I could still make my getaway. I quietly closed my laptop and pulled out the power cord. With my free hand I pushed back the afghan I'd been curled up under. I shoved my feet into my slippers.

"Katie?"

Damn. Not quick enough. I looked up at my roommate/landlord, a half-smile on her face, hair mussed and lips kiss swollen. She was standing at the corner where the hallway reached the kitchen, open to the living room. No sneaking away now. Her hookup stood in the shadows behind her. Not my business and I'd intruded enough, so I dropped my gaze. Laptop in my hands, I stood, ready to hide out in my room. With earphones in.

"Sorry, I should have been in my room already. I'll just —" I threw up a thumb in a dorky move towards my room.

"Katie?"

I froze in place. This voice wasn't Madeline. It was male and impossibly familiar. I never thought I'd hear it again in this lifetime. I'd been counting on that. My eyes opened so wide I must look like Bambi. *What the fuck?*

Hookup guy stepped around Madeline. I immediately regretted every life choice I'd made that brought me to this moment. Most especially the ones that resulted in the hobbit slippers and baggy sweats I was wearing, as well as the hair that needed washing and the lack of makeup. *Damn it.* If I was going to meet Josh again, I was supposed to look hot, in a skintight dress with heels, perfect hair and makeup, not like a hobbit after an extended visit to Mordor.

And damned if that devastated, heart ripped out feeling wasn't trying to make a replay in my chest. Fuck no.

"You two know each other?" Madeline leaned back against the breakfast bar. Even tousled, she was sleek and put together. Josh was wearing a short-sleeved button down with jeans, his brown hair a mess. He was taller than I remembered him, and the shirt didn't hide how broad his shoulders were, or the biceps stretching the sleeves or the sweetness in those brown eyes...

Uugh.

I needed to salvage this situation. I'd only been rooming

with Madeline a couple of weeks so far, and I liked this place, especially the discounted rent. Housing prices in Toronto were stupid. If Josh messed this up for me, I'd throttle him with my power cord.

"Yeah. We knew each other in high school." There was no reason to tell her that we'd dated for two years.

"We went out for two years and then broke up."

Thanks, Josh, for making it as awkward as possible. Madeline looked between the two of us, eyebrows raised. I, however, got stuck on that phrase. *We broke up.*

I didn't want to drag this out. I wanted to hide in my bedroom and try to pretend he wasn't about to hook up with my roommate. But some things I couldn't let slide. "No, Josh. *We* didn't break up. You broke us up. I didn't get a say in it, remember?"

His brow scrunched in his *I'm thinking* expression. I snorted. Madeline chuckled. "Oooh. Drama. I'm here for it."

I didn't know her that well, and I didn't want to air my dirty laundry in front of her. I took a step to slink away but no. Josh was busy rewriting history and not thinking about my situation at all.

"Katie, it was the right thing to do."

I exerted admirable control by not throwing my laptop at his earnest, confident face. It was a close call though. My knuckles showed white as I reminded myself of the cost of a new laptop.

"Was it, Katie?" Madeline asked. I couldn't let him congratulate himself on his wisdom. I'd just clear that up so I could leave, Josh and Madeline could get back to what they'd been doing, and I wouldn't find myself looking for a new place to live.

I narrowed my eyes at my ex, hoping to laser my displeasure into him with my glare. "Josh thought so. He was being scouted for the NHL draft, so I guess he didn't need his tutor anymore."

He made a hurt noise in his throat. Madeline turned to him. "Wanted to be free to fuck around, Josh?"

I could have cheered. Madeline was on my side, even though I wasn't the one planning to give her orgasms. Maybe I should because right now I loved my roommate.

"No!" He almost shouted, which was pretty rich. He was here, precisely to fuck Madeline. The only reason the two of them weren't already naked was because of Claire and Jamie and my stupid decision to watch one more episode.

"Oh, really?" With me and Madeline staring at him, he finally realized just how precarious his position was. He ran his hands through his hair and rubbed his face. I didn't let the familiar gesture fool me into lowering my guard. Or my laptop.

"Okay, this looks bad. And yeah, I've hooked up. But that's not why we–" A growl from me had him course correcting. "Not why I broke up with you."

Madeline looked like she only needed popcorn to be having a full movie experience. "Why then?"

He looked at me, as if asking for permission. I lifted my chin. *Up to you, buddy.* He turned back to her. "It was our senior year of high school. Katie was accepted to a bunch of schools and some of them were offering her scholarships. I didn't want her to make a decision on a school because of me."

There was a moment of silence. Madeline looked at me, and I nodded. "Yep, that's what he said. *In a text.*" The pain of reading that still hadn't faded as much as I wished.

Madeline's eyes rounded.

"Because obviously, having a vagina, I couldn't have made a decision in my own best interests."

"Oh, Josh. You didn't." Madeline shook her head at him.

Josh's cheeks flushed. "I – okay yeah – I should have talked to you. I was afraid I couldn't go through with it if you were right there."

Now I was really angry, and all that hurt and rage could finally be unleashed on the guy who was the source. I no longer cared that I looked like I spent my free time reading romance novels and accumulating cats between visits to the shire.

"Yeah, Josh, you *should* have talked to me. It's not like I didn't know you were going to be drafted. And maybe we could have decided on a long-distance relationship, or maybe we would have broken up, but you could have respected me enough to let me have a say in a decision that affected me."

Josh's jaw fell open. He swallowed. "You would have wanted to break up?"

I rolled my eyes so hard it hurt. "Maybe. We'll never know because *you didn't bother to talk to me.*"

I reminded myself that Josh wasn't cute, he looked like a goldfish. "I just – I never thought—"

Before I could explode again, Madeline patted his arm. "You're not irresistible."

His cheeks heated up as he stared at the floor. "I know."

That seemed like my cue. "Well, I'm going to my room. Have fun."

"Katie?" Josh was wearing his kicked puppy expression. "I'm sorry."

I stopped in my tracks. I deserved an apology, damn it, but the right one. "What are you sorry for, exactly?"

"That I didn't talk to you. I thought I was doing the right thing."

"Really?"

I wanted to cross my arms or put my hands on my hips, but I was still hanging on to my laptop. Instead, I let my tone show just how much I doubted that. "And that's why you started going out with Rhonda?"

He looked down again. "Mom said I needed to make it real."

"That bitch!" Madeline said the words, but they were exactly what I was thinking.

"Yeah, I knew she never liked me." There was an unsettled feeling in my stomach. When he took Rhonda out, I'd been angry and hurt and mortified. Convinced he'd really wanted to fuck his way through the puck bunnies when he got to play hockey. Not that his "best for you" argument was any better. I didn't want to think his mother had manipulated him, that maybe he'd really believed breaking up was in my best interests. I wanted to keep hating him.

"That's not right. She liked you."

I rolled my eyes. Madeline tilted her head in a question. I shook mine. "You dodged a bullet, Katie."

There was an awkward pause. I wasn't going to discuss Josh's mother, and Madeline was waiting for us to entertain her.

"Uh, I'm going to go." Josh's eyes were flicking from me to Madeline to the hallway.

Madeline nodded at Josh. "Good idea."

"And again, I'm sorry, Katie. I didn't want to be an asshole."

He turned and headed to the doorway. Madeline followed and locked the door behind him.

"Wine?" she asked when she came back. I nodded and finally set my laptop down.

She pulled a bottle out of the fridge and reached for the bottle opener.

"They never want to be an asshole, and yet..."

"Exactly."

Thank You

For reading *Playmaker*. Extra thank you's for leaving a review. This hockey series is a new project for me, so I appreciate anyone who spreads the word!

About the Author

Kim Findlay left hockey country, (Canada) to sail the beautiful waters of the Caribbean, finally landing in Sint Maarten (SXM). She balances a husband, dog, writing, reading and accounting, while missing family back home. (Not the weather though)

Website: www.kimfindlay.ca

If you'd be interested in more frequent updates, and would like to help name characters and assign their jersey numbers, join me in my Facebook group: Runaway Romance.   https://www.facebook.com/groups/runawayromance

I'd love to hear from you, so please reach out at kim@kimfindlay.ca.

Also by Kim Findlay

Cupid's Crossing Series, Harlequin Heartwarming

A Valentine's Proposal https://books2read.com/u/ml6A7Y

A Fourth of July Proposal https://books2read.com/u/3Rw6vB

A New Year's Proposal https://books2read.com/u/bWYQOD

A Country Proposal https://books2read.com/u/3y9KwJ

An Unexpected Twins Proposal https://books2read.com/u/br9wAk

MooU (College hockey multi-author series) Heart Eyes Press

Halftime https://books2read.com/u/4E7lYz

Inspirational Suspense (as Anne Galbraith)

Out of the Ashes https://books2read.com/u/bQpyOD

Kidnap Threat https://books2read.com/u/3JLpvJ

Hidden Evidence https://books2read.com/u/ml6ARY

Out of Print: (waiting for reissue!)

Crossing the Goal Line

Her Family's Defender

Coming Next:

Replay (Ducky)

Playoff (Denny)

Played Out (JJ)

www.ingramcontent.com/pod-product-compliance
Lightning Source LLC
Chambersburg PA
CBHW070503160726
48003CB00004B/1397